He kissed her the only way he knew, hard and without tenderness or thought or caring.

Pure instinct—a force he never questioned—drove him to kiss her harder and harder still. Lost in a sea of sensation, it took him a moment to realize what was happening. *She was letting him kiss her!*

Growling angrily, he wrenched his head up and shoved her away. "What the hell are you doing?"

Tenderly she tested the puffiness of her lips. "I give you credit for trying, Mr. MacKenna." Her voice was husky, her breathing uneven. "In your place, I would certainly have tried the same thing. However, you cannot scare me into leaving. I've made a decision to stay, and I never change my mind."

He backhanded the moisture from his lips. "You bitch," he snarled.

"Perhaps," she snapped back. "But I'm not a whore, Mr. MacKenna, and the next time you kiss me, you'd better protect your . . . " Her gaze lowered pointedly. " . . . privates. A knee can be a powerful weapon."

Also by Kristin Hannah
Published by Fawcett Books:

THE ENCHANTMENT

A HANDFUL OF HEAVEN

Kristin Hannah

FAWCETT GOLD MEDAL • NEW YORK

A Fawcett Gold Medal Book
Published by Ballantine Books
 Published in the United States by Ballantine Books, a division of Random House, Inc., New York, and simultaneously in Canada by Random House of Canada Limited, Toronto.

Library of Congress Catalog Card Number: 91-91985

ISBN 0-449-14736-3

Manufactured in the United States of America

First Edition: September 1991
Third Printing: August 1992

To the men in my life, Benjamin and Tucker.
I love you.

And to my mother, who always believed I could
do anything.

Special Thanks . . .

To Rob Cohen and Elisa Wares, who gave me what every first-time author dreams of—a chance.

To Megan Chance and Nadine Miller for their unwavering support and excellent advice.

And, perhaps most importantly, to Andrea Schmidt, who kept my baby boy happy while I worked.

Prologue

EARLY MARCH 1896

"Hey, Stoneyman!"

The guttural shout hung like a foul odor in the tent's chill air. Stone Man MacKenna felt its intrusion in every pore and bone of his body. His big hands clenched, unclenched. Just once, he thought, let me hit the noisy bastard just once. . . .

"You gone deef?"

He lifted his head slowly, pinning an ice-cold stare on the three men huddled around his Yukon stove. Just looking at the pea–brained, loudmouthed bunch made his gut ache. His rawboned face shifted into its customary scowl. "What do you want?"

Midas Magowin grinned, showing off a set of teeth more dead than alive. "You settin' over there thinkin' about how much you'd like to shoot us? Hell, we ain't doin' nothin' but talkin'."

Stone Man's scowl intensified. "That's plenty."

"Not to the Mounties downriver, it ain't. So, if you're gonna shoot us, shoot; and if you ain't, quit your glarin'. It gives me the willies."

"That's the idea."

"We're stayin'. It's colder'n spit out there right now, and you got the best stove in the pasture." Midas leaned back on his stool just far enough to get outside the stove's circle of heat, then he spat. The moment the slimy brown stream left his lips it froze solid. The rock-hard glob hurtled through the air and hit the planked floor with a solid *smack*, shattering into a dozen glasslike shards.

"This is a trading post, damn it," Stone Man growled. "I'm not running a hotel for gossipy, good-for-nothing gold diggers."

Chuckling, Midas rubbed his bony hands together. "Truth is, Stoneyman, you ain't runnin' shit. This here's the sorriest excuse for a tradin' post I've ever seen."

Stone Man's bushy, jet-black eyebrows drew slowly together. Beneath the hairy ledge, eyes the color of aged bourbon narrowed. "You'd best remember where you are, old man." His big voice fell to a whisper. "This is my post. That's my stove. I haven't kicked your butt *yet*, and I've put up with your infernal jabbering. But no half-bald, gnat-sized, older-than-God miner is going to tell me how to run my post. Understood?"

Midas flashed a triumphant smile. "Fair enough."

"H-Hey Stone Man . . ."

With an irritated sigh, Stone Man turned to the speaker. It was the kid, Cornstalk, the gangly newcomer who listened to Midas's mindless chatter for hours on end and imitated his hero's every movement. "Yeah, kid?"

Cornstalk's thin, freckled face broke into an eager grin. "Thanks for letting us stay. It sure is warmer in here."

Stone Man grunted in response. His teeth ground together in a familiar surge of resentment. They'd won. They were staying—again. He couldn't get rid of them until closing time. He knew it; they knew it. Other people depended on the trading post's hours.

He certainly couldn't reason with them. He'd been trying *that* since the moment they'd moved into his peaceful valley, and all he'd gotten for his effort was a pounding headache.

What was it about mining that drew fools like buzzards to a dead elk, he wondered. They came four thousand miles for a golden dream, but most of them never even staked a claim. Instead they sat around, drinking, smoking, playing cards, and yapping.

He shoved a lock of raven-black hair out of his eyes and glared at the motley group. Their raised voices battered his ears, rending a hole in the silence he'd traveled thousands of miles to find. They sounded like a pack of hyenas fighting over a rabbit bone—howling, barking, hissing.

He squeezed his eyes shut and massaged his temples. All he wanted was to be left alone. Was that asking so goddamn much?

"Hey, Cornstalk," Midas's tobacco-graveled voice interrupted his thoughts. "What was I talkin' about before Stoneyman's surly presence interrupted me?"

Stone Man's eyelids felt as heavy as boulders. With supreme effort he opened his eyes and looked up. The first thing he saw was Midas's triumphant, gap-toothed grin. Just once, he thought, glancing at his fists. *Just once . . .*

The old fool started up again. "Cornstalk, I asked you what in the hell I was talkin' about."

"Christ, Midas," Stone Man snapped, "you only talk about two things: gold and ladies. Neither of which, by the way, you'd know from bear shit."

The old man's Cheshire cat grin flattened. Offering an injured sniff, he replied, "That proves what I've long suspected about you, Stoneyman. You're big *and* stupid. I don't talk about ladies. I talk about whores."

"Yeah!" Cornstalk agreed.

Midas affectionately slapped his skinny protégé on the back. "Like I was sayin' yesterday, a good whore's about the best thing that can happen to a man, but a lady—ooee! Hell, I'd rather tussle with mating wolverines than a purebred lady. 'Cause a lady's a fight just itchin' to happen, and once she starts a'talkin', only a heart attack can shut her up." He shot Cornstalk a knowing look. "Hers, that is. Yours won't cause more'n a stutter."

Suddenly the tent's canvas flaps flipped open. Freezing air blasted through the opening, and a man stumbled into the store. Snow swirled in after him, pooling and drifting around his mukluks as he hurriedly re-tied the flaps.

The air settled almost immediately. Hobbling slowly, the stranger moved over to the stove, pulled out a small three-legged stool, and sank onto its hard surface. His whole body seemed to deflate.

After a moment he shook his behooded head. Snow danced off his heavy parka and hit the hot stove in a spray. The hissing and popping of dying flakes filled the tent. Hands trembling, he stripped off his huge mittens and eased the fur-lined hood from his face.

"Old Bill," Midas hollered at the Yukon's only mail carrier. "What the hell you doin' way out here?"

Bill tried to smile and failed. "Damn, it's cold out there," he muttered, pouring himself a cup of coffee. Curling his arthritic fingers around the hot tin, he lifted the cup and let the steam pelt his face.

"Come on, Bill. Whatcha doin' here?"

Bill took a sip before he answered. "I got a letter for Stone Man."

Everyone looked at Stone Man. He felt their eyes drilling through his chest. Mail was scarcer than gold on the Throndiuck River, and gold was damned scarce.

Frowning, he walked over to Old Bill. As he entered the stove's small circle of warmth, an involuntary shiver rattled his bones. "Who the hell would write to me? I've never gotten a letter in my life. It must be a mistake."

Bill reached into his buckskin bag and withdrew a crumpled, dirt-smudged envelope. "It come outta St. Louis, and it's addressed to Cornelius J. MacKenna. That's you, ain't it?"

Stone Man took the letter in his weather-chapped hands and stared at it for a long moment. Whoever had written this letter had taken his time. The penmanship was flawless. Perfect.

It was an honest-to-God letter from someone *out there*.

His strong hands shook. Like the other hard-bitten, lonely souls who wandered the Yukon Territory, Stone Man had left civilization behind long ago. He'd come north because he didn't have friends or family or loved ones. He had stayed because he liked it that way.

And now . . . a letter.

Awkwardly, his big fingers unaccustomed to the task, he opened the envelope and slowly withdrew the letter. The brushed, bumpy paper was folded in exact quarters, the edges aligned with military precision.

Unfolding the paper, he began to read.

Dear Mr. MacKenna,

I take pen in hand to respond to the advertisement

which you placed in the St. Louis Post Dispatch. *As it is now November, I can only hope you are still in need of assistance. If so, I would like very much to be considered for the position of partner in your trading post.*

The terms stated in your advertisement are entirely acceptable to me. I agree to manage the post for one year in exchange for one-half ownership in the post plus room and board.

Although I admit to inexperience in such a venture, you will find me a hard worker, well organized, and willing to work for our mutual success. I will be eagerly awaiting your reply.

Sincerely,
Devon O'Shea

P.S. Should you choose to take me on as your equal partner, could you please advise me as to what I should bring to make my time in the Yukon Territory more enjoyable?

He shook his head in disbelief. "Well I'll be . . ."

"What is it?" came the miners' chorus.

He smiled for the first time in weeks. Why not? He could afford to be sociable. This Mr. Devon O'Shea had answered his prayers. In another few months he'd be left alone again. He wouldn't have to worry about running the post, and he could photograph wildlife to his heart's content. And he'd never, never find himself trapped in a room with chattering miners again.

He closed his eyes. It was almost enough to make one believe in God.

"What is it?" Midas demanded.

"It's a reply to my advertisement."

"What advertisement?"

"When you fools first started straggling into my valley, I ran advertisements in about ten big-city papers seeking a partner in the post."

"Why'd ya do a damn fool thing like that?" Midas cut in. "You're mean as a wet cat. Ain't nobody in the world you could work with."

"I don't want to work with anybody. I want to be left alone. That's why I put the advertisements in. I need someone to protect my investment in the post while I take my pictures."

"Investment. Ha!"

Stone Man ignored Midas completely. "Anyway, it's been a while since I sent the ad. Nobody ever answered, and, hell, I forgot all about it."

Midas slapped his sinewy thigh in glee. "And now you got one? Yee-ha! Crack open another jug o' hootch, boys. This is our lucky day! There ain't a man alive who's meaner'n Stoneyman. His partner has to be an improvement."

"Maybe he plays poker!" Cornstalk chimed in, taking a big, dribbling swallow of hootch.

Midas grabbed the jug and greedily raised it to his lips. "You bet." The words came out in a watery gurgle. "And maybe . . ."

Their voices droned on, running together in Stone Man's mind until he had trouble thinking. They were even worse when they drank, he thought sourly. Then they talked all at once.

The pounding in his temples accelerated. For the first time in years he wished for one of the simpler amenities of civilization: transportation. If the post were in San Francisco or Boston, O'Shea could be at work in a week. But not here, not in Yukon Territory. Stone Man would be lucky to meet the man before the fall colors hit. Even if he wrote a letter hiring O'Shea today, Stone Man would still spend the next few months trapped with a bunch of worthless miners.

The smile slid off his face. It was going to be a long wait.

Chapter One

LATE SUMMER 1896

Willpower alone kept Devon O'Shea seated. Perched on the edge of her berth, she sat stiff as a new nail, her perfectly manicured hands curled into a bloodless ball in her lap.

Ten minutes. That's all she had to wait. In just ten short minutes she'd meet her new partner, Mr. Cornelius J. MacKenna.

Unfurling her fingers, she pressed one slim hand against her churning stomach. Why couldn't she calm down? She knew it was irrational to be so nervous, and Devon rarely acted irrationally. And yet, no matter how often she chided herself, she couldn't stem the trembling in her hands or the racing of her heart.

Today was so very important. It was the day her new life began: a life not shoved on her by adversity but one of her own making. *Her* life.

Sighing softly, she drummed her fingernails against the metal frame of her berth, listening with half an ear to the faintly metallic beat. In the cabin's quiet, it sounded like the cavalry coming.

She sighed again. If only she were more like her sister, Colleen. Colleen wouldn't be nervous now. She'd be far too busy spinning romantic fantasies about Mr. MacKenna to be anxious.

But Devon was nothing like her younger sister. Colleen was spontaneous, whimsical, impractical; Devon was calm, pragmatic, levelheaded. Unlike Colleen, she saw no point in spinning daydreams. Oh, she knew Colleen envisioned Mr.

MacKenna as tall and breathtakingly handsome, knew her sister pictured him alighting gracefully from a jet-black landaulet, doffing a natty top hat, and blathering romantic poetry.

But not Devon. She didn't spend her time wishing for a handful of heaven to call her own. Daydreaming, wishing, pretending, whatever one called it, was a silly waste of time. Mr. MacKenna, whatever he looked or acted like, was her partner for one year. For better or worse.

A knock rattled the narrow stateroom door. "Miss O'Shea? Miss O'Shea? I'm here for your bags."

Her perfectly coiffed head snapped up. *Oh my God.* This was it. The moment her new life began.

She forced herself to remain steady. It wouldn't do for a twenty-nine-year-old woman to go rushing about like a schoolgirl. She had an impression to make. The people she'd meet in the next moments would be her neighbors, her customers, perhaps even her friends.

Rising stiffly, she smoothed her shirtwaist's crisp white front and shook the wrinkles from her pin-striped serge traveling skirt. Her hands ran a quick check of the rust-colored hair that lay coiled at the base of her neck.

Glancing around the tiny cabin that had been her home for forty-four days, she smiled. Not a thing was out of place. Her two trunks were stacked in the corner, their brass corners perfectly matched, their bright metal locks aligned. Her leather gladstone valise shone like a general's boot, and her most prized possession, a bright red bicycle, gleamed. Everything was exactly as she liked it, orderly and spotless.

"Come in," she said. Her voice was low and throaty with just a touch of harshness, like the contented purr of an old tomcat. Its whispery sensuality contrasted sharply with the chiseled, almost austere lines of her face.

The narrow door popped open, and a young man scurried through. Offering a quick, perfunctory smile, he headed for the trunks. Halfway there he stopped dead. It was a full minute before he turned around, and when he did his eyes were as big as quarters. "A durn bi-cycle," he said, shaking his head.

Pride brightened Devon's moss-green eyes. "Isn't it grand?

It's a Royal Worcester Two-Speed Changeable-Geared Racycle—just like Miss Lillian Russell rides. My sister and her husband gave it to me as a going-away gift."

A hard swallow set the boy's Adam's apple to bobbing. "You're wantin' it to go, then?"

A small frown tugged at her perfectly arched eyebrows. "Of course."

"But—"

She cut him off with a wave of her pale, freckled hand. Picking up a book from her berth, she patted its leather spine. "Have you, perchance, read Mr. John McMoffat's *Guide for Alaska and Yukon Gold Seekers*?"

"Nope."

"I thought not. The *Guide* recommends bicycles for travel in the Yukon. As you know," she said smartly, "not many horses make it this far north."

The boy's lips quivered. "McMoffat, huh? Fella must live a fur piece away. Yer sis and her husband, they really buyed it fer ya, fer this trip?"

"They did, and I would take it as a personal favor if you'd stop grinning like that. The *Guide* makes the point that—"

"Thanks, ma'am!" He hefted the bright and shining bicycle onto his narrow shoulders, snatched up her valise, and bolted out of the cabin.

Odd young man, she thought as she moved over to her makeshift crate vanity and sat down. A sharp glance in the hand mirror assured her that she looked as good as a fairly plain, almost middle-aged woman could look. Her freckled skin was clean, and her hair, normally a pile of corkscrew curls the color of old rust, was well-contained.

Pinning her hat just so atop her sternly backswept hair, she plucked up her handbag, gloves, and umbrella. With a quick tilt of the chin, she sailed out of the cabin.

Outside rain fell hard and fast, pinging on the metal overhang above her head and running over the edge in a sheet of undulating silver.

She stood close to the ship's curved metal wall, her Curacoa kid walking boots pressed ankle to ankle and well out of harm's way. Her gloved hands, trembling ever so slightly, were curled tight around the chain handle of her handbag.

The sternwheeler edged toward the ribbon of brownish-gray muck that banked the Yukon River and began to slow.

She frowned. Why were they slowing down? This swampy wasteland couldn't be her destination. She'd expected a town like Circle City; a town with opera houses, dance halls, libraries, lights. A boom town.

She peered through the gloom. There was nothing out there; nothing except a single half-finished log cabin that sat like a skeletal king amidst a shoddy court of grayed canvas tents.

Tents! She shivered, pressing a hand to her breast as she stared at the six tents dotting the boggy pasture. What were they for? Certainly no man could survive a Yukon winter with so little to protect him from the elements?

"Devon O'Shea!"

Her name boomed across the decks, startling her.

"Devon O'Shea, report to the bow."

Clutching her handbag tighter, she popped open her umbrella and moved cautiously down the slick metal stairs. Her high heels clicked atop the wet, puckered metal as she hurried across the deck. "I'm Miss O'Shea," she said to the burly crewman handling the sternwheeler's bow line.

He cocked his head in her direction, looked her over—thoroughly—and then turned his attention back to the wrist-thick rope in his hands.

Nervously Devon tightened her grip on the umbrella. "Sir," she said to his broad back, "I am Miss O'Shea. Is there a problem?"

He turned to face her. Swiping the rain out of his bloodshot eyes, he shook his head. "If you're Devon O'Shea, and heaven help Stone Man if you are, there's no problem. You're gettin' off."

"Not here, I'm not."

Shoving his red wool cap high on his head, the crewman scratched his sweaty brow. "You told the cap'n you was gettin' off at MacKenna's post. Right?"

Her mouth went dry. It was all she could do to nod.

"Stone Man's place is here."

She fought to remain calm. "Who?"

"Stone Man—that's what folks around here call ole Cornelius. Anyway, his post is here."

"Here?" she managed to gasp. "Mr. MacKenna's post is *here*?"

"Yeah. Here."

She looked around. Gray, desolate swampland stared back at her, silent and lifeless. She pressed her small, gloved hand flat against her roiling stomach. For one terrifying moment she thought she was going to be sick.

"You want to sit down, miss? You don't look so good."

Fighting panic, she clamped her mouth shut. She had to think . . .

"Miss? You want to sit down?"

"No," she ground out. "I don't want to sit down. I want to know how much a return ticket to St. Michael costs."

He shrugged. "I dunno. 'Bout a hundred bucks."

She winced. It might as well be a thousand . . . "Okay, I can't go there . . . Then I'll go back to Circle City. Please inform the captain."

"The boat don't go that way again till spring. Come on, lady," he said, "you're getting off here."

She didn't know how long she'd stood on the ragged square of once-red canvas that served as the town's dock, or how long she'd stared, dry-eyed, at the sternwheeler that was now a dot in the distance. She knew only that she was stuck in this godforsaken swamp, bound here by poverty and the vow she'd given Mr. Cornelius MacKenna.

Wrenching her gaze away from the sternwheeler, she resquared her sagging shoulders. There was no use wishing things were different. Crying over spilled milk didn't put it back in the bottle. She slapped a smile on her face and reached down for her valise. Halfway there she froze, her eyes rounding with horror. Her open umbrella slid through her fingers, landing on the rain-slicked canvas with a quiet thunk.

The muddy ground was swallowing her bicycle!

Instinctively she lurched forward, dropping to her knees and scrambling to the canvas's rippled edge. Out of the corner of her eye, she saw the wind pick up her umbrella and carry it off. It spiraled end-over-end like a dancing black bubble and landed in the brown river. With a silent curse she curled her fingers around the icy steel of the bike's handlebars and yanked hard.

The mud fought back. Rain hammered her face, pooling and clogging in her eyes and running in cold streaks down her cheeks. She licked the wet rivulets from her lips and swiped them from her eyes.

Sucking in a big breath, she pulled with all her strength. "Come . . . on." The words came out in two bursts of chattering teeth.

The bicycle popped free. She hauled it onto the canvas and lay it on its side, pushing slowly to her feet.

Panting, shaking with cold, she peeled the mud-blackened gloves from her hands and crammed them into her handbag. Staring at her treasured racycle, its bright red frame mottled with clumps and streaks of mud, she felt tears threaten.

She squeezed her eyes shut. *No.* She had to remain calm. Crying wouldn't help. Besides, it was only mud. What was mud to a Two-Speed, Changeable-Geared Racycle? A little water and the bicycle would be as good as new. One had to keep things in perspective.

Slowly she opened her eyes. Adventures, she thought grimly, were messy businesses.

Tilting her chin upward, she took her first step toward Mr. MacKenna's trading post.

It was the second step that nearly killed her. She plunged into the mud like a falling boulder. The black goo tongued her knees, curling cold and syruplike around her legs. Bits and chunks of it splattered up to her face, mingling with the rain and sliding down her wet cheeks in torrents.

She knotted her fists, fighting the urge to scream in frustration. Gritting her teeth, she plodded through the thigh-deep mud. Her skirts were a deadweight that fought her every step.

After what seemed hours, she stopped. Heaving for breath, wiping the persistent rain from her eyes, she tried to focus. Something loomed in front of her. She blinked hard.

Slowly the blur cleared, and she could see a string of two-inch-by-twelve-inch planks stretched out before her.

"A boardwalk." The word came out in a soft, thankful sigh. She surged forward, stumbling blindly toward the nearest plank. Her foot came down hard on the board's edge, driving it deep in the soggy mud. Beneath her foot the wood shifted and shot forward. With a strangled cry she fell backward, landing flat on her back in the mud.

"Darn it!" she screamed, beating her ice-cold fists in the mud. She wanted to kick the stuffing out of something, anything, she wanted to—

No.

She had to relax, to get control. Taking a deep, shuddering breath, she tried counting. "One . . . two . . . three . . ."

She staggered to her feet. Slinging an arm around the nearest post, she held herself upright. Eyes closed, she tried to regain her breath.

Something cold and wet smacked her in the head. She looked up. Hanging above her were the dirtiest, ugliest, biggest pair of denim pants she'd ever seen. Scrawled across the seat were the words: MACKENNA'S POST.

It couldn't be. Devon's every hope for the future vanished. She eyed the half-finished log cabin at the end of the muddy street, and disappointment settled rock-hard in the pit of her stomach. Her post could at least have been in the cabin.

Reluctantly she brought her gaze back to the filthy, grayed canvas structure in front of her. MacKenna's Post. Her post. The store she'd come halfway across the country and then some to run was housed in a dilapidated tent. A *tent.*

"Perfect," she said with a groan. "Just perfect."

Shoving through the flaps, she marched inside. Dead center she stopped, her eyes scanning the sorry tent in a heartbeat. About the size of an average dining room, it had sagging gray canvas walls, a mishmash of haphazard shelving, a tiny metal stove, and a filthy wood-plank floor.

Against the far wall a mountainous slab of humanity sat hunched behind the most lopsided, disorganized counter she'd ever seen. The thick, sharp odor of unwashed bodies and old food engulfed her. Her fragile control slipped a notch. This . . . this pigsty was the post she had intended to transform into a fashionable store.

"Mr. MacKenna?" she said stiffly, moving toward the

disgustingly unkempt counter—and the even more disgustingly unkempt man behind it.

His head came up slowly. "Yeah?"

She moved in for a closer look at her new partner. Her eyes narrowed with immediate disapproval. He was a grim, angry-looking old man—what she could see of him, anyway.

A wide-brimmed miner's hat was pulled low on his forehead, shielding his entire brow. All she could see was a huge black handlebar mustache and bushy black beard that was shot through with threads of gray. A curtain of straggly midnight hair hung limply from beneath his hat to below his collar.

Reluctantly she looked into his eyes. And froze. He was staring at her. From within the flossy swirl of gray-streaked black hair, his eyes stood out like cat eyes, whiskey-colored and predatory. A chill slithered up her spine, and she took an involuntary step backward. Her heartbeat drummed in her ears. There was something about his eyes that frightened her, an intensity that was almost animal-like—raw, unveiled, and dangerous. The words *I'm your new partner* lodged in her throat.

Something *whooshed* past her hand. She glanced down, her eyes widening as a huge glob of tobaccoed spit hit the floor beside her foot and puddled.

Spit! The hairy ape had spit at her! Her control shattered. "How dare you? You filthy, disgusting—"

He lunged at her. "Get out of my post."

"Your post?" Spitting mud, she rammed her hands on her board-straight hips and glared up at him. "Don't you dare yell at me, you baboon."

"Bab—" His dramatic voice cracked. "Go home."

"I am home."

That stopped him. He stepped backward, eyeing her warily. "You're crazy."

Opening her handbag, she whipped out her letter. When she saw what her muddy fingers did to her perfectly clean, precisely folded paper, she felt another surge of anger. It was all *his* fault. How dare he act as if *she'd* done something wrong. "Did you or did you not place an advertisement in the *St. Louis Post Dispatch* seeking a partner in this post?"

"Huh?"

"And did you or did you not receive a response to this advertisement, which you accepted?"

"Huh?"

She gritted her teeth. *Darwin was right.* "Mr. MacKenna," she said stonily, "are you a man of your word?"

His eyes narrowed almost imperceptibly. "Yeah."

"Then this is our store."

"Huh?"

"Stop grunting at me!"

"All right, lady," he answered in a rich, rumbling voice that sent chills of apprehension scrambling down her rigid spine. "Just what in the hell are you trying to say?"

Her chin popped to a self-righteous tilt. "Unlike others who are, shall we say, lower on the evolutionary chain, *I* speak quite clearly, Mr. MacKenna. I'll say it again: This is *our* store. Yours and mine. I am your new partner."

He snorted. "Do I look stupid to you?"

She studied him for a moment. "Why, yes, Mr. MacKenna, you do."

A low growl burst from his throat. "Well, I'm not, and I wouldn't let any chatter-mouthed woman have half my store. My new partner's a man from Missouri."

She allowed herself a small smile. "He is? And did your advertisement specify that only males need apply?"

"Goddamn it, lady, I've wasted enough time with you. My partner's a man from Missouri, so get out of here."

"You're wrong. I am he."

"Very funny."

She shoved the letter at him. "I'm having a bit of trouble finding humor in the situation myself, Mr. MacKenna. I just traveled thousands of miles to be part owner in a thriving store in a boom town. Imagine my surprise to find that I'm the proud owner of a filthy, disheveled, disorganized, plank-floored tent stuck smack in the middle of nowhere."

He looked at the letter in her hand; then he looked down his nose at the bedraggled, scrawny, sanctimonious fishwife in front of him. "Ho-ly shit. You can't be—"

Her smile was sugarcoated steel. "Devon O'Shea."

Chapter Two

Thick, angry silence encased them. Mr. MacKenna's breathing quickened, punching through the quiet like a fist, spilling across Devon's face in hot, harsh bursts.

"Say something," she demanded. "An apology would not be out of order."

Nothing.

Exasperated, she broke eye contact. Staring at the row of small, nut-colored buttons that lined his tan flannel shirt, she crossed her arms. Beneath the sodden, wrinkled folds of her skirt, her foot picked up a staccato beat.

Darn him, she thought angrily, he wasn't going to be any help at all. Unless, of course, she wanted someone to load her trunks on a dogsled and hand her the reins.

As usual, it was up to her to solve things.

She set her mind to work. Her thoughts sped up one logical path and down another, seeking, probing, searching for a compromise, but every avenue of thought led to the same revolting but inescapable conclusion: They were stuck with each other. They'd both made a bad bargain, and now there was nothing left for them but to make the best of a horrid situation.

"There's no way in hell you're going to be my partner."

She rolled her eyes. "I *am* your partner."

"Holy shee-it!" boomed from the rear of the tent.

Devon spun around, her eyes drawn to the shadows huddled just outside the opening. Eavesdroppers! Snorting her disapproval, she strode over to the opening and flung the flaps back. Three men stared back at her.

"Don't you gentlemen know how rude it is to listen in on other people's conversations? Where are your manners?"

One of the men—a boy, really—yanked off his hat and crushed it to his gaunt chest. The battered felt quivered in his shaking fingers. "I-I got manners, ma'am," he stammered, staring at his own hands. "I-I'm Cornstalk, ma'am. They call me that 'cause o' my yeller hair and my skinny . . . uh . . ."

Warmth flared in Devon's heart. It had been years since any man, boy or no, had been nervous in her presence. "Your height?" she offered.

He lifted his head just far enough to look at her. At her soft smile, he grinned. "Yeah. 'Cause o' my height."

A big, one-armed black man pushed past Cornstalk. He smiled at her, a Santa-like grin that made his bright eyes disappear into folds of flesh. "I'm Bear," he said, tugging at the gray-white tufts of hair that spotted his cheeks and jaw. "So called for the fight I lost."

Her gaze flitted to his baggy sleeve. "I'm sorry."

"Don't be. If you gotta be sorry for somebody, an' maybe you're that type o' gal, be sorry for the bear. That old coot's lying dead as Moses' toes, an' all for an arm he can't use."

Devon couldn't help smiling. Young Cornstalk looked like he hadn't had a decent meal in weeks, and Bear—well, a woman with a good needle and thread probably wouldn't be turned away. For the first time in months she actually felt . . . needed. A ray of hope crept into her soul. Maybe she could make a life here after all. "Cornstalk," she said with a smile, "would you do me a favor?"

"Sure, ma'am."

"Could you run on down to the riverbank and collect my things? I'd appreciate it greatly."

"You bet, ma'am."

She laid a pale hand on his forearm. "You're a real gentleman, Cornstalk."

"Gentleman. Shee-it," hissed the gnarled, bent old man standing beside Bear.

"Midas . . ." Bear's voice was a rumble of warning.

Devon's warm smile faded as she studied the man called Midas. His eyes, buried like bits of gravel in a sea of wrinkles, drilled her with hate.

"Good Lord," she muttered under her breath. In all her twenty-nine years, no one had ever hated her. Now, after just thirty minutes in the Yukon Territory, she had two enemies. And as far as she could tell, that was half the population.

"Go home, lady. We don't want your kind here."

She glared at him, undaunted. "I am home." Without waiting for a reply, she tossed the flaps back in place and spun around.

Her partner hadn't moved an inch.

Bustling toward him, she steeled herself for his close-mouthed contempt. His surliness was not going to rattle her, she vowed silently. She was going to be calm, collected, and rational. There had to be a reasonable compromise.

So he was big, hairy, uncouth, slovenly, and doubtlessly stupid. Everybody had faults. As long as he quit spitting and took a bath . . .

When she was completely calm, she looked up. He was staring down at her. Why, he's not old at all, she realized with a start. His mahogany-gold eyes were clear, and the skin surrounding them was etched by the wind and sun but not by time. It was his soul that was old; deep in his eyes she could see bitterness and disillusionment.

It was a look she knew well, for she herself had aged early. She'd discarded her childhood long ago, choosing instead to don the heavy cape of a mother's responsibility, and though she'd never once regretted her decision to raise Colleen, she couldn't deny the consequences of abandoning her youth. Whenever she looked in the mirror, she found herself staring into the eyes of an old woman, a woman who'd missed her chance to have children.

Yes, she understood the tired sadness in his eyes. For one strange, dizzying heartbeat, she felt almost connected to him. "Mr. MacKenna . . ."

"You've got to go."

The spell snapped so cleanly it might never have been. Devon felt like a fool for letting a pair of eyes get her so off track. Staring hard at his left breast pocket, she tried to figure out a way to communicate with him.

Be friendly, she thought. That might work. What had that crewman called him? Tilting her head to look at him, she pasted a smile on her face. "Now, Rock Man—"

"Stone Man."

She looked at him blankly. "Pardon me?"

"Stone Man, not Rock Man."

"All right, Stone Man." His nickname matched his wit, she thought. "Let's put our heads together and solve this problem."

"I already solved it. You've got to go."

She gritted her teeth. So much for reasoning with a primate. "I'll go, Mr. MacKenna," she said evenly, "when I want to go."

"Then, lady, you'd better want to go right now."

"Devon Margaret O'Shea."

He frowned. "Huh?"

"Another sparkling gem of conversation," she remarked under her breath. "I said, my name is Devon Margaret O'Shea. You may call me Miss O'Shea."

His jaw twitched. "Just start walking. You've got a long trip ahead of you."

"What trip is that?" She smoothed the front of her soiled skirt. "I spent most of my savings on the supplies you recommended. And the two boat trips cost a fortune."

"Two boat trips? Christ almighty! Do you mean to tell me you took the all-water route? What are you, a goddamn queen?"

She stared him down. "Yelling at me isn't going to solve a thing."

"You're wrong!" he bellowed. "It makes me feel better. I *like* to yell."

Her voice took on an edge of steel. "So did my father. I'm used to bullies, so don't think you can frighten me. The solution is easy, Mr. MacKenna. Just give me two hundred dollars, and we'll pretend this unfortunate situation never occurred."

A collective hiss of astonishment came from the canvas trio.

Devon ignored the ill-mannered outburst. "That should be enough to get me back to Seattle. I have enough money for the train trip cross-country."

Cornstalk skidded into the tent. "All done, miss. Your things're in the log cabin Crazy Spike started to build afore he died o' bein' shot in the back. Anything else I can do for you?"

Stone Man pinned a cold stare on the kid. "You can carry her across the Chilkoot on your back."

Devon snorted derisively. "I'm not crossing the Chilkoot Trail, Mr. MacKenna, so you can just put that out of your mind. I'm returning the way I came. By water."

"Oh, miss," Cornstalk said in a rush, "there ain't no gettin' out of here this year, leastways not by water. The only way out of here this late in the year is to walk."

"Get out," Stone Man roared. Cornstalk jumped like a scared rabbit and hightailed it out of the tent.

"Is he telling the truth?" Devon whispered.

"There's a way out, but not by water."

"Oh, my God," she groaned. "I'm stuck. Really stuck."

"No, you're not. You're leaving here if I have to fling you like a rock."

Her head snapped up. "Enough is enough, Mr. MacKenna. This is all your fault. You placed the advertisement, and you accepted my application. You're the one who pretended to have a store and not some . . ." She glanced around in disgust. "Hovel with shelves. So don't you dare threaten me."

"No goddamn woman was supposed to answer. You tricked me."

"Tricked you, Mr. MacKenna? Did you anywhere in that advertisement specify that your partner had to be a man?"

"Lady, I've had just about enough of you."

"Oh, no, you haven't, Mr. MacKenna, not by a long shot. If you didn't want a woman, you should've said so. But you didn't, and so here I am. Broke, stuck in the middle of a godforsaken frozen moose pasture with a store that looks like it burned to the ground yesterday and a partner who looks like he crawled from the rubble this morning." Her eyes narrowed with resolve. "Well, Mr. MacKenna, you wanted a partner, and you've got one."

"I didn't want you."

She smiled, a ghost of a grin that curved her lips without touching her eyes. "You aren't exactly hero material yourself, Mr. MacKenna. But what we wanted doesn't matter a bit. What matters is what we got, and what we've got is each other. I'm here for the winter."

"Over my dead body."

The smile slipped up to her eyes. "That would be preferable, I'll admit, but as it's unlikely, let's not waste time hoping. Now," she said, clapping her hands, "the advertisement said the partnership included room and board. Could you please show me to my room?"

The shadows exploded with laughter.

"W-What's so funny about that?" She glanced nervously at the men huddled behind the canvas wall. "The advertisement did say room and board, didn't it?"

A slow grin slid across Stone Man's bearded face. "Oh, yeah," he said, "it did. Standard room and board for the gold fields. Follow me, *Miss* O'Shea."

He led her to a small wood-framed tent not more than a hundred feet from the post. Easing open the door, he said silkily, "Here it is. Home sweet home for me . . . and my partner."

Devon's eyes snapped up to his. "You don't mean—"

His gaze flicked through the open door. "Take a look at your new home. Yours and mine, that is."

Cold dread killed Devon's retort. Something in his eyes, something painfully akin to glee, chilled her to the bone. He didn't want to live with her any more than she wanted to live with him. So why was he smiling?

"Come on . . ." he whispered in her ear.

Suddenly she was afraid; the last thing in the world she wanted to do was to look inside the tent.

Her hands curled into tight little balls. This tent was her home, and ignoring that fact wouldn't change it. Squaring her shoulders, she turned stiffly toward the door.

One look inside and her legs turned to warm molasses. "Good God," she groaned. "You must be joking."

"Do I strike you as a man with a sense of humor?"

Her stomach did a wrenching flip. The space was so small. She could *feel* him beside her, his big body like a cloud of foul-smelling smoke, hovering, plunging her into the dark of shadow.

He was gloating. She knew it without looking at him. He thought she'd take one look at this . . . this . . . Words failed her. Nothing in her past had provided a word worthy of this place. Filthy rathole was far too kind.

The tent floor, what she could see of it beneath the layer of dirt and mud, was a series of rough-hewn planks chinked with gobs of moss. The planks formed a three-foot-high wall that ended where the taut canvas began. The ceiling sagged sadly, its once-white surface grayed by soot and smoke. In the exact center of the room was a little sheet-metal box perched precariously on wooden slats. If not for the battered metal pipe that rose from its misshapen surface and disappeared through a hole in the tent's ceiling, she wouldn't have known it was a stove.

There were no windows, and the air in the tent, if in truth there was any, was stagnant and fetid. The table was a thick board set on two stumps, and four stumps made up the chairs. Two hooks jutted from the left-corner support pole.

She immediately thought about the two trunks she'd packed so carefully. Then she looked back at the rusty hooks and groaned. Her closet was a *hook*.

It was worse than she could have imagined. Much worse. She scanned the room for a bright spot, a ray of hope. There had to be *some* redeeming quality. She forced a tight-lipped smile. Maybe, with a little elbow grease . . .

She glanced to the left and froze. Every hopeful thought fled her mind. Her mouth dropped open. The word "no" hung soundlessly on her lips. "It can't be . . ."

"Yes," came Stone Man's gloating declaration. "That's the bed."

Her eyes rounded in horror. There was only one bed. A big, rough-hewn bed with a splintery partition down the middle.

One bed for both of them.

She forced herself to meet his triumphant stare. "You mean

to tell me that if I had been a man, I would have slept there? With you?''

His grin expanded. ''Yeah. All us miners sleep that way. It's warmer.'' He turned back to the others. ''Go to the log cabin and get her things, Cornstalk, the lady's going home.''

The tone of his voice struck her with mallet-hard force. Anger surged through her blood. ''Don't move, Cornstalk,'' she yelled. ''And you,'' she hissed at her partner, ''you wait a minute.''

''I'm just helping out.''

''Don't help me,'' she snapped. ''It's your *help* that got me here. Your help that has me standing in the middle of a darn tent, faced with the prospect of freezing my . . . gentle parts for months in a rathole. So don't help me anymore.''

''No, you're not.''

''I'm not what?''

''You're not going to freeze your butt off until spring in my tent.''

''Our tent,'' she corrected grimly.

''My tent.''

She whipped the letter out of her handbag again. ''It's our tent. Unless you're planning to build me one.''

''Quit flinging that damned letter in my face like it was a presidential decree. I wrote it. We both know it.''

Unfolding the letter, she held it up and read aloud, ''As stated in my advertisement, you will be made my equal partner in the trading post immediately upon your arrival. The position requires full day work approximately eight months a year and includes room and board.''

Folding the now-muddy letter back into precise quarters, she placed it in her handbag and glanced up at him.

His face looked hot enough to explode. ''Lady . . .''

Devon rammed her slim forefinger in his barrel chest and met his hard-eyed gaze head-on. ''You don't scare me, Mr. MacKenna, not with your bear voice or your giant size or your eagle eyes. I don't scare easily. Now answer me: Is this our tent, or do you intend to build me one?''

''I can't build you a tent.''

A frown darted across her brow. ''Why not? It seems the simplest solution.''

"There aren't any more stoves up here. Nothing gets to the Yukon that wasn't carried on somebody's back." He eyed her with contempt. "And I don't suppose you packed anything as useful as a stove in those precious trunks of yours."

"I brought everything you told me to," she shot back, "and a stove was not on the list."

"A man wouldn't need one. And I never thought a woman would be stupid enough to answer my advertisement."

At that Devon's whole body sagged. Suddenly she felt every one of her twenty-nine years. She'd come halfway around the world to live in rat-infested squalor with a craggy-faced, foul-tempered mountain of a man. "Criminy sakes," she muttered. "It *was* stupid."

"Don't worry lady," he said eagerly, "we'll get you home."

"Home?" she said dully. "If I had a home, I wouldn't be standing in this dump."

"You've got a home. Everybody's got one."

She lifted her face to his. "Do you?"

He shrugged uncomfortably. "This is it."

"It's not much."

"Maybe not, but it's mine."

"True. It's more than I—" She stopped. She'd been about to say it was more than she had in St. Louis, and that was true. The farm she'd grown up on now belonged to Colleen and her husband. There was nothing for Devon in St. Louis except bad memories, and if she went back now, defeated, she knew she'd spend her whole life as good-old-spinster-aunt Devon.

No. She stiffened her spine. She might not have much, but she did have half ownership in a trading post. And although MacKenna's post might not be much now, it had potential. With a little hard work it could be the best post around. "This home *was* yours," she said resolutely, "now it's ours. I'm moving in for the winter."

"Then I'm moving out."

She brightened. "Perfect."

He snorted. "How does a person so stupid keep breathing? It wouldn't be safe for you to live alone up here. These men haven't seen a white woman in years. And not one'd care if you were willing."

She nipped nervously on her lower lip. That wasn't something she'd considered. "Then you're staying."

"Yeah. You're the one who's—"

"Staying." She stuck her head out of the tent and yelled, "Cornstalk, could you bring me my valise and trunks?"

"Sure, ma'am!" he hollered back, his feet already moving.

Stone Man grabbed her by the wrist and swung her back into the tent. "What do you think you're doing?"

She smiled up at him. "A lady needs her things around her."

"Ladies"—he spat the word—"don't live in the Yukon."

"They do now, Mr. MacKenna."

Chapter Three

Stone Man shoved past Devon. She stared at him in disbelief. He was leaving her—just like that! Lunging after him, she yelled, "You come back here, Mr. MacKenna. We're not finished with this."

He pushed through the narrow door and plunged into the mud beyond. His stride didn't waver, and he didn't look back. Like an angry bull he charged forward, his massive shoulders hunched against the pelting rain, his face tucked into the fleece collar of his mackinaw.

Devon shuddered to a halt at the doorway, her gaze glued to the disgusting quagmire of a street. God, she didn't want to step in it again. . . .

"I mean it!" she shouted.

He kept moving.

"Darn you," she cursed under her breath as he stormed through the trading post's flaps and disappeared from her view. Whirling around, she stomped inside her new "home" and slammed the door shut behind her. The rusty hinges screamed in agony, and the "clothesline" strung above her head shimmied. Muddy work boots, slung over the sagging rope by knotted laces, clunked together, and a pair of wet, filthy red socks fell to the floor with a squishy *plop*.

With the door closed, the tent's stench engulfed her. She smelled wet wool, unwashed feet, human sweat. The disgusting odors wormed into her stomach. Gagging, she clamped a hand over her mouth and flew to the door. Flinging it open, she gulped greedily of the fresh, rain-sweet air.

"Oh, God," she moaned between breaths. She wasn't going to make it. She wasn't strong enough. . . .

Oh, yes, you are. She jerked upright, ramming the heels of her hands into her watering eyes. She refused to be sick.

She patted her soggy, mud-splattered hair and lifted her chin. Determination glittered in her eyes. It was time to start making the best of it. Grimacing, she plunged into the mud and started slogging toward the post.

Stone Man felt sick to his stomach. "Quit staring at me!"

Midas's fist slammed onto the cold Yukon stove. The sheet metal jumped and rattled. "Dang it, Stoneyman, say something."

"What?" he demanded. "We all know she can't go anywhere."

Midas shot to his feet. "She sure as hell can—and she'd sure as hell better!"

"Aw, Midas," Cornstalk chimed in, "she don't seem so bad. Maybe if you'd just give her a chance . . ."

"Don't seem so bad? Son, she's death in a long skirt. And you!" he shouted at Stone Man, "you're the one who oughta hate her the worst. The witch'll talk you into an early grave."

Stone Man's bushy eyebrows drew together, melting into a solid black line. For once the old fart was right. Little miss levelheaded had spent ten minutes in his tent, and not once had she closed her mouth for longer than it took to breathe.

He had to do something to get rid of her. And fast.

"All right, boys," he said, staring right at Midas. "Put your money where your mouths are. It'll take two hundred bucks to get her out of here. How much money have you got?"

Cornstalk pulled out his small buckskin drawbag and peeked at the gold dust inside. "Maybe ten bucks."

Bear patted the lump in his breast pocket then shook his head. "Less."

Midas slammed his scrawny arms across his chest. "We can't send the princess home by water. A boat wouldn't make it more'n halfway to St. Michael before the river froze, and there ain't a man up here'd talk to us again if we stranded 'em with a woman for the winter."

Bear jammed a toothpick in the gap between his front teeth and rattled it around. "He's right, Cornelius."

Stone Man dropped his chin into the rough cradle of his palm and sighed. "I know," he muttered. "Shit."

Midas kicked the stove. The metallic clang echoed through the tent's silence. "Dang it! Don't you go gettin' all bleary-eyed, Stoneyman. Her high and mightyness can walk like ever'body else."

Bear tossed the toothpick over his shoulder. "Naw," he said. "That skinny thing wouldn't last ten minutes by herself. Hell, someone'd have to shoot her halfway to the Chilkoot."

Midas spat a huge glob. "Stoneyman oughta do that anyway. It's the only sensible thing. She's the plague. We oughta kill her now 'fore she has a chance to spread and multiply. Christ, she could infect some of the Injun women with her uppity ways."

"I'm not going to shoot her," Stone Man answered.

"I'm glad to see you draw the line somewhere," Bear remarked blandly.

Stone Man's mouth compressed. "It's not a firm line."

"She's probably paintin' your bed pink right now," Midas mumbled.

Bear grinned. "Tell you what," he said. "I'd be willin' to take her to Circle City. She could winter there and catch a boat out in the spring. I'll take her if she'll leave tomorrow."

"Yee-ha!"

"Don't break out the hootch yet, Midas," Bear said quickly. "I'll only take her if she's willin'. I won't have no woman kickin' and screamin' around my fire."

"She won't go," Cornstalk said to no one in particular.

Bear shrugged. "I don't think so neither."

"Oh, she'll go," Midas promised. "I bet if one of us tried to get a little lovin', a proper lady like her'd run for cover."

Bear lurched across the stove and grabbed Midas by the collar. "You ain't gonna hurt that little gal," he growled.

As usual Midas backed down immediately in the face of a real threat. "I-I ain't gonna try nothin'," he stammered.

Releasing his hold on the miner, Bear snatched up his

battered felt hat and dusted it off. Cramming it down on the grayed cottony tufts of his hair, he pushed to his feet. "Well boys, I gotta go. But before I do, put me down for a buck on the lady."

"I'll take your money," Midas answered. "A buck says she leaves tomorrow."

"I'll bet a buck—" Cornstalk's voice cracked, dropped. He clamped his mouth shut in embarrassment.

"That's nothing to feel bad about, boy," Stone Man said. "It's natural."

Cornstalk grinned broadly, then said, "Looks to me like she's staying."

A scowl crept across Stone Man's craggy features. The thought of spending a winter locked in a two-man tent with a squawking woman was enough to make his blood run cold. "Look again, kid," he said, "and don't blink."

"Blink all you want, Cornstalk. The lady is definitely staying."

At the sound of her voice, Stone Man's head jerked up. She was standing just inside the tent, her muddy hands clasped together, her hat drooping over her dirty forehead like a puppy's tongue on a hot August day. How the hell did she manage to look so prim and proper with mud dripping down her face?

She was smiling like a contented cat. Or, he thought angrily, like she'd heard the boys' bets and wanted to place one of her own.

Shit! How long had she been there? He'd glimpsed enough of her personality to know that if she'd heard the boys' bets, he wouldn't be able to get her butt out of his tent with an axe handle.

He eyed her warily. "How long have you been hiding behind the tent flaps?"

She sniffed, all uppitylike. "I don't hide."

"How long were you *standing* behind the tent flaps?"

"A while."

"How long is a while?"

She shrugged. "More than a moment, less than a spell. I don't know, exactly. Just a while."

"Lady . . ." The word was a warning.

A warning she completely ignored. "You don't scare me one whit, Mr. MacKenna. Now," she said crisply, "where are the cleaning supplies? I want to get started."

In a cloud of silence so thick it made her spine rattle, Devon forced her chin a little higher. Edging past her partner's intimidating form, she glided toward the haphazard array of overladen shelving that cluttered the tent's center. Huge piles of dusty boots lay heaped next to sacks of flour, which slumped alongside mining pans and cans of Campbell's split-pea soup.

She grimaced. Organizing this mess was going to be even worse than she'd thought. The soup belonged over there, next to the—

"Get out!"

The booming command shattered her thoughts. She turned away from the crate of cans and leveled a steady gaze on her partner. "Not until I find what I need."

"What you need is a boat ticket home."

"What I need, not that you would recognize these items, is soap, water, and a bucket."

He took a step toward her. "Lady, you've got about ten seconds to get the hell out of my store."

"Aha!" she cried, clapping her hands together. "Here's the soap—right next to the pickaxes. Why didn't I look there first?" Sweeping the cleaning goods into her arms, she tilted her head to a proud angle and headed for the door.

As she sailed past Stone Man, his hand snaked out, capturing her wrist in a viselike grip and pulling hard. She landed in his arms, her cheek pressed against his chest. The smell of wood smoke on flannel crept into her nostrils.

He lowered his head. "I'll be home for dinner at eight," he whispered harshly in her ear. "Be ready to shut your mouth for once and listen."

His warm breath slid down her cheek, setting off a flurry of butterflies in her stomach. The well-worn flannel beneath her cheek swayed, lifting and dropping like a calm sea. It took her a moment to remember she'd been insulted.

"Shut my mouth!" she hissed, wrenching free. "You listen to me, Stone Man. It was your incompetence and failure to consider all possibilities that got us into this mess. From now on, *you* listen to *me*."

The skin around his eyes flinched. "Never."

She tossed a contemptuous glance around the disorganized store. "This dump is half mine. I'm your partner, and until spring you'll darn well listen to me."

"Never."

She went on as if he hadn't spoken. "Come spring I'll gather my earnings and leave this sorry blight on the earth's face. But until then we're equal partners."

"You won't last that long, lady."

Her gaze turned icy. "Don't bet on it, Stone Man. I have a way of . . . surviving." Tightening her hold on the precious cleaning supplies, she strode out of the tent.

After she'd left, Cornstalk turned to Stone Man. "What's a blight?"

Stone Man's gaze remained riveted on the fluttering tent flaps. "She is, son. She is."

Snapping open his pocket watch, Stone Man glanced at the time: eight o'clock. He couldn't put it off any longer. The boys had been gone for hours. It was time to shut down the post and go home.

Home. The word alone made him tense. Yesterday his tent was a home; today, who knew?

He flipped open the tent flaps and peered out.

The camp was naturally quiet—just the way he liked it. The rain had dwindled to a silvery mist that clung to the gray-blue spruce needles like flecks of crystal. Puddles winked white from the sea of mud. Fogless, the sky was a dull amber-blue fusion of early evening light; the strange, half-lit evening of the autumnal Yukon.

He knew from experience that tomorrow's dawn would be perfect, a day made for photography. He jammed his hands into his pockets, letting the tent flaps flutter shut. He should be getting his glass plates and chemicals together—and what was he doing? Hiding in his tent like a naughty schoolboy, afraid to go home.

"Damn," he muttered. She had him acting like Cornstalk, stupid and nervous.

He rubbed his sweaty palms on the coarse denim of his pants. For the first time since he'd left prison, he wished he were a drinking man. A belt of Scotch would taste good right now. Damn good.

Wait a minute, he thought. Why the hell am I nervous? She was the one who ought to be scared. She was the one who was leaving—somehow. He didn't exactly know how he was going to do it, but he was damn well going to do *something* to make her run from him like a shot-at coyote.

Yes, she was the one who ought to be nervous. In less than twenty-four hours she'd be packing for a trip north, one that the scrawny little thing wouldn't—

Don't think about the hardship. It was her own fault she was up here. If she'd just been a man like she was supposed to none of this would have happened.

He'd just have to convince her highness to leave. How hard could that be? She was only a woman—and a damn stupid one at that. A smart one wouldn't have gotten off the sternwheeler.

He could outsmart her by a Yukon mile.

Smiling, he slipped into his mackinaw and started for home. Nothing to it. By this time tomorrow the little lady with the uppity ways would be halfway to Fortymile.

And good riddance.

He stood outside his own door for a long minute, reminding himself that she was stupid and he was smart. Still, she had a way about her of making a man feel dumb. . . .

Suddenly the door swung open, and there she was, standing right in front of him, her face all flushed and lively. Their eyes locked. He felt his mouth drop open. She'd cleaned up, and she looked . . . younger.

Guilt tickled his gut. The trails weren't kind to a woman her size.

"Mr. MacKenna?"

Her brackish voice ripped a hole through his thoughts. It wasn't his goddamn fault she was a woman. His mouth snapped shut with an audible click of teeth; his eyes narrowed. "You wasted water on a damn bath?" he growled. "There'd better be enough left for drinking, or you'll be the one hauling it."

The startled look froze on her face, and whatever she'd

been about to say vanished. Pushing past her, he barreled into his tent. Two steps in he stopped in his tracks. "What the . . ." He spun around, stabbing her with his eyes. "This place smells like a goddamn hospital."

She met his angry stare without flinching. "Better a hospital than a privy."

"Why you—"

She hurried to his side. "Let's not fight, Mr. MacKenna. I've made us a nice supper, and I would so hate to spoil it. Let's call a truce. Perhaps after eating we can reach a compromise."

He reined in his temper, forcibly reminding himself of his mission. Already he knew her well enough to know that if he antagonized her, she'd only dig her heels in deeper. And her goddamn heels were in deep enough now. "Okay," he mumbled, letting her help him out of his coat. "What's that other smell?"

A pained look crossed her face. "Supper."

"Oh." He watched as she smoothed wrinkles from his old mackinaw and hung it carefully on the lower hook. He snorted. The little priss was probably itching to iron it.

"Sit down, please," she said, waving her hand regally toward the table.

There was a bright red tablecloth on the table and two white cloth napkins. "Christ," he muttered under his breath.

"What was that, Mr. MacKenna?"

"Call me Stone Man. And I didn't say anything." He lowered himself to one of the stump chairs and scooted close to the table.

She buzzed around the stove, lifting lids, stirring, tasting, testing, opening the oven door and closing it. It made him dizzy just watching her.

"So, Mr. . . . uh . . . Stone Man, how long have you been in the Yukon?" Her voice sounded different, nervous. "It seems so desolate and lonely up here. But then, perhaps you're that type of man. I, myself, find that . . ."

Her words mushed together in his mind. She was chattering like a squirrel, and it was giving him a headache.

"How old are you?" he cut in when she took a breath.

A pot lid clattered noisily into place, and she spun to look at him, her pale face flushing. "Sorry, I didn't expect you to—I mean, most men wouldn't ask. I'm twenty-nine."

He studied her for a long moment. She wasn't bad looking, in a skinny, freckled kind of way. There were probably lots of men desperate enough to marry her. "Kinda old to be gallivanting around the country like a girl in short skirts, isn't it? Why don't you settle down, have some kids?"

Her hands were shaking noticeably as she plucked up his plate and started ladling dinner onto the cobalt-blue tin. "I'm not old. And I have no intention of discussing my personal life with you."

Setting the plates on the table with mathematical precision, she smoothed everything—her hair, her cheeks, her skirts. Then she sat down like a princess and picked up her fork.

His gaze dropped to the plate she'd set in front of him. He stared at it, amazed. The food was perfectly placed: the sliced moosemeat smothered with rich gravy was at twelve o'clock, the butter and spice-laced turnips at four o'clock, and the biscuits at seven o'clock.

The aroma made his mouth water. He hadn't eaten since breakfast, and this was the best-looking meal he'd ever seen. Lowering his elbows to the table, he curled his arms protectively around his plate. The action was unconscious, a left-over legacy from prison days, when food was protected at all costs. Taking the flaky roll in his dirty hands, he cracked it open and slid it through the moose gravy, then piled a huge fingerful of turnips on top and shoved it into his mouth. Chewing noisily, he rammed a chunk of meat in his mouth, then glanced across the table.

She was staring at him, agape.

He stopped chewing. "What's the matter with you?"

Her gaze immediately dropped back to her perfectly ordered plate. "Nothing," she said quickly, cutting a thimble-sized bite of meat.

"Good," he said, slogging another hunk of biscuit through his gravy. He lowered his head again but kept his eyes fixed on her through slitted lashes.

He couldn't believe it: She was eating counterclockwise, one food item at a time. She didn't so much as touch her turnips until every bit of meat was gone.

With a snort of disgust, he went back to eating.

"Well," came her whiskey-tenored voice, "how is your meal?"

"Fine," he said, jamming the final bite of biscuit into his already overstuffed mouth. Swallowing loudly, he took a long swig of water, then leaned back in his chair and burped.

At his belch, Devon dropped her fork. The clang of metal hitting hardwood seemed obscenely loud in the quiet room.

He got up and poured himself a cup of coffee. "Now, lad . . . uh, Devon, we've got to solve our problem." His eyes swept the spotless tent in a heartbeat, noticing the shelving she'd built for his books. Until now they'd been scattered all over: under the bed, under the stove, behind the snowshoes—wherever he happened to be standing when he didn't want to read anymore.

Good God, she must have ferreted them out like a miner after ten-dollar nuggets.

He groaned. Midas was right. By tomorrow his bed would be pink, probably with little white flowers on it. She'd been here all of six hours, and already he felt uncomfortable in his own home. He cleared his throat. "We can't live together. It won't work."

She dabbed the napkin at her mouth then set it alongside her plate and looked up at him. "Where will you go?"

His hold on the coffee cup tightened. The woman was goddamn unbelievable. "I'm not going anywhere."

"Neither am I."

"Neither are—" *Slow down. Think.* He hated having to think; he wasn't good at it. What he wanted to do was pick her up by her skinny backside and toss her out of his tent. He remained calm by sheer force of will. "You don't know what it's like up here in the winter. Eighty below zero isn't uncommon. You can't even imagine that kind of cold."

She chewed on her lower lip. "Give me the two hundred dollars, and I'll go home."

"Dammit, Devon, even if I had the money, you can't go home by water. Not this year."

"You can't expect me to walk?"

He dropped into the chair opposite her. "It's not that difficult a trip,'' he lied, staring right into her eyes. ''We've all done it. And Bear offered to—''

''No.'' Snapping to her feet, she swept the dirty dishes into her arms and strode over to the half-full wash basin.

Her back was to him as she flung the plates into the sudsy water, but he didn't need to see her face to know she was furious. Her body was stiff with silent anger.

''Devon . . .'' The rich, warm cadence of his voice floated across the tent.

Her ruthless attack on the dishes didn't dim. ''I'm not walking, Stone Man. Not anywhere. Get that through your thick skull. Here I am and here I'll stay until spring.''

Damn! He slumped in his chair, plopping his furry chin onto his laced fingers. She meant it. She was staying.

There had to be a way to force her out . . .

Suddenly Midas's words popped into his mind. *I bet if one of us tried to get a little lovin', a proper lady like her'd run for cover . . .*

He studied her, wondering.

Would she run from lovemaking?

He swallowed dryly. It was his only hope.

Pushing himself slowly to his feet, he moved awkwardly across the room. Right behind her he stopped. The rain-sweet scent of her filled his nostrils. She smelled of goodness, not like any of the women he'd touched before. He was used to women who reeked of stale tobacco smoke and cheap liquor. He could tell just by looking that her hair would feel like wolf fur: soft and long, and just a bit prickly.

He focused on the pale curve of her neck. Her skin was so light, like a layer of new cream flecked with cinnamon.

He lifted his hand and held it just over her shoulder, staring in amazement at the slight tremble of his fingers. He couldn't remember the last time he'd seen his hands shake.

How did you touch a woman you hadn't paid for? Would she scream? Hit him? Cry?

It didn't matter, he reminded himself, as long as she left. Running his tongue over paper-dry lips, he stared at the milky softness of her skin, wishing, strangely, that his hands were clean.

Then, steeling himself for her response, he touched her.

Chapter Four

His fingers curled around the thin curve of her shoulders, squeezing gently.

She flinched at the contact, but one sharp intake of breath was the only sound she made. Beneath his damp palm he felt a butterfly-quick shudder of apprehension. Then she regained control. Her body stiffened.

His hand inched across the bumpy surface of her serge coat toward her throat. Her breathing quickened, taking on the harsh, uneven tenor of the hunted. He forced himself to continue moving slowly; he wanted to frighten her, not terrorize her.

His dirty fingers slid through the frothy swirl of lace at her throat and crept downward, burrowing past the starched cotton of her collar to the skin beneath. The small indentation below her collarbone was like a bower of milky velvet cradling his callused fingertips. The quick, even beat of her pulse danced against his flesh.

A shiver swept her body, bringing a smile to his lips. His plan was working. Any minute she'd pluck up her rumpled skirts and run for home.

"W-What are you doing?" She sounded edgy, nervous.

Still massaging the base of her neck, he moved closer to her. The soft, worn flannel of his workshirt melted into the prim navy-and-white stripes that ran down her back. With his other hand he pulled out the wiggly little pins that confined her hair.

"Relax," he whispered in her ear as he plucked out the

final hairpin. Even to his own ears his voice sounded strained, raspy.

A waterfall of russet hair cascaded down her board-straight back. Her only response was a small, mouselike whimper.

He couldn't help noticing the way her hair captured the light. Hundreds of red and gold highlights swirled in and out of the heavy, rust-colored curls. A strange and foreign urge seized him. For a heartbeat he wanted to bury his face in her hair, to feel the soft strands brushing his skin.

Mentally he shook himself. He had to remember the plan. So what if she had pretty hair? So did a red fox, and a wilier, more troublesome animal didn't exist. It was just that he'd been so long without a woman.

Remember the plan. He leaned toward her, and as he did, her scent filled his nostrils. She smelled so different . . . so good. She smelled of rain and summer air and homemade soap. He kissed the soft flesh of her earlobe.

A small shiver crept along her skin, vibrating against the callused hardness of his fingertips. Still tasting the sweetness of her skin, he turned her around and gathered her into his arms.

She refused to meet his gaze. Staring straight ahead, her eyes bright and wide, she focused intently on the row of buttons that marched down his shirt. Her lips were pressed together tightly, but she couldn't stop their trembling.

He felt her warm breath sliding through the mat of salt-and-pepper hair that peeked from his open collar. "Devon . . ." Her name slipped from his lips.

She didn't look up. Her small, pink tongue darted out, leaving a trail of sparkling wetness on her lips.

His insides clenched. His hold on her shoulders tightened. His breathing quickened.

Damn. He was acting more like an untried youth than a thirty-nine-year-old man who'd grown up in one of the seediest brothels in New Orleans. His mouth was dry, his hands were shaking.

He had to get control of the situation. Now.

He took her face in his hands. Burrowing his fingers through her hair, he forced her face upward. The dark, rough flesh of his hands framed the milky paleness of her skin, and next to hers, his skin looked obscenely dirty. Shame curled in his stomach.

Their gazes locked. In the depths of her forest-green eyes, he could see a flicker of barely contained fear.

His shame intensified. How often had he sworn never to hurt another human being? And yet here he was, preparing to hurt—

No. He wouldn't hurt her; he was merely going to scare her. She'd leave here with her body intact. With an animal-like growl, he lowered his head and crushed his lips to hers. He kissed her the only way he knew; hard and without tenderness or thought or caring.

Pure instinct—a force he never questioned—drove him to kiss her harder and harder still. His hands roved freely across her shoulders, down her back, pinning her body against his. The warmth of her breasts and thighs seeped through the worn fabric of his clothes. Her breath, fast and shallow, pelted his beard.

The rock-hard shell of his self-control cracked. All thoughts of "the plan" vanished. A shiver rattled up his spine. His hold on her body tightened, became almost an embrace. The assault on her mouth changed subtly, softened. His tongue slipped past the barrier of her lips, tasting, testing, probing. Ah, she tasted so good, so sweet . . .

Lost in a sea of sensation, it took him a moment to realize what was happening. *She was letting him kiss her!*

Growling angrily he wrenched his head up and shoved her away. "What the hell are you doing?"

Her fingers traced the red scratches that were already coiling around the edges of her mouth, the leavings of a wire-hard beard on velvet skin. Tenderly she tested the puffiness of her lips. With no small thanks she realized that although his personal grooming habits were only slightly better than a barnyard pig's, at least they extended to brushing his teeth. "I give you credit for trying, Mr. MacKenna." Her voice was husky, her breathing uneven. "In your place I would certainly have tried the same thing. However, you cannot scare me into leaving. I've made a decision to stay, and I never change my mind."

He backhanded the moisture from his lips. "You bitch," he snarled.

"Perhaps," she snapped back. "But I'm not a whore, Mr. MacKenna, and the next time you kiss me, you'd better protect your . . ." Her gaze lowered pointedly, "privates. A knee can be a powerful weapon."

"Lady, if there's one thing you're in no danger of touching, it's my privates."

She smiled grimly. "And here I was thinking I had nothing to be thankful for."

Green-tinged light emanated from the battered tin lantern, creating a strange, unearthly pall in the tomblike tent. The Yukon stove sputtered and hissed, its metal top clattering at the fire's bright orange onslaught.

Devon was ready to scream. The only human sound in the tent was the ceaseless staccato of her tapping toe on the planks beneath her feet. It drummed in her ears. She and Stone Man had been sitting not more than five feet apart for three hours. In all that time not one word had passed between them. Not a syllable.

Right now, she decided, even a grunt would be a relief.

In all her twenty-nine years she couldn't remember ever feeling so edgy. He was making her crazy. She'd always hated hostile silences. They reminded her of her father.

As a child she'd had no choice about how she lived. But she was an adult now, and things were different—*she* made the rules that governed her life. She refused, positively refused, to live like enemies for ten months. She'd spent her whole childhood walking on eggshells around her father's sullen silences and terrorizing tempers. She'd be darned if she'd do that again.

Her foot stilled. Squaring her shoulders, she lifted her head and leveled a heavy stare on her partner. "What's wrong with talking?" she demanded.

He didn't even look up from the book he was reading.

She shot to her feet and started pacing. It was a struggle not to wring her hands together. Maybe a less shrewish approach would work. "Shall we play cards? Whist, perhaps?"

Nothing.

She tried again. "How about a cup of tea?"

Less than nothing. She yanked hard on the reins of her temper. She wouldn't let him goad her into a tantrum. Forcing her lips into some semblance of a smile, she remarked, "Is that *Treasure Island* you're reading? I must say, I wouldn't have expected a . . . man such as yourself to be—"

He slammed the book shut. "Shut up."

She smiled triumphantly. It might not be much, but it was better than that horrible silence. "I will not."

He flipped the book open again and pinned his gaze to the volume's water-warped pages. "Talk all you want, lady. From now on, I'm deaf as a post to your caterwauling."

Caterwauling! Her hands curled into white-knuckled fists. *Oooh!* He had a lot of nerve, slandering her conversational skills. Him! A big, dirty, disgusting specimen of a man who—

She gathered her wits about her. There was no sense in plunging to his Neanderthal level. Nice, intelligent people could argue without shouting, and she was certainly intelligent. "We are humans, Mr. MacKenna, and humans talk. That's the distinction between us and the animals." Her chin popped to a self-righteous angle, and she peered down at him from her loftier position. "Of course, with some of us, the line blurs."

The barb was delivered so calmly it took Stone Man a moment to realize he'd been insulted. When it sunk in he surged to his feet. "Who the hell are you to find fault with me? I am what I am. If you don't like it, get the hell out. No one invited you here."

Her lips tilted upward in the barest glimmer of a smile. "Not true. You invited me here."

His face turned purple. A small blue vein throbbed at his temple. "Quit goddamn reminding me."

A small sigh escaped her lips. There was no victory in baiting him. It was like taking candy from a baby. The only victory lay in remedying their animosity. Somehow she had to get him to observe the most basic social amenities. Otherwise . . . she shuddered at the thought of "otherwise."

"Mr. MacKenna," she said evenly, "let's try to get along,

shall we? Otherwise it's going to be a long, supremely unpleasant winter.''

His eyes flashed with anger. ''Not for me it won't.''

''Mr. MacKenna, if you could just try to be reasonable, I'm sure we could reach a compromise.''

''If you'd stop flapping your jaw for five seconds, you'd hear me. I don't get along with people. I steer clear of them. Got it?''

She counted to ten and tried again. ''Mr. MacKenna—''

''Quit goddamn calling me that! I'm not the king of England.''

''A relief to Englishmen everywhere, I'm sure.'' The observation slipped out before she could stop it.

''That's it!'' He flung his book toward the makeshift bookrack. It missed, thudding into the sagging canvas wall and landing on the floor with a soft *thunk*. Without sparing a glance at the fallen book, he stood up and peeled off his shirt.

Every muscle in Devon's body tensed. She stared at him with bulging eyes. ''W-What are you doing?''

His pants slid to the floor, puddling around his ankles. His eyes met hers, and there was a wicked glint in the golden orbs. ''Dancing,'' he answered as he bent to untie his workboot laces. Kicking off his boots, he peeled off his stinking socks and tossed them over the sagging clothesline.

Devon had to jump out of the way to avoid getting a faceful of filthy sock. She glared at him, her hands pressed tight to her hips.

He'd peeled down to the dirtiest pair of red long johns Devon had ever seen. Scratching his sweat-stained underarm and bulging groin, he said, ''Night, lady,'' and climbed into bed.

Devon stood rooted to the floor, her mouth agape. It was one thing to decide logically to share a divided bed with this man all winter. It was quite another to crawl between the sheets.

Moving nervously, she plucked up his discarded pants and shirt and hung them up.

He stretched out, the movement strangely graceful and feline for so big a man. With his broad back to the wall, he propped his head in his hand and watched her. In the darkened corner his eerie, whiskey-colored eyes glimmered.

"Quit fussing," he commanded.

She swallowed hard, unable to tear her eyes away from him, from the bed. The scratchy iron-gray blanket covered him like a layer of dirty snow.

The blanket concealed his beard and mustache, but she knew he was smiling at her discomfort. Not a humorous smile, of course. His eyes were as hard as glass and twice as cold. Beneath the blanket, she knew, his smile was a tense, angry slash of lips and nothing more. It was probably the only type of smile his lips knew.

His lips. Without warning she remembered the kiss, remembered how his lips had started out so cold and tight—and how they'd suddenly turned soft, almost welcoming. God, he wasn't planning on trying it again, was he?

"Are you going to wear that dress to bed?"

She stiffened. "A gentleman would turn away."

This time the smile was unmistakable. "Would he?" he drawled. "How dull."

She scanned the tent, looking nervously for a corner of privacy. There was none; no nook or cranny that would shield her from his prying, penetrating eyes. She swallowed dryly.

"No sense putting it off. You strip here, in front of me, or outside—in front of all of them."

Walking stiffly across the tent, she blew out the lantern. It helped a bit. The light went from eerie green and flickering to a dull and dingy brown. Lines blurred in the shadowy gloom, becoming a series of indistinct shapes. His body became a range of mountains and valleys sheathed in metal gray. His breathing, soft and even, blared in the tent's thick quiet.

"When does it get dark around here?" she muttered.

"September," came his answer from the darkened corner of the bed. His voice was rich, deep, mocking.

Gathering as much courage as she could find rattling around in her soul, she shimmied out of her skirt, shirtwaist, and jacket, then slipped a white cotton nightdress over her head and wiggled out of her undergarments.

Letting the lace nightdress flutter around her ankles, she

looked around for her hook. Barely able to make it out in the shadowy gloom, she felt her way along the stove and table to the support beam she was seeking. Careful to shield her corset and petticoat beneath her clothing, she hung her belongings on the hook.

It was time. With one sharp, indrawn breath, she squared her shoulders and headed for the bed. She moved slowly, her bare feet padding silently across the moss-chinked floor. Gingerly she lifted the blanket. A shudder tiptoed up her spine at the thought of sleeping in this bed with this man. Squeezing her eyes shut, she clambered up the rough-hewn plank sides and slithered under the blanket.

She gasped. Good heavens, there were no sheets on the bed. The blanket felt worn and dirty, and it made her legs itch. And it smelled. First thing tomorrow her beautifully embroidered bed linens got unpacked.

She lay stiff as a switch, the blanket clutched up to her chin. Beside her, he settled deeper into the flat, ghastly-smelling mattress. His breathing slowed.

She let out her breath in a long, relieved sigh. He was going to sleep. She was safe. Squeezing her eyes shut, she started to pray. *God almighty, bearer of all light—*

Something scurried up her naked leg. She let out a banshee scream and scrambled out of bed.

He snapped upright. ''What the hell!''

She stared at the bed. ''Insects,'' she whispered. In her imagination, she could see the blanket moving.

Oh, God. She could handle disorder, animosity, filth, but not bugs.

''Christ, is that all? If you're still here next week, you won't even notice them.''

She stood beside the bed for a long time, her eyes glued to the bunched-up blankets. All she could think of were her lovely sheets folded away in her chest and her soft, fresh-smelling bed back home. A wave of hopelessness washed through her. Her body started to tremble.

''You won't make me cry,'' she mouthed to the mountainous man on the bed. ''And you won't make me leave.''

He answered with a soft, even cadence of breath. As she

listened to the sounds of his sleeping, she felt her own eyelids grow heavy. Goodness, it had been a long, exhausting day.

Slowly she inched her back onto the musty, flat mattress. Edging as far away from Stone Man as she could, she pulled the dirty, scratchy wool blanket up to her chin. She lay stiff and unmoving, trying to will her lower lip to stop trembling.

Please God, she thought, let this all be a dream. A horrible, horrible dream.

Devon wakened reluctantly, groggily. The inside of her mouth felt like an old shoe, all dry and caked with sand. For the first time in her life she hadn't brushed her teeth before going to bed. Why?

Memory slapped her in the face. Groaning, she pushed herself to her elbows and blinked, opening her sleep-gritted eyes painfully.

A pair of legs came into focus. Naked, pale, and thin, the legs lay scissored atop a metal-hued wool background.

Good heavens! They were her legs! A sharp cry of dismay shot past her lips. She scrambled upright, shoving her nightdress to her ankles. As the material ballooned around her legs, she brought her knees up and wrapped her arms protectively around her shins.

Cautiously, keeping her lashes lowered, she peered to her right.

He was gone. She straightened, scuttling backward. She hit the rough-hewn spruce headboard hard, feeling it rattle along her spine.

"Morning."

The soft word landed in her lap like a rock. She stiffened instinctively, shooting a nervous glance to her left.

Stone Man was sitting at the table, slurping something from a battered, blue-speckled tin cup. The smell of coffee, strong and pungent, wafted to her nostrils. She breathed deeply, letting the wonderful, familiar scent warm her. "Good morning," she said cautiously. "How long have you been up?"

Rising, he poured a second cup of coffee and offered it to her. "Long enough to do some thinking."

She didn't say what popped into her mind. Instead she

smiled and took the cup of coffee from him. Her fingers curled around the tin. The warm metal had a strangely calming effect. She felt her heart slow down, her breathing normalize.

"Mi—" His big, chiseled face screwed into a tight frown. "Hell," he muttered, "I'll be damned if I'll call you Miss O'Shea."

Devon smiled. "Fair enough. You may call me Devon."

"Whatever. The point is, I've thought and thought about the problem—not something I'm good at, mind you—and I can't see a way out. You can't leave; I can't build you a tent. We're stuck together for the winter."

She sighed. "I know."

"I suppose you think you made a bad deal. God knows, I got shit."

She opened her mouth for a stinging retort.

"Hold your horses," he cut in. "That's not what I mean. Aw, hell, all I wanted was a partner to run my post so I'd be free to come and go as I pleased, to take all the photographs I want to. And what did I get? A damned woman who can't be left alone."

"I'm not an imbecile. I've been on my own since I was fourteen years old. I can certainly manage a few hours a day in your, I mean our, trading post."

"Being on your own in St. Louis—" he said the word like it tasted foul on his tongue "—isn't like being on your own in the Yukon. You're the only white woman for miles, and the valley's filling up faster than a whore's bed. You're not safe alone."

Her chin edged up. "I can take care of myself."

His laugh was harsh, mirthless. "Right. Lady, you can't protect shit."

Her chin dropped into the crevice between her knees. Much as she hated to admit it, he was right. The thought of being alone with men like Midas made her blood run cold. "So what do we do now?"

Pushing suddenly to his feet, he grabbed his mackinaw from its hook and slung it over his shoulder. "You stay out of my store and out of my way. That's what we do."

"Now just a blessed minute, you can't . . ." She stopped. He wasn't listening to her.

Without sparing her a glance he jammed a battered felt hat on his head and stormed out.

She bounced out of bed. Ramming her fists on her hips, she glared at the still-shaking door. Stone Man MacKenna better think twice if he thought he could tell her what to do. She'd come all this way for a chance to start her life over as a post operator, and she was darn well going to do it.

Tossing down the last sip of coffee, she got dressed, snatched up her cleaning supplies, yanked open the tent's narrow wooden door, and marched through the doorway.

The sight that greeted her stopped her dead. She felt like Alice just stepping through the looking glass.

It was a whole new world. There was no trace of yesterday's boggy, stinking, fog-shrouded dung heap. The ground beneath her feet was barely even mushy.

The sky was like she'd never seen it: a deep, sapphire blue that reminded her of a bottomless lake. And the greens! Every tree and bush and shrub shone green in the golden sunlight. Here and there the first spots of autumn color peeked through.

She sucked in her breath, awed. The land was wild, free, beautiful. Tightening her hold on the bucket's handle, she hiked up her skirts and headed for the post.

He was sitting behind that disgustingly lopsided counter again. As before, his head was bowed forward, and he was studying some squares of pale-green glass. His coal-black hair hung limp and dirty around his face, and his blunt fingertips kept up a steady thrumming on the counter. The stove was cold, uninviting.

In one efficient glance she appraised the store.

Her stomach sank. It was even worse than she'd first thought. There were rows and rows of sagging, half-filled counters. Items were clustered together without apparent rhyme or reason, and atop it all lay a thick, grayish haze of dust.

She took a deep breath and immediately wished she hadn't. The tent smelled like rotten food, dirty socks, wet wood, and kerosene.

She tried to hold her breath and talk at the same time. "I've come to work."

His head jerked up. He stabbed her with narrowed, angry eyes. "Go home."

"Shall we have this discussion again?" She trailed her forefinger along the nearest shelf top. A thick layer of dust stuck to her finger.

"Just go."

She walked up to the counter. Blowing the dust off her finger, she smiled as the cloud poofed in his face. "No more talking. I'm here to work."

He eyed her daisy-sprigged dress of lavender muslin and snow-white apron with contempt. "Doing what?"

She patted her bucket. "Cleaning."

"No."

"Yes."

His fist slammed hard onto the lopsided counter. A jar of penny nails crashed to the floor. The glass shattered on impact. A dozen or so rusty nails clanged against the weathered floorboards then rolled into the muddy cracks.

Devon flinched.

"No!" he roared. "My tent already smells like a goddamn hospital. You aren't going to do the same thing to my post."

"Our post." She marched over to the huge cask of water sitting just to the right of the counter.

"You can't use that water for cleaning. That's for drinking. You want water for cleaning? Then start hauling it."

She splashed a ladleful of water into her bucket. Then another.

"Goddamn it," he bellowed. "Don't you listen to anyone?"

She flashed him a smile. "No. It appears to be the one thing you and I have in common."

He must have recognized the determination in her eyes, because he scowled and then plopped his furry chin in his big palm. "Clean all you want," he hissed, "but say one word and you're out." He waited a minute before adding, "Cold."

Chapter Five

She was humming off-key. Way off.

Stone Man hunched his shoulders higher and burrowed his chin into his chest. Christ. She sounded like a throat-shot wolverine, whiny and pitiful.

It was giving him a headache.

He tilted his face just enough to skewer her with his eyes. His gaze was hard, angry. Whoever decided it was wrong to punch a woman hadn't met Devon O'Shea.

He let out a long, low sigh, wishing again that he was the kind of man who used his fists easily. Plopping his elbows on the counter, he eased his chin onto his steepled fingers and wondered why she couldn't at least be normal. Women were supposed to be stupid, sociable, easily intimidated by men.

All he'd wanted was someone to manage the post so he could take photographs. And what had he gotten? An obsessively chatty woman who picked up his boots before they hit the floor and thought like an army general.

Christ . . . He was more tied to the post now than he was before.

He tried to drag his gaze away from her but couldn't. Of their own accord his eyes kept seeking her out. He couldn't help staring at her; she was so damn out of place.

He ground his teeth. If only she knew how ridiculous she looked, with her flowery dress and her curled-up hair. The throbbing in his temples intensified then slid down to the base of his skull and hammered.

Once she'd started cleaning she was like a tornado in the tent, her movements so fast they became a blur of motion. First she'd torn down all his shelving. The second she'd finished that, she'd set about separating the whipsawed planks from the solid wooden blocks that formed the shelving's support. Squares on the left side of the counter, planks on the right.

Then she'd scrubbed down the planks, her small hands whirling on the wood, never stopping or slowing. He'd watched, awestruck, as splinter after splinter lodged in her lily-white flesh. He'd waited expectantly for her shrieks of pain, and again she'd disappointed him. Not once had she complained. Not once. In fact, other than that godawful humming, she hadn't said a word.

Her refusal to talk was starting to bother him.

Frowning, he wove his blunt-edged fingers through the wiry pile of gray-black hair at his chin, tugging thoughtfully. Who would have thought silence could be so irritating?

Extricating his fingers, he snapped open his pocket watch and glanced down at the plain face. One o'clock. She'd been cleaning for four hours already and only half the tent was clean. Clean enough for her highness, anyway.

He groaned aloud. *Shit.*

She peeked up from behind a now-glistening shelf. "What was that, Stone Man?"

"Nothing," he grumbled.

She straightened slowly, pressing her hand to the small of her back and easing the kinks out of her spine. Her small breasts strained against the stiff cotton of her apron. Dark, damp patches of fabric hugged her breasts and circled her underarms.

Stone Man's breath stumbled. She looked different, not nearly so uppity. A few wayward strands of her hair had come loose, curling haphazardly across her sweat-dappled brow. A single bead of sweat slid down the swanlike curve of her throat, disappearing into the ruffled lace at her collar. The fabric clung to her neck like a second skin.

She glanced around, looking for something. "Shall I make some coffee?"

Stone Man yanked down the brim of his hat. His gaze

plummeted, landing hard at his crossed arms. "Do what you want."

He could hear the little *click, click, click* of her pointy heels on the dried plank floor as she bustled up to the stove. Unwanted, a picture of her legs as he'd seen them this morning flashed in his mind. Long and pale, they had looked almost ethereal against the harsh wool of his blanket.

The clicking had stopped. He tensed, waiting for her to break the silence with another of her stupid observations. When she didn't say anything, he reluctantly peeked out from beneath the dirty brim of his hat.

Immediately he wished he hadn't. She was staring right at him, and a small smile was playing at the edges of her mouth.

"Shall I light the stove? Or would you rather do it?"

Something sour swelled in his stomach. *Shall I light the stove?* She sounded like one of those rich English biddies talking to her scullery maid. And that look—it was enough to set his blood boiling. One more of those "I can wrap you around my little finger" smiles and little miss perfect was going to find herself ass-deep in Yukon mud.

"I'll do it," he growled. "It's my stove, I'll light it." Hauling his big body out of his comfortable chair, he shambled over to the cold, forlorn little stove. Taking a match from the tin box nailed to the main support post, he lifted the metal lid and started the fire.

She sank onto the little three-legged stool near the stove and sighed wearily. "I must say, cleaning this . . . tent is proving to be quite a challenge." She patted the coil of hair that had slid sideways and now rested loosely above her ear. "I like challenges. Don't you?"

He grunted in response, lowering himself slowly onto a stool beside her. He watched her out of the corner of his eye. She was starting to wilt. Poor little thing, he thought with a sneer, all that cleaning was too much for her. She probably wouldn't try it again for weeks. Thank God . . .

She popped up. "Well," she said, smoothing the dirty front of her apron. "I'd better get back to work. I couldn't sleep tonight knowing our post was a pigsty."

He stared at her, dumbfounded. "You've got to be kidding."

"Do I look like a woman who jokes about dust?"

His lips pulled into a tight grimace. "No. Or anything else, for that matter. What about the coffee?"

She offered a smile that left him feeling like a child. "That was for you, silly." Then, before he had time to answer, she started it again. Humming.

He snapped to his feet, instinctively taking a fighter's stance: legs braced apart, arms at his sides, hands coiled. *Silly.* She'd called him—*him*—silly.

Enough was goddamn well enough. He grabbed her shoulders and spun her around to face him. He was gratified by the flash of fear in her eyes. Good, he thought. Let her be afraid of me for once. Lowering his face to within inches of hers, he said harshly, "Your half of the post is clean. Leave mine alone."

The fear transformed magically into triumph. "Sorry, Stone Man. I cleaned your half first."

His hold tightened. His mind whirled. What now? Knock her unconscious? That sounded good. Really good. No, too temporary.

The seconds ticked by. They stood inches apart, staring into each other's eyes, his fingers anchored in the softness of her shoulders. Their breath mingled into a harsh, loud duet in the tent's thick quiet.

"Oh, hell," he muttered finally, releasing his hold. He didn't want to hurt her. He just wanted her to shut up. "Just quit the goddamn humming," he added as a pride-soothing afterthought.

"All right."

He tensed immediately, waiting for the follow-up. With her there had to be a but. He waited and . . . nothing. A relieved smile curved his lips. He'd done it; he'd won a round.

When he glanced over at her, she shot him a bright smile—and broke into a rousing, ear-jarring, rendition of "When the corn is waving, Annie."

He stared at her in amazement and slowly started shaking his head. He couldn't help feeling a grudging respect for her gumption. She was smart. "All right," he capitulated. Hum, dance, do card tricks. Just stop that godawful singing."

She practically skipped over to her bucket and plucked it up. "Don't mind if I do."

Devon took a deep, satisfying breath. It was done. The store was spotless. Everything was in its new place; the shelves were orderly and organized.

She dropped the soggy rag into the bucket, wincing as grayish water sloshed over the sides and slopped across her freshly scrubbed floor. Sighing, she pushed slowly to her feet and walked toward the door.

She flipped open the flaps and peered out. "What time is it, Stone Man?" It was the first time she'd spoken in four hours.

He didn't answer.

Turning, she caught sight of her partner and smiled. "You can take the earmuffs off now," she yelled, stomping hard on the floor to get his attention. "I'm done humming."

"Promise?" he shouted. At her swift nod he pulled off the beaver fur muffs.

"What time is it?" she asked again.

He checked his watch. "Five o'clock."

She glanced back outside. "It's so beautiful here," she said, more to herself than to him. It was still full daylight outside. The only hint of the hour was the strange pinkish haze that outlined some of the faraway trees.

"You think so?"

For once Devon detected no sarcasm in his voice. She turned around, facing him. Their eyes met. "I think it's one of the prettiest places I've ever seen. It's so wild, so free. I can see why you'd want to photograph it."

His face seemed to relax, and he almost smiled. "Not many people understand what I see in this land," he confessed in a quiet voice. "I don't think the wildness will last long. So many people are coming in, trampling—"

Suddenly someone rammed into Devon, and she found herself stumbling backward. She caught sight of a dirty tan mackinaw and got a good whiff of body odor laced with whiskey.

"Well, well, ain't this a cozy little scene?" said Midas Magowin when he came to a stop in the center of the tent.

Righting herself, Devon stared at the hunched-over little hobgoblin, her smile fading. The little man was looking at her over his shoulder, studying her contemptuously.

She stifled a sigh. The last thing she needed right now was to face the old man's hatred. It had been a hard day.

"So, Stoneyman," he said, still staring at Devon. "I guess we lost our bets. The bitch is staying."

Devon felt a flash of anger. She waited pointedly for Stone Man to say something. He didn't.

"Are you going to let him talk to me like that?" she demanded of her partner.

Stone Man shrugged. "You want protection? Get a dog."

"Why, you . . ." She clamped her mouth shut. Silently counting to ten, she regained composure then focused a steady stare on Midas. "Are you here for a reason?"

Midas turned his back on her. "Stoneyman," he said pointedly, "I need some soup."

"So, get it."

Midas's banty legs moved like eggbeaters as he stomped over to where the soup used to be. "What the hell . . . Where's the damned soup?"

Devon hurried across the tent.

Stone Man followed Midas. "Just because the place is a little cleaner, Midas, doesn't mean . . ." His words ground to a halt. He stopped dead, his eyes widening, scanning the counters. "What the hell? It's supposed to be here."

Devon could hear the rumble of anger in his voice, and she flinched. Some people didn't like change—at first. She figured Stone Man was one of those people. "H-Here it is," she said, pointing to the last row of shelves.

Both men walked over to where she was standing. They couldn't seem to keep their eyes off the perfectly organized, spotlessly clean expanse of shelving that lay between them.

Stone Man stared down at her. His whole face seemed clenched. "What is it doing over here?"

He was going to like it. He was. Once he got used to the system . . .

"Answer me!"

She wet her lips nervously. "Waiting to be purchased."

"What was wrong with the soup waiting where it was?"

"It was hard to find."

"Not to me. Or my customers."

"Well, it'll be easier for everyone from now on."

Stone Man slammed his beefy arms across his chest. "And why is that?"

Devon couldn't contain her proud smile. "Because everything is in its place. Alphabetically."

A hoarse laugh shot out of Midas's mouth.

"Alphabetically?" Stone Man's voice was a low growl of disbelief. "You organized my store alphabetically?"

A frisson of discomfort crawled up Devon's spine. Why didn't he look pleased? "Y-Yes. It'll make things ever so much easier," she said, knowing she was beginning to babble but unable to stem her words. She always babbled when she was nervous. "You see, the soup is between the soap and the snow glasses. How could it be any simpler? Of course, it was difficult to decide whether the glasses belonged with the G's or with the S's, but I decided—"

"*Most of my customers can't read!* They wouldn't know a *G* if it rose up and bit them on the butt."

Devon's mouth dropped open, and her hand flew up to cover the opening. "Oh, my God, I never thought . . ."

"Get out!" The words were a lion's roar.

She forced her chin higher and squared her shoulders. "No. I made the mistake, and I'll rectify it. All I have to do—"

"*Now.*"

"No."

His cheeks reddened. His eyes bulged. In one move he swept Devon into his arms and barreled for the tent flaps. "Stay here, Midas," he flung her over his shoulder. "I'll be right back."

Midas cackled gleefully. "Okay, Stoneyman. I'll start writin' the ABC's on the walls while you're gone."

Devon kicked and screamed in his arms as he lumbered across Front Street. At their tent he snagged the latchstring in his big hand and yanked. The door flew open, hitting the side support beam with a resounding *thwack* as he barreled through.

She pummeled his hard chest with her fists. "Darn you," she cried, "let me down."

"I'd be glad to."

Before she could find a breath to answer, she was flying through the air like a sack of potatoes. She hit the bed hard, sinking deep into the worn mattress. Dust poofed up from the filthy sheets, stinging her eyes, tickling her nose. She scrambled to her knees, crouching. Every instinct in her body screamed for primal release. She wanted to smack his leering face, to scratch his eerie gold eyes out. Her hands curled into hooks as she glared up at him, her eyes narrowed, angry, her breath coming hard and fast. "You—" she hissed.

He swooped down on her, taking her wrists in his hands. Her words died in a gasp. His hold burned, twisting her fingers until they relaxed. "Don't even think of doing battle with me," he said harshly, his eyes glittering like topaz shards. "I'm not like the men you've known in St. Louis. I don't follow society's stupid rules." His voice dropped to a hush. "And I step on people who do."

His words were like a bucket of icy water on the fire of her anger. He meant it, she realized grimly. He *would* step on her, and up here no one would care.

It was sobering and frightening to realize how powerless and alone she really was. She was a woman unused to being afraid, a woman used to being in control. With effort she forced down her pride. This wasn't the time to react on a gut level. She needed to think, to analyze her predicament and devise a reasonable compromise.

"All right," she said shakily. "I won't do battle with you. I concede your greater strength. Now would you please let go of my wrists?"

His fingers flipped open. She jerked her hands back then laced her fingers together and laid them in her lap. Her neck bowed. Staring at her hands, so small and white against the wrinkled cotton of her apron, she took a deep, fortifying breath.

"Devon?"

She didn't look up. She wasn't ready to meet the mocking triumph in his eyes.

His forefinger found the hollow triangle beneath her chin and forced her chin upward.

The look in his eyes wasn't what she'd expected. He looked old, and infinitely sad. And almost sorry. Her heart skipped a beat, and she couldn't help feeling a spark of hope. But then, she reminded herself, it never had taken much to give her hope. She'd always been an optimist—even during the bad days of her childhood.

"Devon," he said softly, "don't make us any worse enemies than we have to be."

She looked directly into his eyes, seeing for the first time the tiny mahogany flecks that darkened the amber orbs. "Why must we be enemies at all?"

The sadness in his eyes vanished, and they once again turned cold and distant. "It's my way. I don't like people."

She answered without thinking. "That doesn't make sense. I don't like beets, but when my Aunt Edna used to serve them on Thanksgiving, I ate a whole plateful."

He jerked his finger back as if burned. "*I* don't make sense?" he asked incredulously. "I don't even know what you're babbling about half the time."

Devon realized her error instantly. *Darn!* What was it about him that disconnected her brain every time she opened her mouth? If she wanted to get through to him, she had to jam lots of meaning into a few well-chosen words. Babbling about Aunt Edna's beets was definitely a tactical error.

"I don't care whether you choked on every one of your aunt's slimy beets at Thanksgiving. I just want you to shut up. Is that asking so much?"

A question! He'd actually asked her a question. Now they were getting somewhere. She beamed. "Well, since you've asked, let me answer. You're my partner and my . . . tent-mate; we can't spend seven months in total silence. I rather enjoy talking, and . . ." She stopped. He was looking at her as if she were a rabid dog.

"Keep away from me, Devon, and keep away from my store. In fact, if you take one dainty little step into my post again, you'll find yourself swimming in the Yukon River. Am I understood?"

She gritted her teeth. Enough trying to be polite and civilized. It was time to set down some ground rules. "I understand you, Stone Man. The question is, I imagine, whether you understand me."

"Understanding things is your game, lady. I don't give a shit whether life makes sense. All I want is to be left alone."

"You're right, I do like things orderly, and if you think a few sharp words and bed-tosses will allow you to set the tone of this relationship, you're sadly mistaken."

"Relationship?" The word popped out of his mouth like an unexpectedly lost tooth. He stared at her for an interminable second, his eyes glittering dangerously. His mouth opened, and he pointed at her accusingly; then his mouth slammed shut. "Forget it. You're not worth the trouble." Spinning on his heel, he stormed out of the tent.

"Go ahead and run, darn you," she muttered after him, jumping off the bed. "You can't go far enough."

She stomped her foot in frustration. They'd come close, that moment when his eyes had been so sad, so lost. If only they'd been able in that second to say the right things to each other.

She was normally so good at communicating. Everybody said so. At home people had come for miles just to get her clearheaded advice.

That was the root of the problem, she decided. She was used to understanding people, and she couldn't make heads nor tails of Cornelius "Stone Man" MacKenna. Why was he so angry all the time? It didn't make any sense for him to hate her so. In truth she was the one with the grievance. She was the one who'd traveled thousands of miles to share a filthy hovel with a man who never bathed and talked less than a cedar tree.

She was the one who ought to be mad, darn it.

He'd gotten what he wanted. He had a partner and one more capable and trustworthy than most. What had he expected when he placed the advertisement? Had he thought a partner wouldn't change his life at all?

Suddenly everything became clear, the way it always did when she reasoned a problem out. She was taking the wrong tack. She would never get through to Stone Man by being calm and logical, because he didn't respond to reason. It was instinct that guided his life and his actions.

The answer was simple. All she had to do was make his life a living hell. Make him beg for a compromise.

A smile curled her lips. He was like a reluctant mule, and everyone knew a mule would move sooner or later. You just had to get his attention.

Chapter Six

Devon's scream of pain bounced off the sagging canvas walls. Cursing, she threw her hammer. It spiraled through the air, end-over-end, and cracked into the rough-hewn spruce table, leaving a deep, half-moon–shaped indentation in the wood before it clattered uselessly to the floor.

She stared at her battered thumb. Pain shot in streaks up to her wrist.

It was all *his* fault, she thought grimly. For the past week she and Stone Man had lived like soldiers in an armed camp. Silent, hostile, wary.

She'd tackled her plan to bring him to his knees with the ambition of a general and the determination of a foot soldier. For seven interminably long days she hadn't spoken. Not one single word. Even when he grunted some unintelligible syllable to her, she hadn't responded. She hadn't spoken or smiled or even glanced his way.

And who had noticed her sullen silence? She had.

She'd also tried—subtly, of course—to poison him. Every meal she'd cooked had been worse than pig slop. Last night's supper, in fact, had been the worst meal she'd ever served: hard-as-a-rock pilot bread, cold canned beans, evaporated apricots, and gooey, half-cooked rice. It had been disgusting enough to make her gag.

He'd wolfed down two helpings, burped loudly, then picked up his book and started reading.

Pain brought her mind back to the present. She sucked lightly at her thumb's throbbing tip. At the rate she was going, she'd be thumbless before she finished building her armoire. She couldn't seem to get the thing balanced enough to stand up on its own.

The hell with this, she decided suddenly. Why was she wasting her time trying to get the stupid thing balanced? What did she care? It wasn't as if an unbalanced armoire would ruin the tent's decor.

Why not just nail it to the wall and be done with it? Once she'd decided she moved quickly, shoving the rickety, four-planked structure into the tent's corner.

She pushed the right side smack against the tent's half-wood, half-canvas wall. When it was perfectly aligned she retrieved her hammer and nailed the plank in place. Then she stood back, swiping the sheen of sweat from her brow and eyeing her creation.

Not bad. Normally, of course, one wouldn't consider four planks nailed together an armoire. But then, nothing was normal in the Yukon.

Later, with her clothes carefully hung on her new cloth-covered hooks and her shoes and underclothes hidden in burlap-lined boxes, she felt better.

Her life was in order. The books she'd brought with her were shelved, her hats were boxed, the bed was fitted with fresh linen, and the food, stored outside in a heap Stone Man called his "cache," was organized faultlessly. She had folded, scrubbed, beaten, built, and boxed until her fingers were raw.

It was time to move on. Time to get the rest of her life in order.

She knew what she had to do. Living with Stone Man the past week had been the worst time of her life. Worse even than living in the shadow of her alcoholic, abusive father.

As a young girl she'd always rationalized her father's verbal abuse. He was drunk, or overworked, or it was his way of showing affection. But she wasn't a little girl now, and she was incapable of lying to herself.

It was a lie to think she could live another day with Stone Man. She couldn't; at least, not the way things had been for the past seven days. Her nerves were frayed.

She'd come halfway across the world to start a new life,

and what was she doing? Reliving her childhood, except that the drunken brawls had turned into silent standoffs.

She'd had enough. She was a post operator, by God, and the sooner Stone Man realized that, the better off they'd all be.

Grabbing a flower-dappled straw hat from her new armoire, she jammed it onto her head. Resolve stiffened her spine and shone in her green eyes as she plucked up her skirts and headed for the door.

The silence was over.

The peace was over.

Little miss levelheaded barged into the post like she owned the place—which, unfortunately, she did. Every muscle in Stone Man's body tensed. Hairs on the back of his neck jumped to attention, quivering like divining rods.

She came to a halt dead center then planted her fists on her hips and leveled a steady, no-nonsense stare on him. Her determination was a tangible cloud between them. There was no mistaking her manner. She was a woman on a mission.

"Hello, Stone Man."

He shoved the battered old miner's hat off his furrowed brow and met her gaze. "I thought it was too good to last."

She studied him warily. "What do you mean?"

He smiled. Shaking her calm was a small victory, but in this war he had to take his winnings as they came. "The last week's been killing you," he said. "Your face has been so red and pinched from keeping quiet, I thought sure you were going to explode."

The grim line of her lips softened. "So, you noticed."

"I'm dumb, not blind."

She moved toward him. "You're not dumb, and I'm sorry for the times I implied otherwise. Shall I make some coffee?"

She was acting slicker than spilled oil, and it made Stone Man's gut clench nervously. But what could a little coffee hurt? He studied her for a moment longer, then answered, "Sure."

Why not? She could make all the coffee she wanted; she could even yap all she wanted. He'd already reached that inescapable conclusion. He couldn't hold her down forever. She was just too damn bouncy.

But this time he was ready for her. He'd been mentally preparing for this conversation for days, knowing she'd ultimately demand her place.

He shivered at the thought of spending the days beside her at the post and the nights beside her in the bed. He'd have a headache all winter long.

"You know, Stone Man," she said, lighting the fire. "I could help you here."

There it was: the offer to help. He swallowed hard, wishing he knew how to pray. This would be a good time to ask the big man for some help.

"Stone Man?"

Her voice wrenched him from his thoughts. He had to say something. Now. Instantly he remembered the plan he'd formulated last night: Plan A. Create a diversion.

He cleared his throat. "How about planting a garden? That'd be good for you. Think of all the dirt you could shove around and then clean up."

"It's almost autumn. Gardening is done in the spring, and besides I'm here to work the post."

He squeezed his eyes shut, trying to ignore the headache that had burst to life at the base of his skull. One sentence and the plan he'd worked so hard on was fodder.

Unconsciously he started rubbing his temples, listening to the pitter-patter of her pointy-heeled shoes on the hard plank floor. The noise was getting louder—she was heading his way. He tensed, trying to remember Plan B.

"I'll make you a deal."

His eyes flipped open. "Ha! I've made enough bad deals with you to last a lifetime."

"Then make a good one," she said, her low, throaty voice thick with challenge.

There it was, that "I can wrap you around my finger" smile. He clenched his teeth. "Like what?"

"Like this: I'll bet you I can improve business."

The coffeepot started to boil. The lid clattered, bouncing atop the aging tin pot, and steam puffed into the dust-laden air. She moved quickly, easing the pot off the direct heat and pouring two cups.

He watched her spare, economical movements, awed. She was a study in self-restraint. He could see it in her motions, in the determined set to her chin. She'd probably never taken a breath or a step without thinking about it, without planning out her next movement.

"Put your money where your mouth is, Stone Man," she said when she'd turned back around. "If I can't do something to improve our business, I'll stay away from the post until spring."

It sounded too good to be true. He eyed her suspiciously. "What happens in the spring?"

"I'll leave when the river thaws. No matter what."

A frown creased his brow. She was outthinking him again, he could feel it. Damn! Why couldn't he think faster? "Who gets to decide whether you've helped business?"

Her eyes met his straight on. "You do."

"Come on," he said, "you're not that stupid."

"Try me."

His head told him to laugh in her face. She had to be outthinking him again. But his instinct was loud and clear: She couldn't win. She was counting on him to act honorably. *Ha!* He couldn't lose. As always, he went with his gut feelings.

"All right, you've got four days to do something that boosts business. If you don't find a way to help, you're out. Fair enough?"

She smiled, a dazzling display of white teeth that made his gut sting with warning. "Fair enough. Now," she said, looking around, "I'll need some supplies. Wax, jars, things like that. . . ."

Stone Man felt all the tension slither out of his spine. A slow grin spread across his face. She was going to cook! He thought about the horrible pastelike rice she'd served him last night. And that pilot bread—one well-thrown chunk could kill a small dog at fifty paces.

She'd cooked one good meal, that first night. A fluke. It had to be; no one *chose* to eat bad food.

Yes, he'd done the right thing. As usual, his instincts were right. The men in the Yukon wouldn't pay for Devon's cooking. He'd choked down her grim suppers to keep her quiet. For him silence trumped taste.

But not to the rest of the men. They might be desperate, but they weren't desperate enough to eat her cooking. Even Midas could make passable biscuits.

He spat a huge wad of tobacco, his grin broadening as it hit the floor and splattered across her pointy-toed blue shoes. In four days his worries would be over. He chuckled to himself. "Here, Devon, let me help you . . ."

The minute Stone Man entered his tent that night, he knew something was wrong. Real wrong. He stopped just inside, his fingers tightening instinctively on the rawhide latchstring that opened the door.

The tent was leaning. A frown creased his brow. "What the—"

"Hello, Stone Man, welcome home," Devon said brightly, helping him out of his dusty old mackinaw. Folding it carefully over her arm, she bustled toward the hook, her skirts swishing atop the wood plank floor. Involuntarily his gaze slid down her ramrod-stiff back and landed at her hips. The rounded curves swayed enticingly beneath her crisp, no-nonsense green skirt.

It took him a moment to remember what was bothering him. He wet his suddenly dry lips and asked, "Why is the tent leaning?"

She stopped short. The lace bottom of her skirt shuddered. "Leaning? The tent?"

He noticed the sudden stiffening of her shoulders, and he grimaced. "Yes, Devon, the tent is leaning. Why?"

She turned around slowly. An unusual pinkness tinged her high cheekbones. "Well," she drew out the word, "it could be my armoire."

He frowned. "Armwaaa? What the hell's an armwaaa? And why would it make my tent lean?"

She stepped to the left, clearing his view. Directly behind her, where his tent corner used to be, there was now a huge, lopsided square. It looked like a half-smashed soup crate that someone had ripped the bottom out of.

His eyes narrowed, sweeping the dilapidated frame. It was nailed to the wall. Nailed. He shook his head, raking his fingers through the morass of black hair at his forehead. How could someone so smart in some things be so stupid in others?

"I was thinking," came her nervous voice, "that a curtain across the front might help, maybe chintz."

"Chintz?" he echoed, gritting his teeth. "Who said you could put up your damn woman shit in my tent?" He spun around, heading for the door.

She threw herself in front of him, barring the exit with her body. "Oh, no, you don't. I've made supper—and you're going to sit down like a gentleman and eat it." Her eyes swept him from head to foot in one desultory glance. "Do the best you can, anyway."

His face twisted angrily at her jibe. Goddamn her for thinking she was better than him! Leaning forward, he planted his big hands on either side of her and lowered his face to within inches of hers. She straightened, meeting his cold-eyed gaze with one of her own. Their fast-paced breathing mingled, synchronized, and pounded through the tent's silence.

The moment multiplied. Neither of them moved, neither backed down.

Devon cleared her throat. "This is ridiculous. Are you staying for supper or not?"

He *felt* ridiculous. How the hell did she do that to him so easily? "Fine," he spat the word.

She twirled out from under his arms and bustled over to the stove where she immediately began her evening ritual, the dance with the Yukon stove, or, as he'd come to call it, the sparrow stuck in a glass box routine. She dipped and dove, opened and closed, tasted and tested, poked and prodded.

All that work for food that tasted like cow dung.

It made him sweat just watching her work. Walking to the table, he lowered himself onto the nearest stump chair and plopped his elbows on the table. A soft, sweet scent caressed his nostrils, and he looked up. She'd put a dented-up soup can full of pink fireweed on the table.

He groaned. *Home Sweet Home.*

The next thing he knew, a speckled blue plate was flying his way. It bumped across the pockmarked table. His hand shot out to stop it, and as he did a half-cooked piece of bacon jumped over his elbow and landed in a greasy streak in his lap.

He slapped the bacon strip on his plate and then looked up. Across the table the very picture of well-bred innocence was smiling at him. "Bon appetit, Stone Man."

They were the last words spoken in the tent for over two hours. By the time she'd finished the dishes, Devon's nerves were shot, shredded to bits by the cursed silence.

Wringing out her dishtowel, she hung it over the clothesline. Smoothing back the curls that had fallen in her face, she glanced at him. He was sitting casually on the big stump chair, his long legs crossed at the ankles. Beside him a small kerosene lantern flickered gaily, painting the drab tent with dancing shards of red and gold. A leather-bound book lay open in his big, dirty hands.

Her gaze lifted to his face. The hard, chiseled planes of his cheekbones were softened by the dim evening sun, and his eyes, usually so hard and cold, were bright. He was staring at the pages of the book, transfixed.

Devon felt something squeeze her heart. He looked almost like a friendless young boy, lost in the adventurous tale of his first story. . . .

A hundred thoughts rose in her mind, but the most important one was *maybe*. Maybe she'd been wrong about him. Maybe he wasn't the Neanderthal, filthy, foul-tempered hulk he appeared to be. Maybe underneath all that dirty, board-stiff black hair and greasy clothes, there was a man, with a man's heart.

She wanted so badly to find some redeeming quality within him; something that would allow them to reach a compromise. Something that would allow them to survive the winter.

She'd try again to communicate with him. In fact she'd keep trying until they reached a settlement. She had to. Her sanity depended on it. There was no way she could survive a winter trapped in this rabbit hole of a tent with a cold, silent hulk of a man.

"What are you reading tonight?" She forced her voice to sound light.

He didn't even look up.

Gliding over to where he sat, she peeked over his shoulder. "Ah, *The Red Badge of Courage.* Rather . . . bleak, don't you think?"

"No."

A start. She touched his hair, letting a long black strand coil around her pale forefinger. "You know, Stone Man, a haircu—"

He belched.

She winced. "Very nice. Anyway, as I was saying—"

"I didn't think interrupting would help."

"You were right. Now then, as I was saying, a haircut and shave wouldn't hurt you a bit. Why, you might even be less . . . uh, I mean more attractive."

He snapped the book shut. "Now that's something I give a shit about. Being attractive." He let out another belch, spat a wad of tobacco onto the floor, then stood up and started disrobing.

Streams of gray-brown spit splattered the crisp lace pleats at the bottom of Devon's skirt. Her eyes widened in disbelief as she stared at the disgusting stains on the fabric she'd labored to iron.

She yanked on his sleeve, using all her body weight to spin him around to face her. "That's it," she hissed at point-blank range. "No more. I've tried to be nice, but now I'm laying down some rules, mister. One more spit on our floor, and you'll be sorry."

He smirked. "Yeah? How's that?"

She smiled. "I'll start singing after every meal."

His smile faded. "You wouldn't."

"Actually, I find my own voice quite pleasant."

"Fine."

"Good. Oh, and another thing. You're not crawling between my clean sheets in those disgustingly filthy long johns."

Anger flashed in his eyes. "The hell I'm not."

She slammed her fists on her hips and glared up at him, her chin jutting defiantly. "The hell you are."

For a long minute they stared at each other; then Stone Man growled, "Fine. You win." Grabbing one of the blankets off of the bed, he swirled the iron-gray wool around his body like a cloak and dropped onto the cold, hard floor.

She stared at him, amazed. "You'd rather sleep on that freezing floor than put on clean long johns?"

He got settled under the blanket. "The floor's warmer than you are, lady. Now shut up and let me sleep."

Chapter Seven

The light hurt her eyes. Devon rolled onto her stomach and yanked the blanket over her head, burrowing deeper into her gray woolen tomb. She didn't want to wake up; lately she much preferred her dream-filled nights to her horror-ridden days.

Then she smelled it: freshly made coffee. She sucked in a deep breath, smelling more musty wool than simmering brew, but her nose was not easily fooled. The aroma was there, hovering just beyond the edges of her nostrils. Her mouth watered.

She inched her way to the headboard. Still under the covers, she shoved her white cotton nightdress to her ankles and sat up.

He was in his usual place, sitting at the table, his long legs crossed at the ankles in front of him, his big fingers curled around a dented blue tin cup. As usual he was studiously avoiding her.

She tugged at the lace stand-up collar of her prim nightgown and cleared her throat. "Good morning, Stone Man."

He looked up, peering at her over the rim of his cup. His eyes were puffed and swollen, and the pupils were red. "Morning," he grumbled.

Devon felt a little trill of malicious humor at his obvious discomfort. Last night had probably been awful for him. Dust in the eyes and nose, a cold, rock-hard floor bruising his body, little creepy-crawly things exploring his flesh. A triumphant smile tugged at her lips. Maybe tonight the clean long johns wouldn't seem so abhorrent.

"Breakfast is ready," he said unexpectedly, setting down his cup and pushing to a stand.

For the first time she noticed that the table was set—in a manner of speaking—with two plates, two forks, and two tin cups. No tablecloth, of course, and no napkins. Still, he had made an effort. She smiled.

Stone Man turned his attention to the big frying pan on the stove.

Thank God. A few moments of privacy. She flung back the blanket, jumped out of bed, and darted to her armoire. Yanking her red flannel wrapper off the hook, she slipped her arms into the puffy, lace-trimmed sleeves and quickly buttoned the twenty-two pearl buttons that marched from foot to throat.

Delving through her well-ordered boxes, she pulled out her worsted bootees and slipped them on. Covered from head to foot, she sighed with relief. She was decent.

"This is wonderful," she said as she headed for the table. Taking her seat, she poured herself a cup of the fragrant, steaming coffee. "It's so thoughtful of you to make breakfast."

"I was losing weight."

Stifling a smile, she took a quick gulp of coffee. "Oh? I'm sorry to hear that."

"Hand me that coffee can, would you?" He pointed to a big red can hanging from the wooden beam that bisected the stovepipe.

She untied the can and let it fall into her hands. Immediately a strange, almost alcoholic odor hit her nostrils. She gagged, shoving the can at him. "W-What is it?"

"Sourdough." He slapped a spoonful of the malodorous dough into his batter. She watched, repelled, as he spooned his goopy mixture onto the flat iron griddle, carefully forming four perfect circles. In a matter of moments the flapjacks had turned a deep golden brown.

He tossed a few flapjacks and a strip of crisp bacon on her plate and handed it to her. "Bon uppitty," he said, practically diving into his own heaping plate.

She lifted her fork, prodding the flapjacks as if she expected them to move. They didn't. She leaned over the plate, sniffing daintily. No odor, either.

"They're flapjacks, not perfume. Just eat the damn things."

Her head snapped up. Their eyes locked. A slow blush of shame crept across her cheeks. He'd been nice enough to make breakfast, and all she'd done was criticize. "Sorry. I didn't mean to offend you. It's just—"

"Lady," he said in a weary voice, "in the Yukon we eat three things in the winter. Beans, bacon, and sourdough flapjacks. You might as well learn to like them now."

Grimacing tightly, she speared a bite-size chunk of flapjack and popped it into her mouth. She chewed hesitantly, then faster, a smile darting across her face. "Why, they're delicious."

"Good." The word came out of his overstuffed mouth as "goo."

She couldn't help staring. He was sitting all hunched over with his big arm slung around his plate as if he expected it to be yanked away at any moment. He'd swirled together all the food, and the result was a gooey pile of red-brown.

A delicate shudder swept through her body. God, he was eating it all mushed together.

His fork froze in midair, and Devon felt his eyes on her. "You got a problem?"

Her gaze plummeted to her own carefully ordered plate. "No."

The fork started moving again. "Good." Shoveling in the last bite, he let his fork clang to the table and pushed to his feet.

She set her fork down silently and looked up at him, wishing desperately that she had a napkin with which to dab her mouth. Just watching him eat made her feel . . . dirty. "Leaving already?"

He wiped the greasy breakfast leavings from his beard and lips with the back of his sleeve. "Yep." The word came out in a grumbling belch.

"Four days from now I'll be coming with you."

His answer was a grunt. Grabbing his summerweight coat

and hat, he started for the door. As his fingers curled around the latchstring, he stopped.

Devon frowned. His eyes were focused intently on the door, as if he were thinking about something. Thinking hard.

"Uh . . . go ahead and wash my other long johns," he mumbled finally. Before the words were out of his mouth, he yanked on the string, jerked the door open, and barreled through the opening.

The door slammed shut behind him, setting off a rattle in the log support beams. Devon smiled to herself. Cleanliness. It wasn't much; but it was a start.

Later, with her hair bundled neatly out of her eyes, her teeth brushed, and the tent cleaned, Devon stared into her armoire, wondering what to wear. Finally deciding on a plain white shirtwaist with a stand-up collar and a navy-blue cotton skirt, she set about dressing.

As her skirt billowed around her head and fluttered to the floor, there was a knock at the door.

She froze. Clutching the shirtwaist over her chemise, she glanced nervously to her right. "Who is it?"

"Father Michaels," came a squeaky male voice.

"Father? As in *Father*?"

The squeaky voice chuckled. "Well, I don't have any wee ones, if that's what ye be askin', lass."

"Just a moment, Father," she said, slipping into her shirtwaist. Tying a little blue bow at her throat, she hurried to the door and opened it.

Her first impression of the man standing on her doorstep was of an abandoned baby bird. He was small—tiny, really—and his little round face was dominated by a long beak of a nose and eyes that seemed far too large.

His deformed body reemphasized her first impression. He seemed to be leaning to the left, and his head, with its unruly mop of bright-red curls, rested stiffly against his raised shoulder. It was as if some unkind hand had simply twisted him.

But it was his eyes that caught and held her attention; they were a bright, lively blue, bubbling with mirth and an unmistakable joy for life. His good humor immediately affected

Devon, dispelling her dour mood of the past few days. She felt as if a breath of spring had washed through her soul.

"Come in, Father. I'm Devon O'Shea."

"And I'm Father Michaels, resident saver of lost and wanderin' souls. I heard about ye the minute I got back into camp this mornin', I did. A lady can't expect to enter the Yukon unnoticed."

Devon's smile faded. "So I've learned. Come in. Would you like a cup of coffee?"

His face crinkled into a big smile. "I would indeed." He limped awkwardly into the tent. The thump of his walking stick on the plank floor vibrated through the canvas walls.

She hurried along behind him, pulling out one of the heavy stump chairs.

"My thanks, lass," he said, sinking slowly onto the hard wooden surface.

As she poured the coffee, Devon confessed, "I'm not a Catholic, Father."

He chuckled. "Aye, and if I were in the Yukon a'waitin' on Catholics, I'd be freezin' me butt—er, backside—off for nothin'. I been up here far nigh on five years, and I don't think I've met a Catholic yet. Although," he said with a wink, "I been hearin' tales that there's a family of them up near Rampart."

She poured two cups and set them on the table, then sat on the stool next to his. "And what brought you up to this godforsaken wasteland in the first place?"

"God forsakes no place, lassie, and ye ought to know better than to suggest such a thing."

She was instantly contrite. "Sorry."

A puckish grin swept his face. "Aye, I know ye are. Anyway, I came up here to find me brother. I found him . . ." His strong voice strained. "He was livin' in that cesspool of a city, Skagway, with an old Indian woman. Clean mad for the yellow muck, he was. He died about a month after I found him, and me, well, I saw plenty of work that needed doin' up here. So I stayed."

She smiled wryly. "I can understand that; I've only been here a week, and already I've seen a few souls in need of assistance."

"How's your own soul, lassie? It's been a hard time of it ye've been havin', from what I hear."

Devon's smile quivered. It had been so long since anyone had asked how she was, how she felt. So long since she'd been allowed to be weak. Inexplicably tears welled in her eyes. She turned away quickly.

His bony hand smothered hers. "What is it, lassie?"

She swallowed the lump in her throat. Her tenuous hold on control loosened; it felt as if part of her soul were thawing. A single tear splashed on the father's hand. "I don't know," she whispered, "I never cry."

"Aah. Then I'll be guessin' that's reason all by itself. We all need a good cry now and then. Even the strongest of us."

She lifted her head slowly, searching Farther Michaels's creased, pointy face. The compassion in his eyes was like a steel band closing around her heart. More tears clogged in her throat. Suddenly the weight on her shoulders seemed crushing, suffocating. She needed desperately to talk.

A little hiccup escaped her compressed lips. "It's been a . . . difficult week, Father. Stone Man and I don't get along well."

His hand squeezed hers once then let go. "I was thinkin' it might be so. Stone Man, he's hard. Hard and lonely."

"Lonely?"

"Aye. What state would ye expect to find a man in if that man had ne'er had a true mother or father, ne'er had a home to call his own, ne'er known peace?"

She sniffled loudly, dabbing at her eyes with her sleeve. "What do you mean?"

Father laid a hand on the table top and pushed awkwardly to a stand. Burrowing through his oversized mackinaw, he pulled out a couple of creased, well-handled photographs and handed them to her. She took the aged pictures carefully.

The first was a picture of an old log cabin in an overgrown field. Her eyes scanned the gloomy picture quickly then shifted to the second one.

Involuntarily her gaze returned to the cabin. There was something about it, something vaguely disquieting. She studied the photograph carefully. The cabin was old, dilapidated, and the flower-laced grass came almost up to the windowsills. She could almost *see* the whisper of the wind in the flowers.

It was abandoned. Somebody had built this cabin, lovingly, with his own hands, and then for some reason he had left. Why? Had he died? Had his family?

The photograph gave no answers.

Uneasy with her discovery, she turned her attention to the second picture. It was a portrait of a well-dressed old woman sitting stiff-backed in her favorite chair. She looked like a queen.

But again something was wrong. Devon's eyes narrowed with concentration. What was amiss?

It came to her suddenly. The old woman was alone; she'd always been alone. There was no wedding ring on her skeletal, dark-veined finger, no pictures of children on the intricately flocked wall behind her. There wasn't even a faithful dog at her side. Had she been alone always? Had she wanted it that way?

Good-old-spinster-aunt Devon. The thought flashed through Devon's mind with lightning speed, bringing with it a stab of pain so acute she almost cried out. The photograph slipped through her shaking fingers and fluttered to the table. *This woman, the look in her eyes . . . It's me. It's my future.*

"Are ye all right, lass? Ye look a wee bit pale all of a sudden."

She barely heard the words. Of their own accord her fingers crept back to the photograph, gliding gently over the woman's gaunt features. She could feel the old lady's pain. She clenched her jaw, refusing to give in to tears.

Most of the time Devon accepted her loneliness, refusing to acknowledge the hollowness in her soul. She would always be separate, isolated; she knew that. It was a choice she'd made long ago, on the day of her mother's death.

And yet sometimes, like now, the need to hold a child of her own swelled, slicing through her shell of self-control like a dagger.

The photograph brought it all back to her, made her ache for all the comforts she'd never have. A husband's soft kiss, a child's toothless grin, a hand to hold hers through the cold, waning years of her life.

She swallowed, tasting the thickness of unshed tears in her throat. Just like the woman in the picture, she was alone and lonely.

"Lass?"

She heard the father's query through the fog of her own thoughts. Snapping herself back to the present, she snatched up the picture and slammed it facedown on the table. "I'm fine, Father. Truly," she answered quickly; perhaps too quickly, for she couldn't quite still the quiver in her throaty voice. "Why did you show me these?"

"Stone Man took them."

"My God, I wouldn't have thought him capable of such . . . depth."

"There's more to Stone Man than meets the eye. He's angry all the time—mad as the dickens, really. But I think it's because he feels things deeper than most folks, and because he's afraid."

She looked at him askance. "Afraid? Stone Man?"

He nodded solemnly. "Aye, he's afraid to need anyone. Such a feelin' makes for a lonely existence. And," he looked at her intently, "for what it's worth, I'd trust him with me life."

She stared at the photograph of the cabin, trying desperately to catch a glimpse of the man behind the camera. It was the most powerful image she'd ever seen and so unlike the man she'd lived with for a week. It didn't make sense. How could the soul of an artist and a poet be housed in the body of an antisocial, foulmouthed Neanderthal?

"Why? Why is he so mad at . . . everyone?"

"God's truth, I don't know." He sank back into his seat. Taking a sip of coffee, he continued. "There's talk, just talk, mind ye, of a woman in his past. A bad woman. And there's speculation on somethin' darker, but I don't know what it is."

"He wouldn't like me knowing this."

The old man shook his head. "He doesn't talk to anyone except Bear, and I don't suppose they talk about feelings. Men come to the Yukon to get away from talkin', and Stone Man more than most."

"Yes," she said softly, "he does value silence."

The priest's head gave one birdlike little twitch, as if it were trying, futilely, to upright itself. When he spoke his squeaky voice was strangely subdued. "Wouldn't ye value silence if ye were afraid of gettin' to know folks?"

She thought about that for a moment. "Yes . . . maybe I would."

He set down his cup with an audible clink and slowly maneuvered himself to a stand. "Well, lass," he said, adjusting the collar of his coat, "I'd best be gettin' along. There's souls aplenty to be savin' in this land."

Impulsively she took his hand. "Thank you, Father. I'll make it work with Stone Man. I will."

A bright smile lit the old man's face. "Aye, I was hopin' ye'd say that. Ye got spirit, lass. It takes a special woman to get to the Yukon." He squeezed her hand. "And an even more special one to stay. God be with ye."

About an hour after the priest left, Devon was ready to begin her quest. She closed the tent door behind her and took a deep breath of the fresh late-summer air. Her lungs filled with the sweet, soft scent that blew along the Yukon River. Strangely, it smelled like spring back home, though the first colorings of fall were already tinting the trees.

Adjusting her khaki-colored felt hat, she lowered the fine white veil across her eyes. The bright landscape muted. Her gloved hands closed tighter around her lard tin's metal handle; the thin wire bit into her palms. With her other hand, she lifted her skirt and headed for the hills.

The lichen-covered ground bounced beneath her feet like a bed of springs. Her footsteps evaporated almost immediately. Though the land was frozen solid no more than twelve inches below the surface, it seemed determined to have a life all its own.

Halfway to her destination, she stopped, setting down her bucket and letting her gaze wander. The hill was a wash of brilliant colors: scarlet, gold, green. Firewood in full pink-red bloom swept across the landscape like the stroke of an artist's brush. And the aroma! She breathed in deeply, savoring the jumbled floral scent.

Even the ground was a palette that looked more like spring

than late summer. Tiny spots of color dotted the greenish-gold lichen moss. Pink, red, blue, yellow—all the colors of the rainbow danced in the soft breeze, scenting the air.

How could she ever have thought it ugly? Or desolate?

When she reached the low-lying shrubs that hemmed the hillside, thrill set her heart thumping. She found what she was looking for.

After seven days in the Yukon and nearly two months en route, the panorama spread out in front of her made her knees weak. She licked her lips in anticipation. Fresh blueberries!

She grinned. Stone Man didn't have a chance.

Smack!

"Darn it!" Devon murdered another one of the little beggars with her hand. Her cheek stung from the impact, and she was certain there were finger imprints on her skin. The Yukon mosquitoes were bigger than buggies. She couldn't hear anything over the drone of their maneuvers.

She gritted her teeth. Why in the blazes had she picked the prettiest netted hat instead of the biggest? The darn gauze was more an invitation than a deterrent. In fact she was certain that a few of the flying combatants were engaged in a rousing game of storm the veil.

Smack! She slapped herself. Hard.

She couldn't take much more. She was getting light-headed from lack of blood. The mosquitoes were taking at least a quart a minute.

She glanced down at her bucket. It was seven-eighths full. Then she looked at the apron she'd also filled.

Good enough. Stone Man hadn't said how much she had to increase business—or for how long. There weren't more than twenty-five men in the whole valley. How much jam could they eat?

Besides, she thought grimly, working the post wasn't worth dying for.

Peeling off her berry-stained white gloves, she carefully knotted the four corners of her apron together and stuck her arm through the gap. Then, picking up her bucket, she headed home.

As she wandered she found herself thinking about the photographs Father Michaels had shown her, about the man who'd taken them. Such moving, aching pictures . . .

Her step slowed. The wind shifted, fluttering through her hair with a soft hiss, and her thoughts drifted with it.

Suddenly she was thinking about the kiss. Their kiss. The one they'd shared that first night together. The memory slipped into her mind, and strangely she had no desire to keep it at bay. It was something she'd wanted to think about for days.

Not that it had been a kiss; not really. But still, when his lips had moved against hers, when his tongue had crept into her mouth, she'd felt something strange and new. A tingling that had spread through her body like a trickle of melting snow. For the first time in her life she'd felt . . . feminine. When his strong arms had closed around her body—

She considered smacking her face again. Good God, what was next? Thinking the man desired her? It had been an assault, no more. He'd simply used his lips instead of his hands. He hadn't wanted her body; he'd wanted her absence.

It was the mosquitoes, she decided. They'd drained her brain of blood. No matter what Father Michaels said, and no matter how good a photographer her partner was, Stone Man was not the type of man a woman could befriend. Not a woman like her, anyway. His female friends, if he had any (which she seriously doubted), would certainly have names like Blaze or Busty.

Still . . .

Forget the photographs. They were the problem. Their images had created the one thing Devon's rational mind couldn't ignore: a puzzle.

Her partner—big, silent, sour Stone Man—had become a puzzle. Never, not once in her whole life, had Devon Margaret O'Shea been able to walk away from an unsolved puzzle. It was like living in a messy house. Things just weren't right.

She gave up trying to ignore the nagging questions that plagued her mind. There was no way on God's green earth she'd get a decent night's sleep until she'd solved the riddle.

But how? Tightening her grip on the handle, she picked up her pace.

There was only one way. She had to get past Stone Man's gruff façade. Somehow she had to glimpse the man behind the icy mask, the man who'd taken those photographs.

Chapter Eight

Stone Man snapped open his pocket watch. He took one look at the time and immediately tensed. Seven o'clock. Just one more hour, he thought sullenly. One more hour of glorious silence before he had to shut up shop and head for home.

"Home." The word came out of his mouth in a disgusted sigh.

He had no home anymore. He had a tent that belonged in one of those damned ladies' books—flowers everywhere, tablecloths, clean sheets. The only thing missing was curtains, and they were only absent because there were no windows. He winced. *Yet.* He wouldn't put it past little miss perfect to cut a hole in the canvas wall. In fact, he could hear her now. *There just had to be a window over the table. The sunlight in the morning is so pretty. . . .*

Thank God it'd all be over in two days.

He couldn't wait. In just two days she'd come barreling in the store with her inedible foodstuffs. And he'd get to throw her out on her ear.

He grinned. In the past two days he'd spent hours fantasizing about the meeting, about the look on her face when he actually said the words "You lose." The two sweetest-sounding words he'd ever heard.

Little miss perfect would probably burst into tears or faint dead away.

God, he couldn't wait.

* * *

Thick spirals of steam pelted Devon's face, tugging at the tight wisps of hair around her face. A few reddish strands popped free from their moorings and curled wildly across her sweaty brow.

Wrapping a towel around the pot's handle, she lifted the heavy iron pan off the stove and set it on the table. She backhanded the moisture from her brow and let out a long, tired sigh. This was the last batch for today. Leaning forward, she peered into the pot.

"Perfect," she said aloud, wiping another big trickle of sweat from her temple. The blueberry-sugar mixture was a deep blackish blue. Careful not to burn herself, she poured the berries into clean lightning jars then poured moose tallow on top as a sealant and screwed the lids tight. When she was finished, she quickly counted today's jars. Thirty-two. With yesterday's work, that made a total of fifty-seven jars of jam. And she still had two days left.

Working quickly, she cleaned up her cooking mess, boxed up her jams, and shoved them under the bed, where they couldn't be seen. Flipping open the nickel face of her pocket watch, she checked the time. Seven forty-five.

He'd be home in fifteen minutes. Sighing wearily, she sank onto the bed, letting her feet dangle lazily over the side. She couldn't cook dinner. Not tonight. She was just too darn tired. . . .

She flopped backward, sinking deep into the mattress she'd restuffed yesterday. The soft, earthy scent of newly gathered lichen moss surrounded her. She stared at the grayed, sagging ceiling, letting her tense muscles relax.

Her mind drifted . . . right into Stone Man's photographs. She squeezed her eyes shut. Why couldn't she forget those darn pictures? Every time she paused lately she found the mysterious photographs hovering at the edges of her thoughts.

She couldn't reconcile the pictures with the man who'd taken them, and it was driving her crazy.

So much disorder. So many pieces out of place.

She'd done a lot of thinking about him over the past two days, and she'd only reached one rather obvious conclusion. There *was* more to Stone Man than met the eye. Somewhere under all that hair and filth lurked a very special soul. A soul capable of feeling the cabin's loneliness and glimpsing the old woman's pain.

The thought softened her. Maybe Father Michaels was right; maybe Stone Man was simply afraid of needing someone. Maybe he was lonely, and maybe—just maybe—he needed a friend.

Her heart did a funny little flip at the thought. If he were lonely, then he needed her, for only a friend could ease the ache of loneliness.

A quicksilver dash of hope shot through her mind. All her life she'd been a caretaker, an organizer of other people's problems. It was a role she felt comfortable in, and without the sense of helping others she felt vaguely lost and adrift.

She glanced around the spotless cabin, remembering the filth that had coated the place the day she'd first walked in. She remembered the bugs, the dust, the dirt, the dried food.

Before her arrival his whole life had been a shambles. She'd remedied that, and soon she'd remedy the post's organizational problems.

The thought brought with it a quick smile. He *did* need her, if not as a friend, then at least as a manager in the post; for she alone could revamp the post into a first-rate store.

Oh, he wouldn't like it at first, she knew that without a doubt. Men never did like change. But when she was finished, and everything in his life ran like a well-oiled clock, he'd see the light; he'd realize that he needed her. That they were a team.

Maybe she could even help him find his way back to the human race. . . .

That was it! That's why God had sent her here. She was the one person who could organize Stone Man's life and help him reenter civilization.

She snapped upright, a determined gleam in her green eyes. Whether he knew it or not Stone Man was about to make friends with his partner.

Even if it killed both of them.

Stone Man paused outside the tent, steeling himself for her caterwauling. Hunching his shoulders, he lowered his head into the protective collar of his lightweight coat and opened the door.

Waves of steamy heat greeted him. Entering, he shut the door behind him, inhaling deeply of the sweet, cinnamon-and-berry-scented air.

A dart of movement caught his eye, and he turned toward it. He was just in time to see his partner bounce off the bed. Even from a distance he could see that her eyes were bright and her face, usually so pale, was flushed. He groaned inwardly. She was up to something. Probably wanted windows . . .

Her small feet hit the floor hard, and she hurried toward him. The dozen or so corkscrew curls that were plastered to her brow jiggled free, nodding up and down with her every step.

"Hello, Stone Man," she said, stopping beside him in a swirl of blue muslin. "May I take your coat?"

He clenched his teeth to keep from shouting at her. He could take his own coat off, but it wasn't worth the hassle. He'd learned that the hard way. If he said no, she'd just run around like a chicken with her head cut off, looking all stupid and wounded. Shrugging his massive shoulders, he eased out of his coat and handed it to her.

She took it eagerly, smoothing away the creases of the day and hanging it carefully on its hook.

He lumbered gracelessly over to the table and sat down. "What's for dinner?"

"Would you like some coffee?" she said quickly, hurrying back to her precious stove.

"Okay." He frowned. Hadn't he asked her a question? Oh, yeah. "What's for dinner?"

She set a pan on the red-hot stove then quickly opened a can of beans and poured the reddish slop into the pot. "Beans and flapjacks," she answered, handing him a steaming hot cup of coffee.

"Good." Even she couldn't screw up beans. Pulling his well-read copy of *Oliver Twist* out of the bookshelf, he leaned back against the tent wall and began to read.

"More coffee?" she said after a moment.

He glanced down at the dregs in his cup. "Uh-huh." Tilting his face, he watched her as she wrapped a dishtowel around the coffeepot's handle and refilled his cup.

"Thanks."

"You're more than welcome," came her cheerful reply.

He took a quick sip then turned his attention back to his book.

Steam jostled the pot's heavy iron lid, hissing into the humid air. Iron clattered on iron. "You know, Stone Man, I can certainly see why you've settled here. It makes St. Louis look so drab and colorless."

He lifted his face to study her. She wasn't looking at him, of course. She was dancing with the stove. Stirring, tasting, testing, pouring, flipping. The heat had loosened her tight little topknot even more, and thick strands of rust-colored hair were curling damply across the side of her face. Her white shirtwaist clung to her curves.

His breathing tripped. He so rarely thought of her as a woman that when he was confronted with evidence of her . . . femininity, he felt distinctly uncomfortable. He cleared his throat and looked quickly away. "Huh?"

She laughed softly. "So we're back to grunting, are we?" She started ladling beans onto the plates. "I thought we'd made more progress than that."

He didn't answer. He couldn't; he had no idea what she was babbling about.

She set the plates down carefully, sliding his across the bright red tablecloth. Then she handed him a glass of boiled and cooled river water. And a napkin.

He shot her a sidelong glance.

"Humor me," she said, still smiling. "Let me pretend you're going to use it."

He bunched the frilly little thing up in his big hand and started eating.

Every once in a while he peeked up at her, just to check, but she was still doing it. Eating counterclockwise, one food item at a time.

"You didn't answer me, you know."

His progress ground to a halt. With the fork tip pressing against his lips, he stared at her. "Huh?"

"I said this land was lovely."

"Oh, yeah, you did." He went back to eating.

She cleared her throat. "I've been out and about a great deal lately, studying the land. I can't wait to see the fall colors."

He rammed a forkful of beans home. "Ish pretty."

Silence fell again, only this time it was strained. He shifted uncomfortably in his seat. It was almost as if they were *supposed* to be chattering like hyenas over a kill. He shook his head. She had him so twisted around, he didn't know what to expect anymore. Without thinking he wiped his mouth with the napkin and went on eating.

Across the table he heard a sharp intake of breath. He looked up. She was staring at the napkin. A slow blush crept up from his beard, and he could feel the color burning across his cheeks. He felt like the village idiot. "Hellfire," he snapped, throwing the napkin to the floor. "Quit staring at me."

Her gaze dropped back to her plate. She picked up her fork again and began eating. "I ran across the prettiest bird today. He was different-looking, kind of a pale gray-white with a black head and bright red beak. He followed me for almost a half an hour, just sitting on the riverbank, twittering."

"Tern," he said, chomping.

She frowned. "What?"

He wiped his mouth on his sleeve and glanced up at her. "It's an arctic tern."

"Oh."

Silence again. Blessed silence.

He heard the tinny clang of metal as she laid down her fork. He didn't bother looking up. An audience would only encourage her to babble more.

"I thought you might like to know a bit about me."

His fork didn't slow. "Nope."

She didn't miss a beat. "I came up here because I needed a new start in life. I had my sister, Colleen, but when she grew up and got married, she didn't need me anymore. I felt sort of . . . lost. I know it sounds silly, but I thought if I found something I could do well . . ." Her deep voice caught, quivered. "I don't know, I guess I thought if I were doing something just for me, something I loved, that I wouldn't be lonely anymore. Can you understand that?"

Stone Man put his fork down. Could he understand loneliness? His head came up; their eyes met. In the green depths, he saw a hint of sadness. A restless longing that mirrored his own.

How could he *not* understand? He'd been alone and searching all his life. "I understand. That's why I . . ." He bit back the confession. It wasn't any of her business what he did or why.

"You take pictures. Wasn't that what you were going to say?"

He looked up at her, surprised. "Yeah," he said after a long minute. "I take pictures."

"A photograph," she said softly, "immortality through art. I suppose . . ." Once she'd started, she kept talking, her voice low and soothing. Her words wove a web of complacence around him. He leaned back in his chair, sipping coffee, listening. A warm, homey atmosphere filled the tent.

After a few moments his head grew heavy and dropped forward. His eyes fluttered shut. There was something so soothing about the sound of her voice. . . .

"Stone Man?"

He jerked his head up. "Huh?"

She was staring right at him, her eyes huge and green in the paleness of her face. She was very close to smiling; he could see it in the tiny quiver at the corners of her mouth.

"Sleepy?" she inquired softly.

He cleared his throat. "Nope. Not at all."

"Do you remember my last question?"

He fidgeted uncomfortably. He couldn't remember a damn thing she'd said all night. Except for something about birds.

"My question was a simple one." Her throaty voice wrapped around him. "Do you think we could be friends?"

He jumped to his feet. Damn her! She'd done it again. Outthought him. And he'd made it so easy. A few hot beans, a soft smile, a few well-chosen words, and he'd actually *listened* to her jabberings.

He ought to shoot himself. Now, before it got worse, before he lost his mind completely. "No," he said through gritted teeth. "I told you once: I don't have friends."

"But—"

"No buts."

She was beside him in an instant. Without a word she laid her soft, white fingers atop his forearm. He felt the heat of her skin through the flannel of his sleeve. Her touch was soft, yet firm. Politely demanding.

"Forget I said that." Her voice was so quiet he scarcely heard her. "We've done well tonight. Let's not go back."

He stared down at her. She stared up at him. Her eyes were big and deadly earnest. His throat was so dry he could hardly swallow. "All right," he said scratchily. "Let's forget it."

"Thank you," she said with a small sigh. Releasing his arm, she smoothed the tight curls off her face and cleared the table.

As she started washing the dishes, he heard the gravelly, off-key strains of her humming. She was humming "I'm only a bird in a gilded cage." Strangely her voice seemed to lessen the strained silence in the tent.

He groaned. He was in big trouble if her humming didn't bother him. "Do you have to hum?" he said harshly.

She shot him an impish smile. "Would you rather I sing?"

"Couldn't you just think about humming?"

"Why, Stone Man," she said teasingly, "that was a joke. Who'd have thought you had a sense of humor?"

"I don't."

"Maybe you just think you don't. Could be you're funny as a stitch inside."

"Unlikely."

"Still . . . you did smile at me—and make a joke. You'd better watch out. You just might be starting to like me."

He squelched a smile just in time. "No chance of that."

Chapter Nine

Stone Man stared at the slow-moving shadow outside the post and slowly shook his head. She was doing it again, trying to ride that damned bicycle.

Click, thump. The shadow lurched forward. The circular shadow of the bicycle's front wheel rammed hard into the muddy, rutted earth and stopped cold. The rider's whole body flew toward the handlebars. When she hit, the little bell bolted beside her left hand tinkled gaily.

"Ouch!"

Stone Man couldn't suppress a smile. He waited, knowing she'd try again. If there was one thing he'd learned about Devon, it was that she never gave up.

She didn't disappoint him. After a few seconds the shadow repositioned itself on the saddle, stiffened, slipped a foot into the rat-trap pedal with an audible *click*, and lurched forward.

Thump. The wheel hit again, only this time she was able to power through the rut. The last he saw of her was a flash of red bicycle and black wheels as she hurtled past the open flaps.

"Thank God," he muttered. As long as she was riding that stupid contraption, she wasn't cleaning, or—God forbid—teaching herself how to cook.

Stone Man was still smiling the next day. Any minute he'd get to say the magic words: *you lose.* Stone Man could hardly contain his building excitement. The words were burning on the tip of his tongue. Any minute now—hell, any second now—Devon was going to walk through those flaps with her inedible foodstuffs.

He smiled. Damn, he felt good.

For the first time since she'd shown up at the post, he had the upper hand. All he had to do was take one bite of her food, and she'd lose the bet fair and square. The men in the Yukon weren't desperate enough to eat her slop.

He flipped open his pocket watch and glanced at the time. Seven o'clock. She was late. Probably tasted her own food and passed out cold.

"Hello, Stone Man."

He looked up. She was standing just inside the flaps, and she didn't have a single jar of food with her. He grinned broadly. She'd probably had to throw the whole mess out. "Forget something, Devon?"

"No. In fact I brought something extra." She peeked out the flaps and yelled, "Come on over."

Bear ambled into the tent. "Morning, Devon," he said, tipping his battered felt hat at her. "Morning Cornelius."

"Come to watch the little lady lose, Bear?"

Bear shuffled over to the table and sat down. "Reckon I'll see somebody eatin' crow," he answered with a good-natured grin.

Devon beelined for the flaps, her dull blue skirt swirling gaily around her feet as she scampered through the opening.

After a moment the flaps parted. A flash of blue appeared. She was coming through butt first! He stiffened, shock widening his eyes as he stared at her softly rounded bottom. There it was again, that unmistakable proof of femininity. Who'd have thought the skinny little thing would have such a nice butt?

Her back and shoulders came into view slowly. She was tugging hard at something, trying to drag whatever it was into the tent.

His gaze traversed her slim, hunched shoulders before sliding down the curve of her spine to the rounded curves of her backside. She wasn't wearing one of those damn things—what were they called, a buttle, bustle? Whatever, she wasn't wearing one. The skirt fell over her little body just as God intended it should.

She started wiggling again.

His response was immediate and unwanted. "Christ," he muttered under his breath, striding toward her and yanking the flaps open to reveal a long, heavily laden toboggan. "What in the hell are you doing?"

She snapped upright. "What does it look like I'm doing?"

Snorting in disgust, he grabbed the rope and hauled the toboggan into the tent. It bumped across the uneven plank flooring, and at every seam the sound of rattling glass rang through the air.

"Stop!" she screamed as a whole layer of lightning jars swayed precariously to the left.

He kept moving. Glass clinked in his wake.

She lunged after him and grabbed the rope, yanking hard. She gave a second good pull, and Stone Man let go. She flew backward, landing on her fanny in a puff of muslin. Dust poofed around her, insinuating itself into her throat and nostrils. She sneezed loudly.

Stone Man's hearty laughter filled the tent. "Sorry I didn't sweep today. It must have slipped my mind."

In spite of herself, Devon felt a small smile tug at her lips. His laughter sounded so good, so genuine. It was almost enough to make her forget he was laughing at her. Almost.

He offered her his hand. "Come on, get up."

Pointedly ignoring his hand, she clapped the dust from her palms and stood up. "Now—" She stopped midsentence to extricate a strand of hair from her mouth. Lifting the wayward lock off her forehead, she shoved it back into her tight little roman knot, and then continued. "Let's get on with it, shall we?"

Stone Man almost felt sorry for her. She was trying so hard. "Are you sure you want an audience?" he asked softly.

She glanced at Bear. "Him? He's not an audience, he's the tasting panel."

Stone Man's smile faded. "I'm the judge."

"I thought you'd like some . . . opinions from shoppers. When I expressed this thought to Bear, he seemed more than happy to help you out. In fact he said something about a 'fair fight.' "

"Oh, he did, did he?" Stone Man shot his friend a wry

glance. "You're kind of old to be putting on armor, aren't you, Bear?"

Bear's grin expanded. "Just trying to help out a couple of friends."

Stone Man grimaced. Christ, if he didn't know she couldn't cook, he might actually be worried. As it was he was just plain irritated. Theatrics weren't something he enjoyed.

"All right," he said gruffly, "what have you got?"

She smiled triumphantly. "Food."

"What kind of food?"

Disappointment flickered across her face. "You don't seem very pleased."

Bear chuckled. "No, he sure don't."

"But don't you think food is a good idea?" she asked seriously. "It's sure to draw business."

"Your food wouldn't draw flies."

Something flashed in her eyes. Anger? Triumph? Relief? He wasn't sure; but whatever it was, it made him uneasy. "What are you looking at?"

This time there was no mistaking her mood. She was happy. In fact, she was goddamn thrilled. Her face had gone all rosy, and her smile was as big as a barn. Even her dusty little hands were joined in a gleeful clapping.

"Stand still," he ordered. "You're making me dizzy."

She settled down. "Sorry."

Her growing smile said otherwise. Stone Man groaned. He was going to regret asking this, but he couldn't help himself. "Okay, why are you smiling?"

"I . . . misled you a bit," she said.

"Misled me?"

"I cooked badly just to bother you."

Stone Man's heart came to a dead stop. She'd done it again; she'd outsmarted him.

Before he could utter a word, she swept her skirts aside as if they were a magician's cape, revealing her treasures. The well-packed toboggan seemed to grow, filling the small tent with its ominous presence.

"What is it?" he said dully.

She ran one efficient finger along the jars' metallic lids. "Preserves, jams, sauces, chutneys." She paused for emphasis then added, "Sixteen blueberry tarts and four canned peach pies."

A groan started deep in Stone Man's throat and slowly rattled upward. "God . . ." He'd been set up good.

In the blink of an eye she was beside him, her small, pale hand resting lightly on his flannel-covered forearm. "The miners will stand in line for this food. Especially come winter, when they're tired of beans and flapjacks. Just think," she said, using her voice to its utmost, "fresh blueberry preserves on your biscuits in January."

He squeezed his eyes shut, trying to ignore the obvious. He'd made a bet—and he'd lost.

"Stone Man?" Her voice held an edge of nervousness.

She was waiting, he could feel it. Waiting to find out what kind of man he was. His eyelids lifted slowly, revealing eyes that were dull and dispirited. "Yeah?"

"Are you going to stick to the deal?"

There it was. The big question. He shot an uneasy glance at the toboggan. The hold on his arm tightened; he felt the tension in her fingers. The grayed fabric walls closed in around him.

The answer to his dilemma was so simple. He knew it. She knew it. All he had to do was laugh in her face. This was his valley, his post, his life. Not a man alive would blame him for reneging on his bet. Not even Bear.

Not a man, that was, except the one in the mirror.

"Stone Man?"

With a heavy sigh he flipped open his pocket watch. It was an unconscious gesture, one he often repeated when under stress. Somehow the steady march of the tiny hands calmed him. He studied the watch's movements for several agonizing seconds, and as he did so, the canvas walls receded. His head cleared. He'd lost the bet, that much was clear. Now it was time to cut his losses.

"You win." They were the most difficult words he'd ever spoken.

She jumped straight in the air, squealing. "Oh, Stone Man, I just knew you were a man of your—"

"Hold it."

She froze, her hands stopping midclap. "But—"

"But nothing. You win, I'll give you that. Now it's your turn to give something back."

She eyed him. "What do you mean?"

"You can work the post eight hours a day, on one condition."

"What condition?"

"You limit your gabbing to ten words a day. The moment word eleven pops out of your mouth, your shift is over."

"That's impossible!"

He smiled. "Look at it this way, you won't have anyone to talk to. How difficult can it be to keep quiet, under the circumstances?"

Her eyes narrowed, focused hard on his. "And if I don't agree?"

"Then you'll win an empty bet. I'll close down the post, pack up my supplies, and move on."

Her mouth dropped open. "That's not fair."

"Nope."

"You wouldn't."

"Try me."

She popped a thumb between her lips and began to gnaw on the stubby nail.

He watched her, fascinated. He could almost see the tiny wheels turning in her mind. She was thinking it through, carefully and from every angle.

When he could stand the wait no more, he said, "Deal?"

She yanked the thumb from her mouth. "One hundred words."

His eyes widened in surprise. The little miss was bargaining! "Twenty."

"Sixty."

"Forty."

"Done," she said grimly.

A sigh of pure relief slid past his lips. He could live with forty, and if he played his cards right, he could trick her into spending them all before noon. "Good."

"Don't get too relaxed, mister. We're not through yet."

Bear's chuckle floated up between them. "Well," he said, pushing to his feet, "I gotta go. It looks like a fair fight to me."

"Thanks, Bear," Devon said to the big man as he shambled through the flaps and disappeared.

"Yeah, Bear," Stone Man called after him, "thanks a whole hell of a lot."

The moment they were alone Devon turned on him again. "Okay, now here are my terms."

"You don't get terms."

"I do if you want me to keep my 'trap' shut."

He thought about that for a minute. He'd pay a high premium to keep her quiet. "Okay. What do you want?"

"You let me organize and clean the post. Every day."

"And if I don't agree?"

"I'll stay longer. Maybe even through next summer."

"You couldn't take it."

One perfectly arched eyebrow shot upward. "Really? Try me."

He groaned inwardly. She could do it, and she would, just to spite him. "Fine, goddamn it," he growled. "Do whatever you want. You always do anyway. Just keep your mouth shut while you're doing it."

She smiled. "I will."

Stone Man groaned, watching her unload her precious toboggan. It was going to be a goddamn long winter. . . .

The next morning Stone Man flipped open his pocket watch and stared dully at the little black hands. It was nine o'clock. Frowning, he re-pocketed the timepiece.

The day yawned before him, a grinning, gaping mouth that alternately laughed at him and threatened to swallow him. They'd only been working together one hour, and already he felt sick. Already he had a headache.

"You know, Stone Man . . ."

An inward cringe clutched him. God, how he'd come to loathe that sentence since he'd met Devon. It was invariably followed by a suggestion on how to improve his nature or his appearance. Or both.

He gritted his teeth and studiously ignored her. As usual, his efforts went unnoticed.

"I could help you rearrange your photograph collection."

He shot her a *back off, lady* glare.

"I haven't seen them, of course," she went on, either blithely unaware or supremely unconcerned about his feelings on the matter. "But I imagine they're . . . disorganized."

He plucked up twenty-three matchsticks, bundled them together, and placed them in a little jar next to the gold scales. The thin wood stems tinkled against the rounded glass sides. Seventeen to go, my little general. The thought gave him some solace.

"If you so much as touch my photographs," he said calmly, "I'll cut your lily-white fingers off."

She blanched. "Well, you needn't be so—"

He picked up another six matchsticks.

"Hold on!" Her gaze shot to the matchsticks in his dirty grip. "That's only five words. Needn't is a contraction. A contraction is only counted as one word."

"Need not. Two words." He plunked the matchsticks into the jar. "I'm not going to count your argument—it was a legitimate dispute. So, you've got a few words left." He leaned forward. "Want to use them now?"

She clamped her mouth shut and went back to the shelves she was organizing.

He watched her line up a row of Campbell's split-pea soup with perfect, military precision, and a quick smile hovered at the edges of his mouth. "Why are you putting the split pea next to the tomato?"

She smiled up at him brightly. "I'm so glad you asked. It was a difficult decision, because—"

"Stop." The word boomed through the tent, severing her sentence. He carefully chose eleven matchsticks. "That's forty. You're done."

"Oh! You!" She glared at him. Stamping her foot down hard on the plank floor, she swept her skirts in her hands and marched out of the tent.

When she was gone Stone Man let out his breath in a long sigh. A slow, easy smile crinkled his eyes. He'd done it. He'd outsmarted her. She was gone for the day, and it wasn't even nine-thirty in the morning.

Damn, it felt good to have the upper hand.

* * *

Two days later, standing in front of her carefully aligned soup cans, Devon pursed her lips. Hard. She'd almost said, "Done."

She'd caught herself in time and compressed her traitorous lips into a straight line. She wasn't about to let herself be suckered again, certainly not by the likes of him. It didn't sit well to have been outsmarted by a man just slightly smarter than an earthworm.

Still she had to give credit where credit was due. He'd outthought her. He'd used her own weakness for talking against her, and two days in a row no less. Yesterday she'd lasted until ten-thirty.

She grimaced at her own stupidity. At the rate she was going, she wouldn't be working a full shift until spring.

He wouldn't outsmart her today, she vowed silently. Today she'd be the best, quietest partner imaginable. Sooner or later he'd have to see that she was an asset to his business. Maybe he'd even lift the talking restriction.

Glancing around the post, she allowed herself a satisfied smile. Everything was perfect. Orderly and spotless. Her pies were arranged in an eye-appealing half circle on the crates behind the old Yukon stove. The tiny tarts bordered the pies on either side, forming a neat rainbow of golden-crusted moons.

The shelves were dustless, level, and the items for sale were displayed with mathematical precision. It was still alphabetical, of course, but with Devon working every day, what did it matter? The men didn't have to know how to read; they simply had to know how to ask.

Now all they needed was a customer.

No sooner had Devon had that thought then the flaps fluttered open and in walked Cornstalk and another man, whom Devon didn't recognize.

"Cornstalk," she cried happily, clutching up her skirts and hurrying toward him. In the background she heard the tiny clink of a matchstick hitting glass. Her smile weakened.

Cornstalk swept the tired old felt hat from his head and crushed it to his chest. " 'Morning, Miss Devon." He swallowed hard as a telltale blush crept up his knobby throat.

She nodded, letting her eyes speak for her.

"This here's my friend, Digger Haines." Cornstalk cocked his head toward the wiry, black-haired man at his side. "He's gonna take me to Circle City for some fun."

Devon turned her attention to Digger. The monkey-faced little man grinned up at her, showcasing a mouthful of chipped, yellow teeth. His gray eyes, sunken in a gaunt, wrinkled face, had the burning gleam of a longtime gold seeker.

"Howdy, miss."

Devon felt a genuine welcome in his warm smile and bright eyes. "Hello, Mr. Haines."

"Mister!" A bubble of laughter shook his throat. "Hell, miss, I'm just Digger." He glanced over toward the counter. "Hiya Stone Man, how ya doing?"

Stone Man didn't look up. "Fine."

Devon tapped Cornstalk on the shoulder. When he looked her way, she shot a pointed glance toward her pies and tarts.

"Holy cow, Digger, look at them pies!"

Digger's eyes rounded as he looked at Devon's display. "God almighty, fresh pies. What do we gotta do to get one?"

Devon weighed each word, mentally culling the unnecessary ones. "Piece is one dollar. Tarts free with ten-dollar purchase."

At that Stone Man's head shot up. "Free?"

She nodded, frowning as ten more matchsticks landed in the jar.

"Holy cow," Cornstalk said, gulping. "There's lots of stuff I need. I was gonna wait and get everything in Circle City, but them pies sure look good."

Digger grabbed the boy's arm. "Come on, kid. Let's stock up for winter."

For the next half hour Devon bustled around after her customers like a mother hen herding her chicks. She clucked, she nodded, she pointed. She did everything but speak, for she was determined to show Stone Man that she could be a useful—and silent—partner. When Digger and Cornstalk had collected everything they needed, she followed them up to the counter.

Sashaying past her partner, she settled in front of the scales.

Stone Man immediately stood. "I'll handle the gold."

She shot him a quelling glance. "No."

They all stared at each other for a long moment. Then Stone Man dropped a matchstick into the jar and eased back onto his stool. "Okay, lady, you do it."

Smiling brightly she turned her attention back to the boys. "Now, what have we got?" One by one she plucked up their purchases, checked the price list, and wrote down the correct price on a piece of cloth. *Bacon, two pounds, 80 cents; beans, five pounds, 75 cents; sugar, ten pounds, 2 dollars and 50 cents; coffee, three pounds, 3 dollars; jam, two jars, 2 dollars.*

The last item was a small bright-orange box. She picked it up, turning it around in her hand as she looked for some indication of the contents.

She frowned. There wasn't a single word on the box. Cornstalk's cough caught her attention, and she looked up. The young man's face was beet red, and his Adam's apple was bobbing uncontrollably. He was staring bug-eyed at the box in her hand.

"Are you all right?" she asked.

He nodded, coughing again.

Digger slapped him on the back. "He's okay, miss," he said, grinning.

Devon turned her attention back to the box in her hand. What was it? She glanced at Stone Man's price list, searching for something, anything, that might aid her.

Cornstalk coughed again. "Them're a dollar, Miss Devon."

"But what are they?"

This time Cornstalk's cough seemed more like an apoplectic fit. She glanced up quickly and immediately frowned in concern. The poor boy was barely breathing, and his face looked ready to explode. "Goodness, Corn—"

Her sentence snapped in half as Stone Man lurched to his feet and grabbed the box from her grasp. "That'll be ten dollars and five cents, boys." He tossed the box onto the pile of purchases.

She bristled. "Now, just a—"

"Trust me."

The strange catch in his voice stopped her cold. He

sounded almost . . . happy. She shot him a sidelong glance, and sure enough his eyes were crinkled up in barely suppressed laughter. A smile hovered in the corners of his mouth.

"Hey, Miss Devon, do we get a tart?"

Smiling at Digger's question, she nodded. "And two free pieces of pie. Just spread the word, boys."

As the two men left the post, Devon heard the sound of matchsticks hitting glass again, but even that couldn't dim her enthusiasm. She'd done a good job; her foodstuffs had increased business.

When she turned back around she found Stone Man staring at her oddly. He was smiling, and there was a softness in his eyes she'd never seen before. Never expected.

"What is it?" she asked uncertainly.

"I'd forgotten women like you existed."

He smiled, an honest-to-God smile that Devon felt all the way down to her toes. "What do you mean, women like me?"

"Ladies," he said softly.

Remembering Midas's diatribe on the evils of ladies, she eyed him suspiciously. "Meaning what?"

His lips twitched. "The orange box was full of gold beater's skins." At her blank look he added, "French letters. You know, little—"

"I know what french letters are!" Crimson splashed her face. Her hands flew to her hot cheeks. She remembered distinctly reading about contraceptive devices in Dr. Cowan's book, *Science of a New Life*.

A groan worked its way up her throat.

Stop it! She jerked her hands from her face. She was a post operator, not some silly husband-hunting socialite. There was no room for feminine sensibilities in the Yukon.

Tilting her chin, she dug deep in her soul for a cool stare. Finding one, she leveled it on her partner. "Gold beater's skins." She forced out the crude words to prove they didn't embarrass her.

His lips twitched again. "Very good."

She nodded smartly. "If you'd had them displayed properly, I would have figured out what they were."

One eyebrow shot up. ''Oh? How's that?''

''They hardly belong between the socks and the gloves.''

''Oh, I don't know,'' he drawled. ''It seems as good a place as any to me. And a damn sight better than most. Where would you suggest? With the hand tools maybe?''

''I should've known better than to discuss logic with you.'' She plucked up her skirts and headed for the shelf nearest her.

His warm, throaty laughter filled the tent. Its rich timbre sent unexpected shivers down her stiffened spine. She forced herself not to look at him, but it didn't do any good. In her mind's eye she held the picture of his face lit up by laughter.

Ignoring him completely, she bundled the orange boxes up in her apron and walked purposely toward the shelf containing P–Z. He was still chuckling as she cleared a space between the picks and the rice.

''Oh, Devon,'' came his warm, lilting voice.

She glanced up. He was waving the jar full of matchsticks. The little wooden sticks were clinking softly against the glass. ''Bye, Dev.''

Darn! She opened her mouth to speak then slammed it shut. Rules were rules.

Without a backward glance she stormed out of the tent.

Stone Man checked the time and smiled.

Chapter Ten

Glancing around the post, Devon frowned. It was so depressingly *quiet*. The only sound in the tent was the impatient tap, tap, tap of her toe.

Oh well, she thought philosophically, at least she hadn't spoken. The jar beside the scales was empty, and it was already eleven.

If only there were more to do. . . .

Suddenly a stranger burst into the post. Stumbling wearily over to the table, he yanked out a stool and dropped onto the hard surface. His shoulders sagged forward, and a sigh escaped his lips. It was a long, low sigh that told the world a chair felt mighty good.

Devon stared in horror at the trail of mud left by the man's filthy gumboots.

He flipped off his hat. "Stone Man, how the hell are you?"

"Well, if it isn't Lying George, back from the dead."

The man laughed, a big, good-natured sound that set his heavy jowls to rocking. "I ain't lying this time. I found it. The big strike."

"Yeah, and I'm president of the United States."

George's quick grin made his long, droopy mustache bunch up under his big nose. Stuffing his hands in the oversized pockets of his coat, he pulled out a Winchester shotgun shell and threw it on the counter. It landed on the wooden surface with a loud *thunk*.

Stone Man stared as if he expected the shell to bite him.

His eyebrows drew together, and a dark frown settled across his rawboned features as he picked it up.

Devon watched, fascinated, as Stone Man tugged the tip off the shell and turned it upside down. Coarse gold flakes streamed onto the counter.

It was a long moment before Stone Man looked up at George. "This gold isn't from a river around here."

"Rabbit Creek."

Stone Man let out his breath slowly. "Shit . . ."

George grinned. "Yep. I staked my discovery claim. Now I'm on my way to find Ogilvy to record it. Just thought I'd pass by here and let you know so's you can pass the word."

"Sure," Stone Man answered in a voice so tired and old Devon barely recognized it. Without another word he swept the gold back into the empty shell and handed it to George.

Devon stood off to the side, uncertain as to what to do. Stone Man obviously didn't like George's news. But why? The discovery of gold in the valley, that was a good thing . . . wasn't it? And a customer with a shell full of gold; well, that simply had to be a good thing.

"Wait," she said as George started to leave, "would you like to buy some tarts or a piece of pie?"

"No, thanks, my Injun wife does just fine by me, missy."

Disappointed, Devon watched him leave. As she headed up to the counter, she noticed that Stone Man hadn't counted her words. That was a first. "Stone Man?"

"There goes Fortymile."

"What do you mean?"

"In the Yukon it doesn't take more than ten minutes to go from deserted valley to boom town. That's why we use tents—they go up and down quickly. Hell, the minute word of George's strike hits, there'll be men pulling up stakes from Fairbanks to Nome. They'll settle in so fast, my peaceful valley—"

"Customers!" Her face lit up. "Our post will be full every day."

"They won't all be miners. A few of the men headed this way will be store owners. By spring this valley'll be a goddamn town."

She chewed on her lower lip. Competition they couldn't

really afford—not with Stone Man's personality. "Well, we'll just have to be the best. I could maybe make some more—"

"That's it," he said tiredly, plunking forty matchsticks in the jar. "Go home."

"But—"

His fist slammed onto the counter. "Now!"

Devon spun on her heels and barreled for the door. Midas entered at the same time, and they rammed into each other. His contemptuous laughter rang in her ears as she stumbled backward.

"Leaving?" he mocked. "So soon?"

Forcing her chin a notch higher, she sailed past him without a word.

His hate-filled voice followed her outside. "Well, Stoneyman, ya got rid o' the bitch early today. Good goin'."

Devon stopped, waiting for Stone Man's response. There was none.

She clenched her fists in frustration. When was that man going to realize that partners stood up for each other?

Sitting across the supper table from Stone Man, Devon watched him push his food around on his plate. He was staring at his supper through wide, unseeing eyes. Not once had he lifted his gaze from the plate.

Her heart went out to him. He was so obviously upset. How, she wondered, could anyone get so upset over a little handful of gold?

But in her heart she knew. It wasn't the small amount found that bothered him. It was what it represented. A thousand greedy men coming to rape the land, and every one of them looking for that handful of golden dust.

For the hundredth time she pondered his prediction. Would the moose pasture be a town by spring? A town with real streets, real stores, real people?

Dare she hope?

"Stone Man," she began cautiously.

He lurched to his feet. Belching loudly, he backhanded the leftover food from his beard and threw his unused napkin onto the table. "I've got to go."

He grabbed his mackinaw off its hook and headed for the door. Devon jumped up and blocked his path. "Where?"

He looked down at her, and she could see a glimmer of something—maybe fear, maybe pain—in his eyes. It flashed for a heartbeat before the well-used shutters slipped back into place.

"Out."

She laid a hand on his shoulder. "Don't go."

He flinched at her touch. "Why not? All you're going to do is babble in my ear. I can't take it tonight."

"I won't babble."

His eyes narrowed. "Promise?"

"I promise. But . . ." Her voice fell to a whisper. "Sometimes talking a problem through shrinks it."

His eyes seemed to bore through her face. The silence in the tent expanded. Their breaths mingled, punching through the quiet like a pair of fists. Outside the wind picked up. The narrow wooden door rattled on its hinges, and the tent shuddered. Rain thumped a hollow tattoo on the sagging canvas roof.

"Please don't go."

The tension eased from his face. His big shoulders sagged. "All right. I don't have anywhere to go anyway. Bear's gone trapping."

Her hand slid down the length of his arm to his wrist. She led him back to the table, pouring two cups of coffee as he sat down. Sitting across from him, she took a quick sip, then ventured, "It's a matter of perspective. All bad things are."

"What do you mean?"

"You think it's bad that your valley will become a boom town, correct?"

He nodded.

"That's because you're looking at it from the wrong perspective. Look at it this way. An influx of people means an influx of customers. More customers mean more dollars, and more dollars mean more photographic supplies."

He took a long drink. "I guess you're right," he murmured. "Still . . ."

"And there's something better than money. You'll be the first photographer here. Your pictures could become the diary of a great strike, and when it's all over you can move on to the next great wilderness."

He glanced up at her. Over the rim of his cup, their eyes locked. "How the hell do you know me so well?"

The warmth of his mahogany-gold stare sent a spider-quick tingle down her spine. She smiled. "You can't live with a man for three weeks and not learn something about him—no matter how hard he tries to shield himself."

"Thanks," he said almost inaudibly.

She studied her cup, staring hard at the dark brown liquid. "Don't mention it. That's what friends are for."

After she'd said it she didn't look up; she couldn't. She could feel his eyes on her. They were like twin balls of fire, burning through her scalp. A slow heat crept across her cheeks. She shouldn't have said it. It was too soon; he wasn't ready to be her friend.

"Then maybe I should have found one sooner."

She hadn't known until that second that she'd been holding her breath, but at his words it slipped from her lips in a long, relieved sigh. He'd almost said they were friends. Almost.

It was something.

Friends . . .

Three weeks later Stone Man was still turning the word around in his mind, still wondering at her use of it.

Did she really think they were friends? Could she truly be that dumb? Any fool knew men and women couldn't be friends. Hell, he couldn't even be friends with men, and he understood how they thought.

He glanced up from the glass plates he was cleaning to look at her. As usual she was hopping around like a bird in search of the perfect worm. Flitting from shelf to shelf, checking, clucking, always moving or straightening some little thing or another.

He sighed, turning his attention back to his plates. At least she was quiet.

"Stone Man?"

Most of the time. He dropped two matchsticks into the jar before looking up at her. "Yeah?"

She had stopped flitting and was now lifting the tent flaps.

Peering outside, she said over her shoulder, "Who said Jack Kelley could come into town and claim Spike's cabin?"

Stone Man let out a tired sigh. Unfortunately he'd been right about how news of George's strike would affect his peaceful valley. New gold seekers arrived daily; new tents sprang up like spring flowers, overnight. And Jack Kelley was the worst of all. He seemed downright dedicated to turning the valley into a boom town.

"Stone Man?" she prompted.

He shrugged. "No one else wanted it."

"It's not fair that he could use that cabin to start up a trading post. He's taking our business."

"I told you, that's what happens when a strike hits. Those damn gold men, they can hear the word whispered on the wind for miles. I imagine the minute he heard about the strike Jack pulled up stakes in Fortymile and hightailed it down here. Hell, and if that's not enough, I hear tell Joe Ladue bought up a bunch of acres along the river and is trying to sell lots at twenty-five dollars apiece."

Her brow furrowed in thought. "I know why Jack's here. But why does he have all the customers? Does a log cabin make that much difference?"

"Naw, not to miners."

She turned around, letting the flaps shudder shut. "Then what is it?"

Four more matchsticks hit the jar before he answered. "Jack lets the boys sit around and talk. And he grubstakes anyone with a beating heart."

She fell silent, and it was all he could do to keep from chuckling. By now he recognized the pinched, constipated look on her face. She was counting.

He tallied quickly; she had five words left.

She tried her usual word-conservation trick—trying to look confused.

She had her usual success. None. Squelching a smile, he studied his plates.

When she couldn't stand it anymore, she said, "Grubstake?"

He peered up at her. "That's where the post puts up all

the supplies a miner needs to get through the winter in exchange for a part ownership in the miner's claim."

Four words.

"We could do that."

He dropped four matchsticks into the jar. "The last thing I want is to be partners with a bunch of grungy, gold-mad miners. No, thanks; I'll take my gold up front. Besides, most of them never find enough gold to pack a pipe, let alone pay back a grubstaker."

She walked over to her precious tart-and-pie shelf, which she'd replenished only yesterday. Her head was bowed, and he could tell she was deep in thought. This was a sign that boded ill for him later.

For now, at least, he could look forward to the rest of the day passing in blissful silence. "Good-bye, Dev."

She was so deep in thought she didn't even look up. "Bye," she murmured absentmindedly as she pushed through the canvas flaps and disappeared.

Closing up for the night, Stone Man found himself thinking about Devon's earlier silence. He cringed, knowing she'd hit him full force with her pent-up thoughts the second he got home.

He was right. As he pushed open the door, she launched into him. "Oh, good, you're home. I've been thinking about—"

He put a hand up for silence. "Wait. Let's get dinner started before you hit me with your new plan."

She walked over to the bucket of water, lifted the heavy metal lid, and scooped him a cupful. Handing it to him, she did a little half turn toward the stacked crates that made up her cupboards. Burrowing through the perfectly aligned bottles and boxes, she pulled out a tin box labeled with black script letters FOLEY'S FAMILY PILLS. She flipped open the lid and extracted two pills. "Here," she said, offering him the tablets, "this should cure your headache."

"How did you know I had a headache?"

She smiled. "Whenever I talk you get a headache, and if you don't have one now, you soon will."

Biting back a smile, he popped the pills in his mouth and

washed them down. Then he poured himself a cup of coffee and sat down. "Okay. Shoot."

"I think Jack Kelley has all the business because no one knows about my baked goods." She peered at him knowingly. "I think Digger and Cornstalk are hoarding the knowledge."

He sighed. He'd wondered how long it would take her to figure it out. "They might be."

"Don't you care?"

"Not particularly. I just appreciate the quiet."

She plopped onto the stool across from him. "But don't you see? You need money for your supplies. There's so much going on at the river. You can't wait to start taking pictures."

"Yeah," he mused unhappily. Things *were* starting to happen and happen quickly. The Thron-diuck had been renamed the Klondike by men too lazy or too stupid to learn the Indian pronunciation, and the lots Joe Ladue had created were beginning to sell. Rabbit Creek had been optimistically renamed Bonanza Creek, and there was even talk of naming the valley after some geologist, George Dawson.

Of course, the old-timers like Digger and Midas weren't falling for all the hype, but the *cheechakos*, the newcomers—they were staking claims like madmen.

"We're here." Devon's words broke into his thoughts. "It's happening. We should take advantage of it."

He lifted his face. Her eyes caught and held him. "How?"

"Advertising."

He started to push out of his seat. "No way, Dev. This isn't—"

"Wait. Just hear me out."

He sank slowly back onto the stool's hard surface. "Talk."

"One sign. That's all I want. Just one sign that lets people know about my pies and tarts and jams."

"It'll look like goddamn San Francisco."

Her lips quivered, tilting upward at the corners. "One sign won't turn your valley into a town. But it might get you all the photographic chemicals you need."

He thought about that. And more. Glancing around his tent, he noticed all the things she'd done for him. His tent and his clothes were always clean. His suppers were always served hot and with a smile. The sheets on the bed were crisp and white, and the mattress was always fresh-smelling and puffy. Hell, he couldn't even remember the last time a bug had scurried up his leg.

"All right. One sign. One little sign."

She leapt to her feet, clapping her hands. "Oh, thank you, Stone Man," she cried. "Thank you. It'll work; you'll see."

He watched her twirl around like a young girl at her first dance, her face all flushed with joy, her eyes as bright as lichen moss lit by the sun, and he found himself smiling. She looked about sixteen years old.

She was so easily pleased, he thought. Not like the other women he'd known in his life: Mibelle, his mother . . .

The bad memories made him jump to his feet. His chair tangled in his long legs, and he gave it a vicious kick. *How could he be so goddamn stupid?* He was actually starting to *like* hearing her talk.

"Enough chatter," he growled. "Let's start dinner."

She froze in midstep, the smile on her face ebbing. The hurt that crept into her eyes stabbed at his heart, but he ignored it. Life was pain. He refused to pretend otherwise.

"There's some stew left." Her voice caught, trembled.

He averted his eyes. "I'll make the bread."

"Fine. I'll go get some canned fruit from the cache."

"Fine." Turning his attention to making biscuits, Stone Man listened to the quiet pitter-pat of her feet as she moved toward the door. He could hear the hesitancy in her step, and he knew instinctively that she wanted to say something to him. Expectancy thickened the air.

Then the door creaked open. The night wind whispered through.

He tensed, waiting.

After a long minute he heard it click shut. He let his breath out slowly. She was gone.

He had to be more careful. He couldn't afford to let his guard down. The last time he'd done it, it had cost him five years of his life in a stinking cell. It was a mistake he wasn't likely to repeat.

And yet she was so easy to like sometimes. . . . So damned easy.

* * *

Devon sagged against the tent's canvas exterior. The wind plucked at her hair, tugging a few strands free to whip across her cheeks. She squeezed her eyes shut, but it didn't help. Tiny pinpricks of moisture burned behind her eyes.

What had she done? She hadn't said anything to wound him, hadn't insulted him, hadn't even babbled. All she'd done was be happy.

A couple of tears slid down her wind-reddened cheek.

She felt so alone out here, so silly and stupid and out of control. Nothing Stone Man did made sense. He hopped back and forth between friend and enemy with the dexterity of a rope dancer.

She brushed the tears away, suddenly angry at herself for being so dumb. She knew better than to get her hopes up. Every time they even came close to being allies, he shoved her away.

A thought struck her. Was it that simple? Could it be that he was afraid of being her friend, of needing her?

Father Michaels thought so. In fact he'd said as much.

She smiled. If that were the case, then maybe tonight's outburst was a good sign. Maybe, just maybe, it meant that she was burrowing a tiny hole through the icy shell that encased his heart.

And if so, maybe they were already friends.

Chapter Eleven

Devon's oldest muslin petticoat, slit from hem to waist along one seam, lay fanned out on the floor. Gnawing on her beleaguered thumbnail, she studied her canvas.

It would work, she decided. Squatting beside the underskirt, she picked up her paintbrush and wedged it between her teeth, then wiggled over to the jars of paint. Two itty-bitty cans of paint were all she'd been able to find in the whole post. One red, one white.

Nervously she cast a sideways glance at Stone Man. He was still cleaning his precious photographic plates, thank goodness. If he looked up too soon, she was in trouble. Not that it was her fault. How could she have known there wasn't enough paint to do the job?

Oh, well. Shrugging off the dilemma, she turned her attention back to the paints. Very, very carefully, she poured the contents of both small cans into one lightning jar. The colors immediately swirled together, giving birth to a shockingly bright shade of pink. Of course, she thought, any shade of pink would seem shocking in the Yukon.

She dipped her paintbrush in the jar and pulled it out slowly. Pink paint clung to the black bristles, dripping in huge globs back into the jar. She cringed, shooting another sidelong glance at her partner. He definitely wasn't going to like this.

She wiggled to the left, using her body to shield the petticoat from his prying eyes, and then set to work. A half hour later, she lay down the brush and stood up.

The bright pink words leapt out at her. FRESH PIES, CAKES, BISCUITS. FREE TART WITH $10 PURCHASE. The letters were perfectly formed, and not a single blob of paint had fallen where it didn't belong.

She took a step backward, eyeing her work. It was a good sign. Good and clean and—

Pink.

"Are you done?"

She jumped like a rabbit at his unexpected words. Her whole body tensed. Turning, she reluctantly met his curious gaze. "I am."

He looped his thumbs through his tired old suspenders and stood up, coming around the counter toward her. "Well, let's have a look."

Every nerve in Devon's body leapt to life. She stared at him, her eyes bugged, as he ambled toward the petticoat. His every step reverberated in her ears. This sign was so important to her. It was her contribution to the post. Her way of being needed. Please God, she prayed, don't let him take it from me.

Four feet from the petticoat he stopped dead. "Holy shit . . ."

She sucked in her breath and held it, her eyes riveted on his stern profile.

"It's pink. *Pink.*"

She gulped, suddenly unable to force a single intelligible word past her paper-dry lips.

He peered over at her questioningly.

"I can explain—"

"I don't want to hear it." He turned his attention back to the sign.

She chewed nervously on her lower lip. Time seemed momentarily suspended. If he told her to throw it away, it would mean he didn't want her help. Didn't need it. The thought made her almost desperate. She refused to be a useless puppet who simply stood quietly at his side for eight hours a day. She'd ventured all this way to be a partner, a participant. Surely he knew that by now.

The silence closed in on her, shredding her self-confidence

with cat claws until she couldn't stand it another second. She opened her mouth to speak.

He turned suddenly and looked at her. She felt the fire in his whiskey-hued eyes burn her face. Her breathing stumbled. The words died on her lips. *He was going to make her throw it away.*

Then he did the strangest and most unexpected thing. He burst out laughing. "Midas always said you'd paint my things pink. I guess the old fart was right."

She stared at him in amazement. He thought it was funny. Stone Man, the humorless hulk, thought her sign was *funny*.

The look on her face seemed to make him laugh harder. "Good God, Devon, your mouth is open and nothing's coming out. Now *that's* a first."

His laughter captivated her, and suddenly it was as if she were seeing him for the first time. The worry lines around his mouth had vanished, and his eyes were crinkled up in the corners and shining brighter than a summer sunrise. She blinked in surprise. Why, he looked . . . nice.

In that instant her every worry for the winter ahead vanished, and for the first time in years she felt young, free. Laughter bubbled up from her lonely soul and spilled past her lips.

Their laughter mingled and filled the tent with a jubilant, happy sound. Without thinking why, she moved toward him. It felt so good, this companionship. Laying her hand in the crook of his elbow, she tilted her face up to his.

The moment she touched him, Stone Man stiffened. His laughter stopped.

Devon immediately felt awkward. Her own laughter trickled into an uncomfortable silence.

He cleared his throat. "Well, you'd best get that sign up."

Her fingers slid off the warm flannel of his sleeve. She searched his implacable profile for a signal, however slight, that the man she'd just glimpsed was real. It was useless; there wasn't so much as a crinkle left around his eyes, and his mouth was once again a tense slash.

"It has to dry," she said after a long pause.

"Oh. Then I guess I'll be getting back to my plates."

"Yes, I suppose so."

Silence surrounded them as they each headed for their respective spots—he to the counter, she to the table. She did her usual things: she made coffee, she rearranged the pies and tarts, she dusted. But time and again her gaze returned to the man seated behind the counter.

More than once she thought of Father Michael's words: There's more to Stone Man than meets the eye.

By the next day their awkwardness with each other had passed. They were back to their silent, word-counting but comfortable routine.

Devon glanced around the post. Everything was as it should be, as it had been every day for the past month. Yet below the surface everything was different.

She felt differently today than she had yesterday. The laughter they'd shared had changed things between them. At least it had changed what she wanted from him. Nonhostility wasn't enough anymore. She wanted that laughter, that moment of caring back.

Maybe, she thought, if she could get him to help her put up the sign, they could find that closeness again. With that in mind, she stood up.

"Devon, sit down. It's still raining."

She plopped back onto her stool. "I know, but—"

"But you think if you pop up and check every ten seconds it'll stop?" He laughed. "Relax, your sign will go up today. It's only a flash rain. Dollar to a dog turd says it's sunny by two."

She smiled. "You'll excuse me if I find myself without a dog turd, I hope?"

He grinned and turned his attention back to his plates.

She cleared her throat. "I'm bored."

He plopped two matchsticks in the jar, then said, "You wanted to be a post operator."

"Maybe I could hum. That doesn't count as talking."

That got his attention. "No!"

"Well, do you have a better suggestion?"

Sighing, he shoved the plates aside. "How about a few hands of poker?"

"But I don't know how to play."

"Good, we'll play for money. Have a seat. Now, let's start with the rules. . . ."

In the next hour the wind picked up, whistling through the patchy copse of aspen trees that bordered the tent. The rain's fury trebled. Hammerbolts of icy water thumped the post's sagging roof and coursed down its canvas walls. The brownish water of the Yukon River burped and struggled against its banks.

But inside it was warm and dry. The little Yukon stove sputtered and hissed, taking the chill out of the storm-dark midday air. The two partners sat across from each other at the scarred spruce table, their elbows resting on the wooden surface as they studied their respective hands.

"Aha!" Devon gave a short cry of triumph as she lay down two queens.

He frowned.

She leaned forward in anticipation. One by one he lay down his cards. Four, ace, four, six . . . four.

She tried to act like a good sport about it. "You win. Again." Then she muttered under her breath, "Darn it anyway."

"Notice anything different, Devon?"

She took the cards from him and started stacking them into four neat piles, one pile for each suit. "No."

"The rain has stopped."

Her hands stilled. Her gaze shot skyward. "It has!" She jumped to her feet and raced over to the counter for her coat. Bundling herself up, she grabbed her petticoat, snagged a hammer and nails, and headed for the flaps.

"Ah, Devon?"

She stopped. "What?"

"Do you remember the day you arrived?"

"Yes. Why?"

"Do you recall being up to your ass in mud?"

"Oh, no."

"Don't worry. We'll get the damn sign up." Grabbing hold of the old table, he hauled it over to the flaps and shoved it through the opening. It immediately sank about six inches into the mud. He waited until it stopped sinking, then he tested it for balance.

"That feels pretty good. Climb up."

She eyed the lopsided table warily. "Are you sure?"

He held his hand out for her. "Trust me."

Devon laid her hand in his callused palm. His fingers curled around hers, the work-roughened skin abrading the soft flesh on the back of her hand. His skin felt warm, comforting.

"Here goes." Hiking up her skirt, she jumped onto the table.

The table immediately started bucking and wobbling beneath her as it settled deeper into the mud. She clung to Stone Man's hand until the movement stopped.

When the table had steadied, she took a deep breath and let go of his hand, then pushed up to her tiptoes. Stabbing a nail through the waistband of her petticoat, she nailed one side of the sign in place.

She spun around to ask Stone Man's opinion. At the shifting weight, the table bucked. Before she could scream she was flying through the air.

She hurtled into Stone Man's chest. The impact sent him reeling. He landed flat on his back in the mud.

Devon landed face-first on top of him. The force of the blow rattled her head and knocked the wind out of her. She lay stunned.

Slowly her world righted itself. Blinking, she wiped the mud from her face. "Oh, my . . ." She caught sight of the eyes staring up at her. That was all she could see—just his eyes. The rest of his face was smeared with mud.

She couldn't help herself. She giggled.

"You think this is funny?"

"N-No, it's just that, well . . ." She tried to school her face into a sober expression. "No."

His hands lifted out of the mud with a sick, hollow sound. She glanced at the two huge balls of black goo then looked back at his face. Beneath the layer of mud, she detected a shifting of the lips. A smile.

"Then you'll find this hilarious." His hands clamped onto her shoulders. Mud squirted through his fingers and slid downward, plopping onto her skirt.

Her eyes bulged. "Why, you—"

"Hey now, this is funny." Warm fingers cased in wet, cold

earth crept up her neck. The contradictory sensations made her shiver. Then his finger was at her mouth, breezing across her lips.

She licked her lips and immediately tasted mud. "Okay, okay, it's not funny."

A low rumble of laughter started deep in his stomach. His muddy beard shifted, tilted, and a dazzlingly white smile broke through the darkness.

It was like the sun breaking through the clouds. Devon smiled back, and before she knew it, they were both laughing like schoolchildren.

"Get . . . up," he said between fits of laughter. "I can't breathe."

Moving was easier said than done. Her legs had slipped apart, and one was on each side of Stone Man's body. She wiggled, trying to wrench her legs out of the mud.

When wiggling didn't work she planted her hands on his chest and pushed upward, unconsciously grinding her pelvis against his hips.

His laughter died abruptly. "Don't move."

The harshness of his command made her freeze. Hands bolted to his heaving chest, legs clamped to the sides of his body, she stared down at him. His breath was coming harder and faster.

Her own breathing quickened in response. She felt the hot weight of his stare on her lips, and suddenly all she could think about was the time he'd kissed her.

She leaned closer until her chin was almost resting on his chest. Her every perception seemed heightened; she could feel the rapid working of his lungs beneath her breasts, she could taste the warm, tobacco-scented rush of his breathing.

She smiled dreamily, thinking about the way his lips had felt on hers. "Are you thinking about our kiss?"

The next second she found herself sitting alone in the mud with him towering over her. She crossed her arms and blinked up at him in confusion.

"Let's get that damned sign up before the rain hits again."

She scraped the mud off her skirts and struggled to stand. "I guess that means you're not," she muttered under her breath.

He shot her a stunning glare. "You're damn right I'm not. That kiss didn't mean anything. Don't start acting like a cow-eyed schoolgirl about it."

He grabbed hold of the drooping petticoat, stretched it to the other support post, and nailed it down. Then he jammed the hammer into the waistband of his pants and stormed back into the tent.

"I liked you better when you were laughing," she said sullenly, following him.

"And I liked you better when the wind was knocked out of you."

After they'd both cleaned up Devon and Stone Man returned to the post and to their respective routines. She, sitting at the table; he, standing behind the counter. By outward appearance, Devon was sewing; but in fact she hadn't made a stitch in nearly an hour.

She was thinking, analyzing, and probing her strange response to Stone Man's body. Obviously she needed to reread Dr. Cowan's *The Science of a New Life*. Especially that section on "Amativeness: the use and abuse of amorous behavior."

What had made her think about that stupid kiss? And what in God's name had made her question him about it?

She groaned inwardly. Whenever she thought about her question, she wanted to slap herself silly. What had possessed her? She could practically hear herself murmuring the words, *Are you thinking about our kiss?*

Oh, God . . .

"Well, well," came a familiar voice, "if it isn't me two favorite people. How be ye both?"

Devon's head snapped up. "Father Michaels!" She dropped her embroidery hoop and raced to his side. "How are you?"

The gnarled little man let himself be guided to the table. "Fit as a fiddle, lass, I am. Thanks for askin'."

She poured him a cup of hot coffee and handed him a canned peach tart.

He shoved the little tart back across the table. "Why lass,

I can't pay for this, ye know. Ye'd best be savin' the goodies for yer payin' customers."

Sitting on the stool beside him, she took his hands in hers. "Take one, please."

"It wouldn't be right."

"They're our tarts, Father, and we'll give them out as we see fit. Isn't that right, Stone Man?"

"Sure, Father, we'd like you to have one . . . or two."

A current of pure electricity careened down Devon's spine. She bolted upright. He'd said we. We, as in my partner and I. "Thank you, partner."

He nodded. Across the tent their eyes met. Almost involuntarily she rose. She moved toward him, her skirts swishing softly atop the plank floor. Her steady gaze never left his face.

She stopped in front of the counter. "You know, Stone Man—" She thought she saw him flinch, and she frowned. "What is it?"

"Nothing."

She tried again. "We can make this partnership work."

"I said the priest could have a tart. Don't make a big deal out of it."

"It's more than that, and you know it. You said we."

"It was a slip."

"No."

He shoved a lock of hair out of his eyes and sighed. "Okay, I said it; I meant it. Don't make me sorry about it."

A smile hovered around her lips. "I won't. In fact, I intend to make you very, very happy."

He groaned. "That's what I was afraid of."

Just as she started to turn around she noticed that the little glass jar alongside the scales was empty.

Her mind swept through the events of the day. Between the sign and the poker game, she'd said hundreds of words. She glanced up at Stone Man. "Where are the matchsticks?"

He shifted uncomfortably. "Gone."

"Gone? What do you mean?"

"I mean gone, goddamn it. I've gotten used to your blabbing. But if you make a damned opera out of it, I'll start using them again."

Devon heard Father Michaels's cackle in the background. She had to bite down hard on her lower lip to keep from grinning. Through sheer force of will, her face remained impassive; not a hint of triumph glinted in her green eyes. She couldn't risk embarrassing him, not now when things were going so well.

"I won't," was all she said.

Chapter Twelve

Midas Magowin stared up at the billowing petticoat, his beady gray-black eyes narrowed in concentration. *Fresh pies, cakes, biscuits. Free tart with $10* . . . He frowned. What was that word?

His pointy features pulled into a grimace. "Damn woman," he muttered under his breath. Who did she think was reading her sign—a bunch of uppity schoolmarms like herself?

"Come on, boys," he hollered to Digger and Cornstalk, "let's have us some fun."

The three men burst through the tent flaps and headed straight for the warm stove, their bootheels clicking a steady beat across the wooden floor.

Midas grabbed hold of the nearest stool and yanked it toward him, planting his scrawny backside on the wooden surface. His eyes did a quick sweep of the place, but he didn't see hide nor hair of the little woman. Must be out paintin' more pink signs on her underwear.

"Hey Stoneyman," he yelled, pulling a jug of hootch out of his coat, "where's the bitch?"

Hidden behind the counter where she was dusting, Devon froze, waiting breathlessly for Stone Man's response.

There was a long silence, and then Stone Man said, "Go away, Midas."

Sighing disappointedly, Devon rested her forehead on the clean shelf in front of her. When would he stand up for her?

"Now, Stoneyman, is that any way to talk to a customer? I come in for my free tart. Where is it?"

"There aren't any *free* tarts. So get your scrawny ass off my stool and move on."

Devon pushed tiredly to her feet and stepped out from behind the counter. "Now, Stone Man," she said evenly, "there are free tarts, it just takes a purchase to get one."

"That ain't what the sign says!" Midas sputtered.

Devon stared at the old man. "It isn't?"

"No, it ain't, damn it. It says free tarts."

"It says free tarts *with a ten dollar purchase*."

Midas's beady eyes squinted. "That's trick advertising." He glared at Stone Man. "You gonna stand behind a woman's thinking?"

"I don't see that it's a question of sex, Midas. The sign says what it says."

Midas slammed his sinewy arms across his chest. Jutting his chin out, he stared sullenly at Devon. "Damn woman can't even paint a decent sign."

Digger Haines shrugged. "I dunno, Midas. The sign looks good to me. I didn't know what it said till now, but it's mighty . . . colorful."

Cornstalk sent her a shy smile. "Bear said just yesterday how it livened up the place."

Their kindness dispelled some of Devon's depression. "He did? Why—"

Midas snorted in disgust. "Bear's dumber than a hundred head of sheep."

Stone Man shot Devon a look that said *ignore the old fart*.

She tried to. Walking to the stove, she wrapped the edge of her apron around her hand and grabbed the coffeepot's tin handle. "Coffee anyone?"

Digger nodded enthusiastically. "Yes, please."

Pouring, she asked, "How are things up at Bonanza Creek?"

Digger gulped down his coffee. "I dunno, but I hear the gold's petering out. If you ask me, that strike of George's ain't gonna amount to a hill of sh—er, dung."

"Midas says the same thing, Miss Devon," Cornstalk chimed in.

"Really?" she asked conversationally, "and why is that?"

"None of your business," Midas snapped. "You make me sick, lady, with your uppity ways and your tryin' to fit in. Well, let me tell you something, you'll never belong here. Never."

Devon paled, taking an involuntary step backward. Was he right? she wondered desperately.

She felt an immediate, almost overwhelming urge to run to Stone Man, to fling herself into his strong arms and let herself be comforted.

She didn't move, of course, for she had no idea how one went about the business of seeking comfort. All her life she'd been the giver of solace, the rock to which others clung. Good old sensible Devon. She had no idea how to turn the tide.

It was just as well, she told herself. Certainly Stone Man knew as little about giving comfort as she knew about receiving it. And there was no one else to whom she could go, no one whose arms felt right around her.

"Never," Midas repeated spitefully.

"Shut up, Midas." Stone Man's command burst through the tent. "You've got no call to talk to my partner that way."

My partner. Devon's knees went weak. Her heart swelled, and tears clogged in her throat. He'd done it! He'd stood up for her.

Her eyes sought him out. He was looking right at her, and there was a softness in his eyes that was new. It wrapped around her heart with bands of warmth. "Don't let him get to you," he mouthed.

His support was all the strength she needed. She snapped her chin to a proud tilt and marched right back up to the table. Towering over the shrunken old man, she grabbed the jug of hootch out of his bony hand and slammed it on the table.

"Hey, you can't do—"

Her hard-eyed glare stopped him cold. "Yes, I can, and the sooner you realize that, the better off we'll both be. This is my post, and I have as much right to make my home in the Yukon Territory as you do."

He squinted up at her. "You got no rights."

She leaned closer, stabbing him with her eyes. "I have every right, Midas. I'm a Yukoner now, and all I ask is to be treated like any other Yukoner. I want to be left alone."

Midas swallowed hard, his knobby Adam's apple sliding up and down his thin throat. His eyes wore the wary, cornered look of a schoolyard bully who'd met his match.

"She's got you dead to rights, Midas," Digger said. "That's the code of the Yukon, and you gotta live by it. We don't harass each other. Hell, if we wanted people sticking their noses in our business, we'd live in San Francisco or Boston."

Midas jerked to his feet. Wrenching his precious jug out of Devon's grasp, he hugged it to his gaunt chest. His eyes flashed with unconcealed hatred. "Lady, you want to be left alone, you got it. I wouldn't spit on you if you were on fire. And I wouldn't eat one of your tarts if I was dying of hunger." He turned to Digger and Cornstalk. "Let's go, boys."

Digger grinned, his yellowed teeth glinting gold in the tent's early-afternoon sunlight. "Naw, I think I'll just hang around a while."

Midas harrumphed. "Cornstalk? You comin'?"

Cornstalk stared hard at his own hands. "I . . . I reckon I'll stay, too."

"Then stay, damn you!" Midas yelled as he stormed out of the tent.

Devon smiled giddily. Stone Man had finally stood up for her! She chanced another glance at him. He was still staring at her. She felt his eyes, as liquid as maple syrup, envelop her. Pride shone from their golden depths. Very, very slowly, he nodded at her.

His silent salute touched her heart. She couldn't remember the last time someone had been proud of her. When she was a child it had been her dearest dream that someday her father would look at her like that.

She offered him a bright smile. He smiled back, and she felt an almost blinding sense of joy. With effort she turned her attention back to Digger and Cornstalk. "So, boys, what was it you were going to say about Bonanza Creek? I really do want to know."

Cornstalk grinned. "Oh, boy, Miss Devon. There isn't any gold in that durn creek!"

"Really?" she heard herself say, "and why is that?"

"Well, the valley's too wide—"

"The willows don't lean the right way—"

"Everyone knows George's strike is on the wrong side of the Yukon . . ."

Devon tried to concentrate on the men's theories but couldn't. After a few minutes she gave up even trying. All she could think about were Stone Man's eyes and the way he'd nodded at her in a silent acknowledgment. In that instant, that heartbeat when their gazes had locked, she'd seen past Stone Man's unkempt façade to the soul that lay within. In his eyes there had been pain and, more than that, there had been understanding. An understanding of what it meant to be left out.

Father Michaels was right. Underneath Stone Man's gruff, dirty exterior beat a heart lonely and aching.

A heart like her own.

At closing time Devon left the post's warm interior and stepped outside. It took her eyes a moment to adjust to the dusk-shrouded street.

She glanced left. A lonely copse of aspen, their bright-gold autumn leaves cloaked by descending night, huddled together against the wind. At the other end of the street, Joe Ladue's new sawmill/saloon stood silhouetted against the charcoal sky, its lightning-jar windows glinting silver in the moonlight.

A cold blast of air cut down from the hills, sweeping through Front Street with a howling sigh. She pulled her woolen cloak tighter around her chin, mentally thanking Stone Man for making her bring it. He was right again; autumn was melting into winter. The nights were getting longer and colder.

Thinking about Stone Man made her frown. He'd acted strangely this afternoon, and the change in his demeanor bothered her. After he'd stood up for her against Midas, he'd gone into one of his deep silences. He'd stared at her for the remainder of the day, but not once had he spoken or smiled.

There'd also been something different about the way he'd looked at her. As if he were seeing her in a new light.

It had been odd indeed. Even stranger was the fact that he'd left her. As soon as Digger and Cornstalk had departed, Stone Man had mumbled an inane excuse about "having something to do" and bolted out of the post.

Devon stepped gingerly onto the makeshift boardwalk and headed home. When she got to the tent it was dark and empty. Feeling her way along the bookcase, she hung up her cloak and quickly built a fire.

The stove chased away the night's chill as she lit the kerosene lantern and set it on the table. Golden light wreathed the small area. She set down their plates and utensils then put on her apron and started supper.

Stone Man approached the tent silently. At the door he stopped, his eyes fastened on the rawhide latchstring.

God, he felt like a fool. Why in the hell had he done it? His hand moved up to his face, feeling the whiskerless line of his jaw. He winced. The skin felt red, raw. Exposed.

His eyes slid shut. She was going to crucify him with questions. Shit.

It's too late to turn back. Squaring his shoulders, he lifted his chin and took a deep breath. His big chest puffed out, straining the seams of the blue flannel shirt he was wearing. Before he could talk himself out of it, he jerked down on the latchstring. The door swung open, smacking into the support beam with a resounding *thwack*. The tent shuddered. A soggy red sock plopped to the floor.

The first thing he saw was Devon's back. She was standing at the stove. He slipped inside, closing the door quietly behind him.

"You're home!" she cried.

He tensed, his hands curling into white-knuckled fists at his side. Unconsciously he moved into a fighter's stance, legs planted firmly on the ground, hands balled at his sides, chin high.

Metal clanked on metal as she set a lid on her cast-iron pot. Running a hand through her hair, she spun around, heading straight for him.

"I'm so . . . ooh!" She stopped dead. Her hand flew to her mouth.

The silence thickened and stretched between them. Stone Man felt it ping down every vertebrae in his back.

"Stone Man?"

The words were spoken so quietly he barely heard them. A lump of something huge and paper-dry lodged in his throat. He swallowed thickly, nodding.

Her hand dropped. Her jaw followed suit. She took one hesitant step toward him. "Is it really you?"

He licked his lips. Never in his life had he wanted so badly just to bolt. It took every scrap of courage he possessed to stay there, rooted to the floor. He felt like an exhibit in Phineas Taylor Barnum's famous freak show. "It's me, but don't make a big deal out of it. Please."

A soft, tremulous smile shaped her lips. "May I take your coat?"

His eyes fluttered shut in a moment of silent thanks. When he opened them again he found himself staring directly into her eyes. He could see the little flecks of cinnamon that were scattered across her nose, smell the soft fragrance that clung to her clothing. She smelled like a late summer night, soft and flowery and full of promise.

"Sure," he said throatily. Shrugging out of his mackinaw, he handed it to her. Their eyes met again. He looked quickly away. "What's for supper?"

"Caribou stew. Evaporated peaches. Biscuits. The usual things. I didn't realize tonight was . . . special."

He snorted. "Nothing's special. I shaved and took a bath. It's no big deal. I always shave before winter sets in."

"From what I hear, winter's still three weeks away."

He shrugged uncomfortably. "Any coffee?"

"Certainly. Sit down." She bustled back to the stove. He took his place at the table, watching her through lowered lashes as she poured two cups of coffee. Her lithe, graceful movements reminded him of a hawk soaring on the wings of the wind.

"That looks good," he commented as she ladled stew onto two enameled tin plates.

"Thanks." In one quick, efficient motion, she served up

two side bowls of peaches, plopped a biscuit on top of each plate of stew, and sat down.

Stone Man stared at his plate. Carrots, onions, and potatoes peeked through a rich brown sauce, beckoning him, and a mouth-watering aroma wafted upward. His stomach growled in response.

He started to reach for his spoon then stopped. *No.* He had a plan, and he meant to stick to it. One night; that's all it had to be. Just one night and then he could go back to his old self. He put both hands in his lap and waited patiently for her to begin eating.

She edged the napkin out from underneath her fork, shook it open, and then smoothed it across her lap.

He grimaced. It was now or never. He grabbed the napkin's tiny white corner between his thumb and forefinger and tugged. The fork rattled. He froze, his gaze darting across the table.

She wasn't watching. She was staring intently into her stew. Probably trying to figure out which vegetable to eat first.

He tugged again. The napkin sailed free, fluttering into his lap like a truce flag. He sighed with relief. Mission accomplished.

He watched her pluck up her spoon, oh so daintily, and scoop out a teeny amount of stew. She lifted it to her lips and ate it soundlessly.

Whoever heard of eating stew soundlessly? Thank God it was just for one night. He picked up his spoon and started eating, slurping as little as possible.

Devon's whole body felt warm. He was trying to copy her table manners! Oh, he wasn't doing a very good job (a darn poor one, in point of fact), but he was *trying*. Really trying.

She looked across the table at him. Their eyes met. Warmth tingled through her body for a heartbeat; then he turned his attention back to his food.

He wanted her to pretend nothing was different. He felt uncomfortable with the change, and so she was to ignore it. But how could she?

Her eyes caressed the soft folds of blue flannel that sheathed his chest and arms. It was such a treat to see him in something other than that bland golden-tan workshirt he always wore.

Her gaze moved to the small vee of skin where his collar lay open. His flesh was nut brown from the summer sun, and a smattering of curly black hairs made it appear even darker. She wondered fleetingly what those hairs would feel like. Soft? Wiry? A blush crept across her cheeks at the unladylike thought.

Flickering lantern light curled golden fingers through his hair, turning it into a shimmering curtain of midnight. More light filtered through his downcast eyelashes, fanning in spider-leg strands of amber across his tanned cheeks.

He was almost *handsome*. Without the aging grayness in his beard he looked ten years younger. Her eyes feasted on the clean, rugged line of his jaw and the sharp, straight nose that perched proudly above the nicest lips Devon had ever seen on a man. Lips that had once tasted her own . . .

"What are you looking at?" The words were a growl, deep in his throat.

She looked quickly away. "N-Nothing. Would you like some pie?"

He brought the napkin to his lips. "No, thanks."

As she watched him wipe his mouth, a strange sensation spiraled through her blood. She felt light enough to float. He was trying so hard.

Why? she wondered suddenly. Why was he making this change? "Why?" The word whispered past her lips.

Stone Man felt compelled to look up. There was such an ache in her voice, such a need. Their eyes met.

The lantern's tremulous golden glow wreathed them. Behind her the tent no longer existed; it was a series of charcoal-shaded lumps, a lightless void. The world had dwindled to just the two of them, and he was lost in her eyes.

"Why?" she asked again.

He licked his lips. She had a right to know, and for some strange reason he wanted to tell her. But the answer—because you didn't deserve Midas's crap—stuck in his throat. Years of training made it impossible for him to force out the words.

It was always a mistake to reveal too much. He'd learned

long ago it was better to shield one's thoughts and dreams. Especially from a woman.

He shrugged. "It was almost winter, and I can't stand a frozen mustache and beard."

Her smile flattened. "Oh. I thought . . ."

The disappointment on her face made him feel awkward. Cowardly. *Damn it.*

He'd planned this evening for her, to give her some of the warmth she'd given him. Why then, when it came time to actually give her something tangible like the truth, did he find himself slinking back into the comfortable darkness of detachment?

"No, that's not true." The words slipped out.

She looked up at him, surprised. "Oh?"

He wished like hell he had a beard to tug on right about now or to hide the heat he felt creeping along his jawline. Now was the time to tell her the truth. To make the kind of confession he hadn't made since he was seventeen years old; a confession that he cared.

"I shaved and all because I thought—after Midas—you might need some cheering up. He was wrong to yell at you like that, and . . . well, I know how much you care about shit like that, and I . . ."

"Yes?" she prodded.

"I didn't want you to feel bad."

Tears lurched into Devon's throat. She swallowed the lump, trying to dislodge it. He'd done it for her. For *her*. She felt special for the first time in her life.

She noticed the blush that stained his cheeks, and an almost aching tenderness unfolded inside her. He was so big, so rough around the edges; but inside, where it counted, he was as frightened and vulnerable as she.

"I don't know what to say. . . ."

Stone Man jumped to his feet. "Thank God. Then let's do the dishes."

He grabbed the large metal washbasin off its hook behind the stove, filled it with preboiled river water from the cistern in the corner, and set it on the table. Adding the potful of water Devon had already heated, he dropped in a bar of lye soap and swirled his hands in the water until it was a murky gray.

Scooping up the dirty enamel dishes, he tossed them into the washbasin. Grayish water splattered over the basin's curled rim, forming big blotches of darkening black on the tablecloth. He shot Devon a sheepish glance. "Sorry."

She smiled. "What's a little water? You want to wash tonight?"

"I guess."

Grabbing her dishtowel, Devon sidled up to him. Her skirts swayed softly, buffeting her ankles. She stared down at the washbasin, fascinated by the quick, sure movements of his hands as he washed the dishes. A patch of milky soap clung to the tiny black hairs on the back of his hands then slid slowly back into the water.

"You mind taking this plate before my hands prune up?" His voice held a suppressed laughter she hadn't heard before.

She giggled. "Sorry."

They washed the dishes and talked of little things; of their day, of the Yukon, of the madness that made grown men muck for gold so far from their homes. Every so often the sound of their mingled laughter filled the tent. Devon couldn't remember when she'd felt so good. It was as though the simple declaration that he cared for her had freed Stone Man. His icy detachment and surly defenses were gone. He was simply her partner, her friend.

She dried the last cup reluctantly, afraid that the spell would be broken when they stepped apart. She needed a plan to keep them together, and she needed it quickly.

As he hefted the washbasin and carried it to the door, she brushed past him.

"Where you going?"

"The cache," she answered, disappearing into the small canvas-covered enclave.

She barreled back into the tent in less than a minute, a green tin box clutched to her breast.

"What are you up to?"

"You'll see." She hurriedly put water on to boil then set a big cast-iron pot on the stove's red-hot surface. She plopped a dollop of bacon grease into the pot.

As the grease hissed and popped, she grabbed Stone Man's arm and led him to the bed. "Sit up there. Those stump chairs are too darn hard, and—"

"Don't bother explaining. I can tell you've got a plan here, and I'm not about to get in your way. Now, you want me up there?"

She nodded. He lifted the heavy partition off the bed and laid it on the floor, then climbed into bed. Leaning against the headboard, he watched Devon's fluttery movements, a wry smile tugging at his lips.

In a matter of moments he heard the telltale pop-hiss-pop of popping corn. His smile deepened. She was making a party out of it.

Devon scooped the popped corn into an old red coffee can then set it aside as she made two cups of steaming tea laced with milk. She carried her bounty carefully toward the bed. Handing Stone Man his cup, she tucked the can under her arm, and wiggled onto the bed beside him.

Like two adolescents they sat next to each other, eating popped corn and sipping tea and talking about everything from the weather to the newest inventions. Everything but themselves.

Within an hour a chill seeped into the tent. Even the hardy stove couldn't keep the cold air completely at bay. Without saying a word Stone Man got up from the bed and pulled a black fur blanket from the chest near the bookcase. Crawling back onto the squishy mattress, he tucked the blanket up under Devon's chin and around her shoulders.

"Wait," she said, "you need it, too. Move closer and we can share."

Sidling up to her, he tucked the black wolverine blanket around both of them. She half turned, tilting her face up to his. In the shimmering light of the kerosene lantern, her skin looked almost golden, and her eyes were black.

It seemed the most natural thing in the world to put his arm around her, to draw her close. She melted against him. The top of her head rested just below his chin, and he could smell the fresh, clean scent of her.

He leaned back against the headboard, taking her with him.

"What shall I tell you about now?" she asked quietly. "Mr. Marconi's amazing wireless telegraph?"

He thought for a moment then said, "Tell me about your family. I feel like hearing a happy story."

He felt her stiffen. "Then you've asked the wrong question."

Stone Man went very still. For some reason he'd always assumed she'd had a picture-book life. Little miss perfect. Could there be pain in her past as there was pain in his? The thought was unsettling.

His hand moved to her hair. Absent-mindedly he stroked the flyaway mass, drawing it back from her face. He didn't intend to ask her about something as private as her pain. It was none of his business.

The thought gave him pause, and incredibly he realized that he *wanted* it to be his business. He wanted to be a part of her life.

He didn't analyze the thought. He simply accepted it. It would frighten him tomorrow, he knew, but for once in his life he felt the need to really get to know another human being.

He heard himself say, "Is it something you want to talk about?"

Her answer was a long time in coming. "Yes, I think it is."

Chapter Thirteen

Yes, I think it is. Devon couldn't believe she'd said it. What on earth had possessed her? She never talked about her past. She never even thought about it. At least she tried not to.

Yet hadn't she waited for years for someone to ask? As a young girl she'd ached to talk about her pain to someone. She'd always been able to shield Colleen from their father's meanness, and as a result Colleen hadn't seen the ugliness and hadn't asked about it. Neither had anyone else. Devon supposed it was because she was always the caretaker, the problem solver. Good old sensible Devon. Certainly *she* didn't have any problems.

She snuggled closer to Stone Man. Being wrapped in his arms made the past seem somehow . . . smaller, less frightening. This was her chance. Here, in his strong arms, she could purge her soul and begin to heal. She could allow herself to be weak.

Lord, how she wanted, just once, to be comforted.

But she was afraid. A long time ago she'd boxed up the memories and buried them in her heart. Never once had she taken them out of storage and examined them with an adult's eyes. She was afraid to open them, afraid that once she started crying she might never be able to stop.

He stroked the hair out of her face. The warmth of his touch soothed her, calmed her fears. God help me, she thought, I *need* to open the box . . .

She drew a shaky breath then pulled out of his arms and looked up at him. "If I tell you about my fa—about when I was a little girl, will you promise not to interrupt me? I don't think I could start again if I had to stop. I have to tell it all at once."

He smiled crookedly. "Me, interrupt you?"

She cuddled up against him again, mentally preparing herself for the ordeal of talking about her father. It would be easier, she decided, if she kept herself detached from the story. Pretend it was someone else's life; then she could just say the words, let him hug her, and everything would be fine.

"My father started out a good man, or so my mother used to say. They met when they were both young, not past nineteen, and they wed on a lark. No doubt my father only wanted to get as far as the bedroom, but my mother, being a lady, made him walk to the altar to get there.

"Mother didn't realize the magnitude of her mistake, of course. All she knew was that Paddy O'Shea was the handsomest, liveliest man she'd ever met. He swept her off her feet. Everything went swimmingly, I'm told, until mother conceived me."

Her hands curled into tight fists. Her lower lip trembled. *It's someone else's story.*

"Paddy didn't want to be a father, you see. 'Too much responsibility,' he said. 'Too expensive.' He demanded that my mother 'take something for it.' I know because he told me every chance he got."

She rushed ahead to keep from thinking about that part of it. "When he was sober my father wasn't so bad. He was . . . orderly. He liked things organized.

"I always did my best to put everything exactly where it belonged. But every time he came home he wanted things in a different place. He'd say that a good daughter would know where things belonged. But I didn't, I could never be good enough." Her voice cracked. "I tried so hard."

She made her voice sound lighthearted. "Of course, father wasn't sober often."

A surge of painful memories accompanied her admission. She squelched them quickly, refusing to dwell on things that couldn't be changed. She wished fleetingly that she could just stop talking, but she couldn't. She'd started, and now there was nothing to do but finish.

"When father was drunk, he was mean," she said matter-of-factly. "He would scream and yell and rage. And there was the strap. . . . "

The strap. She hadn't meant to say that, hadn't meant to think about it. But suddenly it was there, in her mind, and she couldn't dispel the picture of it.

She squeezed her eyes shut, trying desperately not to remember. Memories hurtled one after another through her mind: her mother, broken in mind and body; herself, huddled in a corner, watching it all and crying, always crying; her father's drunken, leering face and high-pitched holler. And the strap. Always the strap.

An uncontrollable shiver swept Devon's body.

Stone Man's hold on her tightened. "Did he hurt you?" His voice sounded angry, almost predatory.

Devon flinched. "I told you not to interrupt."

"Did he hurt you?"

She could tell he'd keep asking until she answered, so she did. "He didn't beat me."

It was the answer she'd always given herself, and it was true. He'd never beaten her, except in discipline, and then only when she'd deserved it by being a bad daughter. So why was it that whenever she thought of him she got a sick, hollow feeling in her stomach?

Such a pat, well-thought-out answer, thought Stone Man. The simple sentence tore at his heart. She was trying so hard to be calm, to be perfect. He felt a white-hot surge of anger at the man who'd taught her that only in perfection could she find love.

He didn't beat me. The sentence was a shield, an automatic response she'd come up with to keep her analytical mind from digging any deeper.

But the pain was still there, buried just beneath her calm, rational exterior in a box marked DO NOT OPEN. He knew because he was thirty-nine years old, and he had the same pain locked away in his own soul.

She couldn't go on pretending she hadn't been hurt. If she did, she might end up like him, bitter and alone. He didn't know why the thought bothered him so intensely, but it did.

He had to help her. But how? Nothing in his life had prepared him to take on the role of comforter. He reached out to her in the only way he knew; he tightened his hold on her body. Before he knew it he'd said, "Fists aren't the only way to hurt people."

She drew in her breath sharply.

"Let it out, Dev. I'm right here, I'll take care of you."

Amazingly she believed him. For the first time in her life she felt protected.

"He hated me." The three tiny words slipped from her mouth, and the moment they did they freed her.

Tears coursed down her cheeks. She wept; for the father's love she'd never known, for the mother's caring she'd done without, for all the times she'd stopped herself from crying. She cried until her soul was parched and dry, and there were no tears left to cry. When she was finished, she felt stronger. Whole.

She pulled a wrinkled-up handkerchief from her apron pocket and blew her nose. Cautiously she looked up at Stone Man. He was looking down at her, and there was a tenderness in his eyes that stole her breath.

The moment stretched between them, and slowly Devon became aware of how she must look. Her hair had come loose and no doubt looked like a lopsided bird's nest. And her eyes! Lordy, her eyes felt like sun-baked mud puddles, all dry and cracked and red.

Smoothing the hair out of her eyes, she tried to smile. "Well, that was fun."

"Thanks for trusting me," he said softly.

That lump came back to her throat. She nodded, feeling the tears return to her eyes. The words "thank you" stuck in her throat. If she said them, the waterworks would start again.

Embarrassed suddenly, she groped for something to lighten the mood. To do something with her hands, she brushed the hair out of his eyes. That was it! Eyeing his hair, she scrambled to her knees. "Could I cut your hair?"

He didn't know what he'd expected her to say, but it sure as hell wasn't "Can I cut your hair?" He smiled. Leave it to Devon to spill her guts and then turn to cleaning.

"Please?"

He shrugged. At that moment he couldn't have denied her a thing.

She leapt off the bed. Beaming, she rushed over to her armoire and returned with a big pair of silver scissors.

"Here," she said, patting the back of the stump chair, "sit down."

He did as he was told. She swept a dishtowel around his neck and clamped the two ends together with a clothespin.

"Collar length all right?"

He eyed the scissors uneasily. "No shorter."

The snip, snip, snip of the scissors filled the quiet tent, accompanied now and then by the sputtering flame of the lantern. Stone Man sat perfectly erect, his only movement the sporadic tapping of his foot on the hard wooden floor.

She edged sideways. Her left leg snuck up between his, burrowing past his knee and settling comfortably along his thigh. The contact jolted him upright.

"Sit still," she ordered.

He froze, his gaze glued to the softly swirling mass of skirting between his legs. He felt the heat of her leg through the wool of his pants. A jet of pure electricity shot up his thigh, landing hot and hard in his groin. He shifted his weight.

"Stone Man, sit still."

Was it his imagination, or was her voice huskier? Was she feeling it, too, this burst of sensation? He tilted his head back. Immediately he wished he hadn't. Her breasts were a hand's width from his face. He sucked in his breath hard. He held it as long as he could then let it shoot past his lips. It fluttered through the lacy edge of her crisp white apron.

The soft, slim fingers of her left hand slid under his chin, exerting pressure for him to look up. He fought it, forcing himself to look straight ahead—right past her breasts to the sagging canvas wall beyond.

"Look up."

Reluctantly he did and found himself staring right into her face. For the space of a breath he felt like he were drowning in her eyes. It took a supreme effort to wrench his gaze away.

Her nearness was giving him all sorts of ideas, ideas he shouldn't be having around a woman like her.

He broke out in a cold sweat. What the hell was he thinking? She wasn't a whore. . . . She was a lady. What in God's name did a man do when he wanted a lady?

The answer came swiftly. Run.

He jumped to his feet, wincing as his left boot heel came down on the scalloped edge of her underskirt. The sickening sound of rending cotton hissed through the tent.

Caught off balance, Devon stumbled into his chest. The scissors clanged to the floor amidst a shower of night-black hair. She flung her arms around his neck, clinging to him for support.

He felt her nipples harden, felt them push against the worn flannel of his workshirt like twin pebbles. Struggling for control, he stared at the ceiling. Concentrating on each breath, he willed his traitorous body to relax.

He felt the quick, almost birdlike movement of her head. She'd lifted her face to his.

Oh God . . . He grabbed her by the shoulders, intending to push her away, but as his fingers curled around the softness of her flesh, he felt his control waver. Slowly, slowly, he pulled her to him.

When he looked down into her huge, expectant eyes, he was lost. In the deepest recesses of his tired, bitter soul, something warm and bright and almost hopeful unfurled.

"Cornelius?" Her voice was a throaty purr that slid down his ramrod-stiff spine like melted butter.

She was on her tiptoes now, her face within inches of his. He could feel the soft vibrations of her breath against his throat. Her lips were one quick movement away. . . .

She wanted him to kiss her, the little fool.

The realization that he wanted the same thing hit him like a lightning bolt. He swallowed dryly. He couldn't remember the last time he'd wanted to kiss a woman—a quick roll between the sheets, sure, but a kiss? An honest-to-God, lip-to-lip kiss? Never.

"Devon, don't be stupid." He tried to stifle the harsh, almost desperate tenor of his voice but couldn't. "You don't know what you're starting here."

She stared up at him unblinkingly. He was wrong. She wanted him to kiss her, wanted it more than she'd ever wanted anything in her life. In his arms she felt it all; comfort, security, warmth. All the feelings she'd never known. Yet it wasn't enough. She wanted more. She wanted, just once, to know passion.

She pulled a few useless hairpins out of her hair. Her ragged topknot collapsed, melting into a fiery spray of waist-length curls. "Then show me," she whispered.

"Oh, God, Dev . . ." He groaned, taking her face in his hands with a gentleness he didn't know he possessed. Anchoring his hold at the base of her neck, his thumbs grazed the velvet skin of her cheeks. She was so damned soft. . . .

She smiled up at him, and the look in her eyes captured his breath. He lowered his head to kiss her. She reached up, meeting him more than halfway. His mouth slanted possessively over hers.

He moved slowly, not wanting to frighten her. His tongue slid along her parted lips, seeking without demanding, until slowly, timidly, she opened her mouth. The unspoken invitation made his heart hammer inside his chest. His hold on her body tightened, and before he knew it he was clinging to her like a drowning man. After all the years alone it felt so good to be in someone's arms, to be held and kissed and cared for.

His eyes squeezed shut in a silent prayer. For the first time in his life he'd found something real.

Something real. A chill swept through his body at the thought. With a deep, shuddering groan he dragged his lips from hers and buried his face in the crook of her neck.

He was a fool, a goddamn thirty-nine-year-old fool.

How could he be so stupid? A man like him didn't find happiness, and certainly not in the arms of a woman like Devon. A lady.

She touched his face. Her palm felt warm and moist against his skin, reminding him forcibly of other, more intimate parts of her body. He groaned.

"Cornelius?"

He succumbed to the pressure of her voice. Pulling back, he looked down. She was staring at him through love-filled eyes.

He fought a wave of despair. He'd waited all his life for

that look, but now it was too late. He was too old to build a white picket fence and too set in his ways to live inside one. He was a Yukoner, a loner. Always had been, always would be. With the realization came a sense of loss so profound it made his knees weak.

"Kiss me some more," she murmured dreamily. "It made my toes tingle."

What she said was "kiss me," but all he heard was the creaking shut of that damn gate. She might be naive enough not to know where this kiss was going, but he damn sure wasn't. A man couldn't make love to a woman like Devon and then walk away. At least he couldn't. Unless he wanted to live inside that white picket fence, he had to stop what was happening between them.

Before he could talk himself out of it he grabbed her by the shoulders and shoved her backward.

"Oh, for goodness' sake," she said with an impatient sigh. "What now?"

"Lesson's over."

She frowned. "Lesson? What lesson? I just want to be kissed some more."

"Find someone else."

The first glimmer of hurt crept into her eyes. "I don't want someone else. I want you."

That simple admission almost did him in. Christ, he thought desperately, if he didn't leave right now, he was going to pull her into his arms and give her what she was so innocently asking for.

With a low growl he grabbed his mackinaw off the hook and headed for the door.

"Wait, Cornelius, please. Let's talk about this."

He stopped. Schooling his features into the scowl he'd worn for twenty-two of his thirty-nine years, he glared at her. "Don't call me that. I'm Stone Man."

And that, he admitted to himself as he stormed out of the tent, was the biggest lie of all.

Devon winced as the door slammed shut. Damn him! She was getting sick and tired of him running away every time things got interesting.

She stared at the door for a long time, trying to will him

to return. When he didn't, she went to the stove and made herself a cup of tea. Sitting down with her tea and her book, she proceeded to wait for his return.

"You can run, but you can't hide," she said in a quiet, determined voice. "We *will* talk about this."

At the moment, however, in the tent's lonely solitude, the thought was paltry solace indeed.

Stone Man stood on the banks of the Yukon, his arms wrapped tightly around his chest. The dead, pock-faced moon cast its skeletal blue fingers along the murky water. He watched through narrowed, unseeing eyes as the season's first chunk of ice floated down the river, its awkward triangular shape illuminated by the moon's wan glow.

A late-night drizzle began to fall; slowly at first, then building. Nail-sharp shards of rain bit at his whiskerless cheeks and forehead, shooting in cold streaks down his neck. Swiping the wetness from his face with an impatient hand, he flipped up his fleece collar, burying his chin in its woolly warmth.

The icy onslaught captured his attention for no more than a heartbeat. He had one glorious moment of freedom, and then he was back in the mire, thinking about Devon.

He'd never wanted a woman so badly in his life.

Why? he asked himself for the hundredth time since leaving the tent. Why did he want her?

He'd learned long ago to live without sex. Growing up in The Painted Lady, he'd learned that sex was nothing more than a couple of quick grunts and a poke in the dark. Nothing to mess up a life over.

And if New Orleans's most famous brothel hadn't taught him the lesson well enough, prison certainly had. Hell, even after five years in that hellhole, he'd never had any difficulty ignoring a troublesome woman.

But Devon was different. More and more often lately he'd found himself watching her and worse yet listening to her. He liked the way she talked—so calmly—and he liked the way she looked at him. Not like he was a dirty, no-account drifter, but like he was a somebody. Like he mattered.

He did matter to her, he knew that, and for some strange reason she mattered to him.

That was precisely the problem. He'd known, of course, that he was beginning to care for her, but until tonight he hadn't realized how much.

Time and again he'd told himself that she was just a friend, a partner, a fellow Yukoner, but he couldn't lie to himself anymore. Not after that kiss. Now he had to face the truth: She was a woman, and he wanted her.

God, was he in trouble.

Fortunately he knew how to deal with trouble. He'd been dealing with it all his life, and always in the same manner—by running from it.

It was time to get the hell out of Dawson City.

A loud knock on the door woke Devon from a sound sleep. She opened her eyes slowly. Scarred planks of wood filled her vision. She blinked. Where in the world—

She remembered in a rush. She'd fallen asleep at the table, waiting for Stone Man.

Lifting her head slowly, she cast a bleary-eyed glance at the bed. It was empty.

Her stomach sank. He hadn't come home last night. *Darn.* He was doing a pretty good job of hiding after all. Wearily she brought herself upright in the chair and took a sip of long-cold tea. The cool liquid helped wash away the sour taste in her mouth.

The knock came again. Louder this time.

She wiped the sandy vestiges of sleep from her eyes and called, "Who is it?"

"Bear."

Every trace of exhaustion vanished. She smiled. Bear was just the person to talk to about the confusing events of last night. Bear was the only person in the world who really knew Stone Man. She jumped to her feet. "Coming!"

Racing to the crockery bowl she kept filled with water, she splashed her face and brushed her teeth, then quickly plaited her hair. Feeling almost human again, she smoothed her horribly wrinkled skirt and hurried to open the door.

"Good morning, Bear," she said brightly, "what a wonderful surprise."

"Morning, Devon."

She frowned at his rather subdued greeting. Normally when Bear came to the post he was grinning from ear to ear. Taking his arm, she led him to the table and pulled out a chair for him. "Here, sit. I'll make us some coffee."

He did as he was told.

At the stove she cast him a sidelong glance. He was so quiet. And he looked tired. "Are you all right?"

"Cornelius sent me."

His tone of voice chilled her to the bone. The coffeepot slipped through her fingers, hitting the stove with a resounding *clang*. It took her a moment to gather the courage necessary to ask, "Why?"

"He left. Said he was goin' up to Rabbit Creek to take pictures of the minin'. There's talk that strike of Lyin' George's might just pan out after all."

For one heart-stopping moment Devon thought she was going to burst into tears. Then she got control of herself. It wouldn't do any good to cry in front of Bear; it would only make him feel uncomfortable. She went to the table and sat down. Squeezing her eyes shut, she counted silently to ten.

She opened her eyes and found Bear staring at her. The sadness in his big brown eyes almost severed her hard-won control. Tears threatened again.

"He could have said good-bye." She'd meant the words to sound angry, but they came out croaked and desolate.

Bear scooted close. She thought for a moment he'd take her hand, but he didn't. Instead he said, "Maybe not."

"Struck mute, was he?" she said with unaccustomed bitterness.

"Now, missy, don't get all snappy with me. I'm liable to snap right back but good."

Devon heard the smile in his voice and immediately felt like a spoiled child. "Sorry."

"Maybe Cornelius couldn't say good-bye. Maybe it took all his guts just to go."

"Oh, my, yes. It certainly takes courage to run away."

"Ah, Devon, I'm disappointed in you. Cornelius always said you was smart as a whip."

She bristled. "I am smart."

Bear wedged a dirty toothpick between his two front teeth and leaned back in his chair, studying her. "Then answer me this, miss smarty-pants, why do most people run away from somethin'?"

Devon thought about that for a moment. "I don't know. I left St. Louis because I was afraid of what I'd become if I stayed."

"Aha!"

Devon sighed impatiently. "Don't look at me like you've just solved my every problem. So what if I ran away because I was scared of staying. What does that have to do with Stone Man? What on earth does he have to be frightened of?"

This time Bear did take her hand. His voice dropped to a whisper. "Gettin' hurt."

Devon was stunned into momentary speechlessness. If anyone else had suggested such a ridiculous notion she'd have laughed in his face, but not Bear. He knew Stone Man too well.

"Stone Man has to know I'd never hurt him," she said finally.

"He ain't a thinker like you, Devon." Bear leaned closer, looking her right in the eyes. "You ever seen a lone timber wolf?"

"No."

"Well, if you had, maybe you'd understand Cornelius a mite better."

"Help me to understand him, Bear. Please."

"Sometimes a wolf gets shunned by the pack, and he has to wander the woods alone. When he sees a campfire, he draws close. He can smell the roasting meat and knows he can kill the poor fool sitting by himself. But the wolf don't move; he just stands in the dark, waiting and watching."

"And that's Cornelius? Drawn to the fire and yet afraid of it?"

"Something like that. Remember, missy, Cornelius lived alone a long time. He's lived by gut instinct so long he don't question it. When his gut says run, he runs."

"And somehow I frighten him." She sighed. "But I would never hurt him." This time the words were spoken with an aching softness.

Bear smiled at her. "I know that, missy. When Cornelius figures that out, he'll be back. A man can only howl at the moon so long."

Devon tried to laugh. "I hope he figures it out quickly. Patience has never been one of my strongest traits."

"Well, I wouldn't get all twisted up over it. He'll come back when he comes back." He winked at her. "You think he'll figure somethin' like this out quickly?"

Devon smiled involuntarily. "No, I don't suppose so."

"Well," Bear said, "I'm here for you till he does. I'm gonna come by every mornin' to walk you to the post, and I'll be keepin' my eye on you durin' the day."

"Oh, that isn't nec—"

"It was to Cornelius. He said I was to watch over you like you was my own kin."

Devon's heart tripped. "He did?"

"He did."

She felt light enough to fly. He *did* care about her, and that's why he'd left. Because he was scared by his own emotions.

She hoped he was scared to death.

Stone Man huddled under the sagging, shivering branches of a half-naked tree, watching rain pummel the Yukon River. Tugging the fleece collar of his mackinaw closer around his stubble-coated chin, he hunched his shoulders against the biting wind. As he skuttled backward, searching blindly for the tree's trunk, a huge blob of rain plunked in his open eye.

"Damn it," he hissed, wiping his eye. Damn the rain, damn the cold, and damn her. Most of all, damn her.

He felt like a frozen pile of dog crap. Just thinking about her made him mad.

All his life he'd been moving, drifting, but this was the first time he'd ever run from anything. And he was running from a goddamn woman. Where was the self-respect in that?

Worse yet it wasn't going well at all. He'd been gone less than twenty-four hours and already he was tired, cranky, and sore. He was too damn old to be gallivanting around the countryside in the shadow of winter, too old to be playing the self-reliant mountain man. Hell, if he'd wanted to spend his nights hunkered down in the mud he wouldn't have built a nice, cozy tent.

Nice, cozy tent. Unbidden an image of home flashed in his mind. Not the sagging, stinking tent he'd built ten years ago, but the home she'd made for him out of clean sheets, good meals, quiet laughter, and wildflowers. It was the first home he'd ever known. Oh, he'd had lots of places to hang his hat, lots of roofs over his head, but he'd never had a home. A place where he belonged. A place he missed when he wasn't there.

No. Those were precisely the type of thoughts he was freezing his ass off to forget. He didn't belong there, didn't belong with her. He didn't belong anywhere, and he didn't want to. He was a loner, a recluse. Through the eye of his camera he observed the building of life by others. He took no part in building one of his own.

The only consolation was that he'd left in time, before she wormed her way into his life. She may have sneaked into his post and into his tent and (he was forced to admit) into his affection, but she damn well hadn't become a necessary part of his life. Not yet. He was still his own man, ruled by no one, accountable only to himself. Hadn't he proved that by walking away from her so easily?

He'd simply had a momentary lapse of judgment—and even that hadn't been his fault. She'd tricked him. She'd made him feel so comfortable he'd let down his guard. But no more. From now on his guard was up. All he had to do was break the habit of liking her.

How tough could that be? he wondered. She was just a woman. It couldn't be any harder than giving up whiskey—and he'd done that in a single day.

Yep, he figured he'd meander up Bonanza Creek way, take a few photographs, kick Devon from his thoughts, and then return home the same man he'd been before she stepped into his life. It shouldn't take more than a day or two. Three tops.

Pulling his hat lower on his brow, he folded his knees up

to his chest and wrapped his arms around his legs. Eyes closed, he leaned heavily against the tree trunk.

Yep, two days away from her and he'd be as good as new. "Stone Man" MacKenna.

But his last conscious thought before drifting off to sleep was of a pair of green eyes.

Chapter Fourteen

Devon curled her gloved fingers around the tin cup, drawing some small bit of warmth from the metal. She took a sip, sighing contentedly as the hot tea slid in a river of warmth down her throat.

From her seat beside the stove she glanced idly around the post. It was perfect, spotless. There was absolutely nothing to be done. Nothing.

Darn it. Stone Man hadn't been gone a week, and already she was bored to tears. And lonely.

"Hiya, miss."

Devon's startled gaze flew to the tent flaps. Digger Haines was standing just inside the post, and for the first time since she'd met him he wasn't smiling.

"Hello, Digger. Would you like some tea?"

He shuffled over to the little stove and pulled out a stool beside her. With a heavy sigh he slumped onto the hard wooden surface. "Call me Marvin. I don't feel much like Digger today."

Devon leaned toward him. "What's the matter?"

"Nothing much," he said with unusual bitterness. "I just made about the biggest discovery of my life, and I can't do nothin' about it. That's all." He stripped off his thick winter gloves and laid them on the floor in front of the stove. "Yeah, guess I'll have some o' that tea after all."

Frowning, Devon poured him a cup. "What do you mean?"

He took the cup greedily, wrapping his stubby fingers

around the hot metal. "I—me, Marvin Joseph Haines—found a mistake on Eldorado."

"A mistake, on the creek?"

"Yep. You know how each man's claim is fifty feet long along the banks? Well, I found a place where there's a fifteen-foot gap." He stared at her hard for emphasis. "Fifteen whole feet on Eldorado. Unclaimed. Think on it, miss. It's worth a fortune." His shoulders slumped suddenly. "To someone, that is."

"Why not to you?"

"Well, I claimed it, o' course, but now there ain't nothin' I can do but sell."

"Sell? But that's crazy, Digger. You're a miner yourself. Why don't you just—"

"Can't afford it, miss. I'd have to work all winter without making a nickel. No trapping, no hunting, nothing. Just digging. See, up here you gotta pick a place on your claim and start digging for the gold. You light a fire every night and let it burn till morning. Then in the daylight you dig till you hit ground that's still froze. The diggings get all piled up, and the durn pile freezes solid. You don't know if you got a dime or a million till spring."

"It sounds difficult, but you're strong and—"

"Strong don't put beans in your belly. I need a grubstake."

"Jack Kelley—"

"Is tapped out."

Devon took a sip of her tea. Stone Man wouldn't like what she was thinking. *He's gone, darn it. If he were so all-fired concerned about how she ran the post, he should have stuck around.* A small smile curved her lips. It was her post now. And her decision. "Digger, I'd be proud to grubstake you."

He gulped hard. "Oh, no, miss. I couldn't let you do that. Stone Man, he's got some mighty firm ideas on grubstaking. Fact is, he thinks its only slightly better'n stealing."

"Do you see Stone Man here?"

"N-Nope."

"Have you seen him here at all in the last six days?"

"Nope."

She smiled. "Then it's safe to say that I'm running this post, and as operator I'm deciding to grubstake a friend."

Digger wet his lips nervously. She could almost see the battle raging in his mind. Half of him wanted desperately to take her up on the offer, but the other half was scared spitless of Stone Man's wrath.

"Well?" she prodded.

Greed won out. "Well, durn it, okay. I'll let you grubstake me, but only 'cause I know this is the big one. It ain't no risk at all."

"Good!" She walked briskly to the counter. Extracting a piece of snow-white linen from her embroidery bag, she lay the material flat on the counter and retrieved her Cross Stylographic fountain pen from its stand under the counter. She dipped the silver tip in the blue ink, shook off the excess, and carefully printed the words, "MacKenna's Post agrees to exchange winter supplies for a forty percent ownership in . . ."

She glanced at Digger. "What's your claim number?"

He hurried over to the counter. "Ogilvy recorded it as fourteen A."

She penned that in then handed the receipt to Digger.

He took the linen scrap from her. Dirt seeped from his fingertips into the material, leaving a scalloped pattern of dull black smudges. "What's it say?"

"It says that this post is a forty-percent owner in claim number fourteen A, Eldorado."

"Most folks're chargin' fifty."

"I know. But forty's plenty for me. After all, you're doing all the work."

Pride puffed out Digger's scrawny chest. "I won't let you down, miss."

She smiled. "I know. Now," she said, clapping her hands together. "Let's get your grub together. You've got work to do."

Long after Digger had gathered his things together and left the post, Devon was still smiling. If Stone Man heard that she was grubstaking miners, he'd hightail it home.

Fortunately Digger Haines just *loved* to talk.

* * *

Devon clamped her chattering teeth together. Shivering, she edged closer to the hot stove, her trembling fingers splayed above the sheet-metal top. The thought of taking off her woolen nightgown was positively repellent.

Unfortunately she had no choice. Men depended on the post's hours. Grimacing, she whipped off her nightgown and hurriedly donned four layers of wool; stockings, vest and drawers, underskirt, and overskirt. Buttoning up her boucle jersey, she strode briskly to the door and peeked outside, gathering in a glance the information she needed.

After a fortifying sip of coffee, she sat down at the table and began to write.

First December 1896.

Weather today is crisp and clear. No new snow last night—buildup remains at approximately eighteen inches.

Several miners seen milling about the saloon this a.m.—apparently it's now too cold to be on the trail. Hard winter is close, and the men who have spent months mining Bonanza Creek are returning home.

The pen trembled in her hands, and she lifted its tip from the paper. The entry was wrong. Not all of the men were returning home. Not the one who mattered.

Tears misted her eyes. It had been forty-one days since Stone Man had left, and every day she missed him more. And all because of a single kiss.

It had changed everything, that kiss. One brief touch of the lips and the guise of platonic friendship had been stripped away. They'd been left naked and vulnerable, unable to pretend they didn't care for each other.

Stone Man, being Stone Man, had run from the truth.

Devon, being Devon, had analyzed it. She'd thought and thought about the kiss—clinically, objectively, and passionately. She'd read and reread Doctor Cowan's book. Nothing helped. She simply couldn't rationalize away the fact that she wanted more from Stone Man than a single kiss. God help her, she wanted more.

It didn't matter that he didn't love her; it didn't matter that Dr. Cowan would label her a wanton. For once in her life all that mattered were feelings—the feelings she had for Stone Man. She wanted, just once, to be loved as a woman should be loved, and Stone Man was her last and only chance.

She was dreaming, of course, but what was wrong with dreaming? And besides, she told herself, she wasn't asking for much—all she wanted was one golden memory to take home with her.

She'd made that decision weeks ago, and every day it grew stronger. Now all she needed was for him to come back.

A knock at the door shattered her musings. She wiped the haze from her eyes and plastered a smile on her face. Thank God for Bear. The friendship that had sprouted between them in the past month was her lifeline. Without him the long days in the post would have been unbearable.

She put on her fur-lined denim parka and winter gloves then opened the door. A blast of ice-cold air slapped her in the face. She staggered backward. Bear grabbed her arm and hauled her close, sheltering her from the wind.

"Pull your hood up," he hollered.

She flipped the wool-lined hood around her face and tied it in place. Bear's hand curled around her padded waist, and together they plunged into the arctic wind, slamming the door shut behind them.

"Look at the river this mornin'," Bear yelled.

She lifted her face just far enough to peek at the Yukon. Huge, battered chunks of ice churned in slow motion through the barely moving water. An eerie, netherworld groan accompanied the river's icy death.

"Won't be more'n a day or two till it's froze solid," he noted.

When they reached the post, Bear immediately went to the stove and started a fire. Devon rushed past him, excited to check her Yukon thermometer. On the counter Bear had set up four bottles, one each of quicksilver, whiskey, kerosene, and Perry Davis Painkiller. Devon figured out the temperature in a glance. Only the quicksilver was frozen.

"It's only forty below," she informed him smartly.

"Better get me a bathing costume."

Giggling, she grabbed the coffeepot and headed outside to fill it with snow.

"Uh . . . don't put no coffee on for me."

"What?"

He cocked his head toward the table. "Sit down, Devon."

She felt a sudden, sharp pang of apprehension. Never in all the days they'd spent together had Bear used that tone of voice with her. He sounded like a father about to mete out punishment. She moved swiftly to the table and sat down. "Okay. I'm sitting."

"And I'm leaving."

"To your tent, I hope." There was the barest of quivers in her voice.

Pushing slowly to his feet, he shuffled over to the table and sat down, taking Devon's small white hand in his own. His eyes were sad. "The post'll only be open for another two or three weeks. After that it's too damn cold. All us Yukoners do in the winter is sit in our tents, drinking to stay warm and wishing to hell we were somewhere else for Christmas."

"Stay, please." Desperation deepened her already husky voice. "I'll plan a Christmas you won't forget. We'll have—"

He squeezed her hand. "Hush, now. I ain't leavin' for good; I'm just gonna find Cornelius. He's shirked his responsibilities long enough, and it's time he came home. . . ."

A lightning bolt came right out of the sky and slammed into Devon's chest. *It's time he came home.* Her heart started beating so hard she could hardly hear.

Bear started to rise. "Well, I'd best be—"

She clung to his hand. "No! I don't want to get him back this way—kicking and screaming all the way."

Bear smiled. "Don't worry. If he starts screaming, I'll knock him out."

"It's not funny," she said miserably. "He won't want to come back."

The twinkle slipped out of Bear's warm eyes. "Nope, he won't."

She tried to smile and failed. Her vision blurred. "I . . . I want him to come back because he misses me—not because he's unconscious."

"I know, but we can't wait no more. You won't survive alone, and I can't move in with you." He stood, holding his arm out. "I'm gonna miss our morning talks, missy."

She flung herself at him. His arm curled around her, creating a harbor of safety. She pressed her cheek against the worn flannel of his workshirt and blinked hard, trying to keep the mist in her eyes from turning into a puddle. "I-I'll miss you, too."

He tightened his hold. "I won't be gone longer'n a lick. I 'spect I'll find Cornelius already on his way home."

She sniffled loudly. "Be careful, Bear."

"I'm always careful, missy. You just get that Christmas dinner ready. I'll be there."

His arm fell away from her body, and she pulled away slowly. "What will I do without you?"

"Don't worry none. Father Mick got home from the Indian camp yesterday. He said he'd watch out for you."

"It won't be the same."

"Thanks." There was an uncustomary catch in his gruff voice. "It's nice for a big old hulk like me to feel special once in a while."

She smiled shakily. "Oh, Bear . . ."

He cleared his throat uncomfortably. "You take care now, and don't you go forgettin' what I told you: Stone Man may be big and more'n half ugly, but the man has a heart bigger'n the whole Yukon Territory. He just don't know it."

Devon sighed miserably. "Then he's the slowest learner I've ever met."

Bear grinned at that. "Don't surprise ya, does it?"

Reluctantly she smiled. "No, I suppose it doesn't at that."

Stone Man's breath came hard and fast, shooting past his blue lips in bulbous clouds of mist. Pausing, he looked skyward. Snow pummeled his unprotected cheeks, stabbing his skin in a thousand pinpricks of fire. He blinked hard, trying to locate the sun through the leaden sky. It was impossible. The heatless globe was sulking somewhere to the east, just inches above the Arctic horizon. He hoped like hell he was still trudging atop the frozen Yukon toward Dawson City.

He grabbed hold of the rope at his waist and lurched forward. The hemp strained, biting into his gloved fingers. Gritting his teeth, he lurched again. This time the heavily loaded toboggan on the rope's other end slid out from its rut in the snow and glided behind his labored steps.

Hours later the snow ebbed. The moon winked in the velvet sky, its blue-white light shimmering softly across the new snow. The ground sparkled like a layer of crushed rock salt.

He slowed his pace, scanning the deserted shoreline for a place to camp. Something in the trees glinted at him. Wiping his tired eyes, he looked again. A trembling finger of moonlight flicked at something metallic—the gray barrel of a stovepipe.

With a thankful sigh he surged through the thigh-deep snow. At the tent he flung back his hood and hollered, "Anybody home?"

No answer. He pulled his toboggan close to the tent and peeled back its icy canvas cover. Burrowing through his belongings, he extracted his sleeping bag, a can of beans, and a can opener.

He entered the cold, quiet abode, feeling his way through the shadowy interior. He found the Yukon stove quickly. His fingers crept along the stove's sheet-metal surface, feeling for a box of matches, which he found. Striking a match, he used the moment of light to peer around.

He saw it in an instant and he smiled. The tent belonged to an old-timer who lived by the unwritten rules of the Yukon. The absent owner had left a pile of wood and a can of beans for whomever happened along.

Stone Man lighted a fire, and in no time the tent felt like home.

What a lie that was. For the first time in his long, lonely life he knew what a real home felt like, and the feeling had nothing to do with a warm fire and a full can of beans.

Home was a place where you belonged. A place you missed.

There it was, the thought he'd spent the better part of six weeks trying to outrun. It was always just below the surface, waiting to pounce at the first sign of weakness. Every night, as he sat alone in the middle of a cold dark nowhere, he'd grown weaker.

Running hadn't helped a damn thing; if anything it had made the problem worse. For weeks now he'd been alone, and, if he allowed himself to admit it, lonely. He missed the strangest things—the husky, sensual sound of her voice, the lilt of her laughter, the way she handed him his napkin, the tiny, mewling sounds she made in her sleep.

Admit it, you coward. You miss her.

No! He was just sick and tired of running, that was all. That's what had turned him toward home last week. Pure exhaustion.

And if you believe that, old man, I've got a train line from Skagway to Dawson City to sell you.

Damn it! He refused to waste any more time thinking about her. Snagging the can of beans, he stabbed the pointy tip of his can opener in the metal lid and wrenched the thing open.

After he'd set the can on the stove, he searched the tent for a coffeepot. Finding one, he packed it with snow and put it on to boil. After a few moments steam spiraled slowly from the pot's mouth. It collected on the grayed, sagging roof and froze solid.

He stared at the icicles for a few minutes then grabbed the bean can and shoveled a huge bite of the half-frozen, red-brown sludge into his mouth. Just as he was about to ram home a second bite, he heard a noise. Moving cautiously toward the door, he lifted the flaps and peered outside.

"Cor . . . ne . . . lius . . ." The shouted word echoed through the valley.

"Bear?" he yelled back, "is that you?"

"Who . . . the . . . hell . . . else . . . would . . . look . . . for . . . you?" came the echoing reply.

Stone Man grinned. By God, for once it would feel good to have someone to talk to. It would keep his mind off Devon.

Devon. Stone Man's smile vanished. Fear chilled his soul. Oh, God, not Devon. A man like Bear didn't make social calls. Especially not in sixty-below weather.

Bear burst into the clearing. "Holy God," he wheezed, stumbling up to the tent, "it's colder than—"

Stone Man grabbed Bear. "Is she all right?"

Bear looked up at him through baggy, bloodshot eyes. "Fine. Now get me something hot."

Stone Man swiveled back into the tent and poured two cups of hot water. Bear took the cup gratefully, wrapping his half-frozen fingers around the warm metal. "I-I w-was about to give up on finding you. I been lookin' for more than two weeks. I must of walked forty miles. Figgered I'd find you two miles from camp."

"Why are you looking for me? You should have known I'd come back. Fact is, I'm on my way now."

" 'Bout time."

"To you, maybe."

When he'd warmed up, Bear planted one ankle on his knee and leaned back in his chair, studying Stone Man through narrowed, knowing eyes. "What's that mean?"

"Just small talk."

"You never made small talk in your life, Cornelius. Now what the hell's going on in that peanut brain of yours?"

I like her. The damning words burst to life in Stone Man's brain. He wanted to tell someone, and Bear was the only one he *could* tell. But years of training were hard to break; he had no idea how to start talking. So instead of saying what was on his mind, he slammed his lips together and sat mute.

"Okay, let's start simple. Why are you headin' home?"

Stone Man shifted uncomfortably. "I got responsibilities at the post. I figured it was time to get back to them."

Bear pulled a toothpick out of his pocket and jimmied it between his gaping front teeth. "I guess you ain't heard."

"Heard what?"

"Digger Haines took over your 'responsibilities.' He and Devon are shacked up in your tent, happy as—"

Stone Man leapt to his feet. For an instant the urge to punch Bear's fleshy face was almost overwhelming.

Rising slowly, Bear placed his hand on Stone Man's chest. "Old pounder's beatin' like a kettle drum. Guess there's more to it than 'responsibilities,' huh?"

Stone Man sank back into his chair, feeling suddenly old. It was pathetic what she'd done to him. He couldn't even hide his feelings anymore. He wore them on his sleeve like a damned bridegroom. "It's not true, is it?"

" 'Course not." Bear leaned toward him. "Cornelius, we

ain't game-playin' men, you and I. If you got somethin' to say, say it."

Stone Man stared at the only friend he'd ever had. Bear was right; the words needed to be said. Maybe if he heard them aloud he'd even be able to laugh them off. It was worth a try. Unspoken they were killing him. He screwed up his courage and said quickly, "I miss her."

The moment the horrific words were out of his mouth, he tensed, waiting for the familiar sense of desperation to engulf him. Yet amazingly this time he felt no despair at the admission. In fact he felt almost freed.

"I figured you did. And just in case you wanted to know, she misses you, too."

"She does?" For a moment he felt an almost blinding joy. Then came the fall. He was acting like a fool, pretending there was something in his future besides a cold tent and a camera. If she'd told him once she'd told him a thousand times: she couldn't wait to leave the Yukon. He wasn't entirely sure what he wanted from her; but he was damn sure he wasn't going to get it. He shook his head. "Bear, old friend, I'm in a world of hurt."

"No, Cornelius, you're just in the world. Welcome back."

For the next few hours the two old friends sat at the table, drinking hot water. Not more than ten words passed between them, and neither felt a loss.

When the water ran out Stone Man stood, stretching his tired muscles. "Want more water?"

"Naw, I think I'll head on to bed," Bear answered, reaching under the table for his fur bedroll.

As Stone Man reached for his own sleeping bag, the tent flaps shuddered. He cocked his head toward the canvas door, listening intently. He heard the sounds of labored breathing and the unmistakable stomp of snow-laden boots.

He and Bear rose at the same time, intending to welcome the visitor in.

Before they could reach the flaps a young man burst through the opening. Stone Man could tell in a glance he was a *cheechako*, a newcomer to the Yukon. He looked tired, hungry, and lost. "Here's the fire, kid. Come on over and—"

The boy whipped a gun out of his pocket and aimed it at Bear's chest. "Don't move!"

Bear lifted his hand into the air. "We ain't armed. This is the Yukon, young fella, not San Francisco. If you want something, all you gotta do is ask."

Stone Man took a cautious step toward the *cheechako*. "Look son, if you're hungry—"

"I'm hungry all right," he hissed, "but not for your left-over beans, old man. I'm hungry for gold."

The weapon wobbled in the kid's hands. Stone Man stared at the filthy skin curled around the firearm's handle. The finger hooked through the trigger was trembling.

They were in trouble.

"Come on, boy—" Bear started.

"Shut up! If I'da wanted to talk I'da gone to Skagway. Just give me your damn gold."

"We're not miners," Stone Man said. "We don't have a speck of dust on us. If you don't believe me, go check our packs. They're outside."

The boy cast a nervous glance behind him. "N—No gold?"

"No gold." Bear took a step toward the boy. "If you'll—"

The earsplitting crack of gunfire shattered the sentence. A light spasmed in the darkness, and out of the corner of his eye Stone Man saw Bear stagger backward.

With a bellow of pure rage Stone Man charged the boy.

The light flashed again, and a volcano of pain erupted in Stone Man's body. He blinked to get his bearings. He tried to localize the pain, but he couldn't. It was everywhere. He blinked again, and the boy was gone.

Everything slowed; the world around him spun. He tried to remain on his feet, but his body suddenly seemed twice its normal size, bloated and misshapen. His limbs felt leaden. He crumpled.

His knees hit the floor hard. Pain shot up his thighs. A groan tore past his lips as he pitched, face-first, onto the cold floorboards.

"Bear . . ." he called hoarsely, sending his hand scouting across the rough wooden planks. His fingers slid through something warm and sticky and wet. Almost immediately the goo turned slick with ice. He wondered briefly what he was lying in, then forgot that train of thought.

"Bear . . ." His voice this time was weaker, scratchier. He licked his thick, dry lips, wishing, inanely, that he had a glass of lemonade. A buzzing ripped through his head, setting off a huge, throbbing headache.

He planted his slick palms on the floorboards and tried to push himself upward, but the strength in his arms evaporated and a wave of nausea consumed him.

He was already unconscious when he hit the floor.

Chapter Fifteen

Stone Man was wakened by a high-pitched buzzing in his ears. *Damn bees.* He shifted position, trying to get comfortable. His knee edged upward. At the movement a fire-hot pain shattered his thigh.

Everything came rushing back.

"Bear?" The word slipped through his swollen, cracked lips. He planted his palms on the floorboards and tried to get up. Something slick and frozen made his hands shoot out from underneath him. He crashed downward, landing in a frozen pool of his own blood.

A cold sweat crawled across his forehead. Panting, he tried to get to his knees.

The world lurched. Bile swelled in his throat, daring him to move again. He clamped his teeth together and concentrated on breathing. When the nausea subsided, he crept, inch by painful inch, across the floor. The fire had long since died, and the tent was a cold, dark tomb.

He hit the table and stopped. Curling his fingers around the rough-hewn spruce leg, he hauled himself to his knees.

An excruciating pain erupted in his upper thigh. The nausea came back, clawing at his stomach. He clutched the table edge with whitened fingers. Sheer determination brought him to a stand.

"Bear?" he croaked again.

His fingers crept across the scarred tabletop for the box of matches. Finding it, he struck one. Tenuous red-gold light flared in the tent's void, illuminating Bear's prone body.

Stone Man's blood ran cold. Lighting the lantern with shaking fingers, he moved laboriously across the tent. With each dragging step, pain gripped his leg. It seemed to take hours to reach Bear's body.

"Bear?"

No answer; not even the rustling of breath. The silence closed in on him. Dread curled in the pit of his stomach. He eased himself back down to the floor.

"Damn you, Bear, wake up."

He grabbed Bear's wrist, feeling desperately for a pulse. The flesh beneath his fingers was icy cold.

A crushing weight settled on Stone Man's lungs. The pain in his leg was momentarily smothered by the blinding pain in his heart.

He stared at his dead friend through achingly dry eyes. *This isn't the way it should have ended for you. Of all of us, you deserved better.*

He stopped himself. *Don't start thinking about what he deserved. . . .*

He staggered painfully to his feet. He'd think about his grief later, if ever. Now he had to concentrate on keeping himself alive. For himself. For Devon.

It flashed through his mind that he had changed. Up until a few months ago he might have laid down beside his old friend and gone to sleep. Until recently life hadn't meant enough to fight for it.

Now things were different. For the first time in his life he had something waiting for him at the end of the line.

All he had to do was get home before he bled to death. How far had Bear said they were from home? Two miles? He could make that. He had to.

He pulled his parka off the back of the chair and eased himself into its fur-lined warmth. Then he untied the bandanna at his throat and wrapped it around his upper thigh, tightening the makeshift tourniquet until his entire leg was throbbing.

Long ago, prison had taught him that pain didn't recede until it was ignored. Drawing a deep, rattling breath, he turned his bleary mind to the problem facing him. Or, rather, lying at his feet.

What was he going to do with Bear? The frozen ground, icy temperatures, and snow prevented burying, covering, or burning of the body.

A wave of dizziness almost brought Stone Man to his knees. He leaned heavily against the table, waiting for his equilibrium to return.

He had to make a decision. Now.

He could leave Bear in the tent, but if Stone Man did that his friend's body would be devoured by predators—either now or first thing in the spring.

Stone Man couldn't risk it. With his wounded leg there was a possibility he wouldn't make it back in the spring, and the thought of wolves eating Bear's body was too sickening to contemplate.

There was only one thing he could do. He'd have to lash Bear to the toboggan and drag him back to Dawson City.

He hobbled to the flaps, wincing as pain sluiced through his leg. He kept moving, step by excruciating step. When he bent to tie his snowshoes on, a wave of dizziness assailed him.

He staggered backward, coming down hard on his gunshot leg. The limb exploded with pain. A raspy howl shuddered past his lips. His body crumpled, landing in a heap alongside the toboggan. He clung to consciousness with grasping, desperate fingers until it crumbled and fell away. Blackness engulfed him.

A few minutes later he wakened with a start. *Damn!* Yanking his gloved hand out of the snow, he grabbed the toboggan's well-tied load and hauled himself to his feet.

By the time he'd laid Bear's big body on the toboggan, covered it with canvas, and lashed it down, Stone Man was exhausted. With trembling, uncooperative fingers, he tied the frozen rope around his waist, flipped up his warm hood, and tried to move.

The sled wouldn't budge. He gritted his teeth and tried again. This time the toboggan lurched forward. Dizzy and weak, he lifted his good leg to take a step. Pain exploded in his wound. He wobbled and fell.

The snow felt icy-hot on his face. Clenching his jaw, he staggered to his feet again. After a long, panting moment, he took one agonizing step forward. Then another. And another.

By dawn his breath was coming hard and fast. His ribs ached from the cold, and he couldn't feel his face at all. His leg felt frozen and on fire at the same time.

But he kept moving, knowing that if he lay down once it was all over. He'd never get up again.

Devon kept him going. In the last hours her visage had become his beacon. He didn't see the snow heaped all around him, nor the velvet sky blanketed with pinpricks of light, nor the trees lined along the bank like spectral wraiths. The image that filled his mind was her face as he'd last seen it—her eyes as bright as lichen moss lit by a summer sun, her mouth moist and waiting for his.

If he died, he'd never have the chance to kiss her again. And God in Heaven he wanted to kiss her.

Please God, he thought desperately, let me make it home. It's not asking so much—home can't be more than a mile away by now.

A soundless, mirthless laugh rattled his throat. The blood loss was affecting his mind. God had never answered one of his prayers. Not once. What made him think He'd answer now?

Devon poured herself a nice hot cup of tea and opened her book, *The Portrait of a Lady*.

Without warning the tent door flew open, smacking hard against the support beam. The whole tent rattled, and a blast of icy air swirled through the opening, bringing with it a flutter of snow.

Devon snapped to her feet. "What in the—"

Stone Man staggered through the doorway.

Her breath caught in her throat as he stumbled toward her. He looked like death. The only color in his face was in his eyes, and the whiskey orbs were dull and unfocused. Snow clung to his bushy eyebrows and jawline stubble. His mustache was a solid block of gray ice.

The cup slipped through her fingers and clanged on the floor. The eerie sound reverberated through the silent tent.

Stone Man opened his mouth to speak. No words issued from his cracked, swollen lips.

Devon rushed to him. Wrapping her arm around his waist, she pulled off his gloves and flipped back his hood. His arms came around her body, and she could feel the tremble in his hands as they closed around her, drawing her close.

Dear God, she thought in a panic, he feels like a block of ice.

"Dev?" The word was whisper-soft, raspy.

She looked up. He looked down. His lips grazed hers in a butterfly-soft landing of pure ice. Then he stilled. His eyes slid shut.

She waited a moment then pulled back. "Stone Man?"

He crashed to the floor.

"Oh my God! Stone Man? Get up!" She dropped to her knees, feeling his wrist for a pulse. Finding one, she drew a ragged, relieved breath.

She clamped hard on her rising panic, refusing to give in to it. With shaking, desperate fingers she tried to peel the frozen parka off his body. His lifeless body fought her at every turn, a deadweight she couldn't lift.

"God, Stone Man," she moaned, "help me . . ."

He didn't answer. She popped to her feet and raced to the cupboard, flinging a dozen knives to the floor in her search for the bowie knife. Finding it, she cut the parka off his body and threw it across the room.

"Okay, Stone Man," she wheezed, "we're going to stand up now." She burrowed underneath him, using her body as a lever to push him upward. He felt like a frozen sack of potatoes against her back.

"Okay, on the count of three . . ." She counted to three then dug her palms into the floorboards and shoved upward.

A groan escaped his lips.

"Help . . . me," she wheezed, lurching upward again. "Oh, God, I can't do it. Oh, God . . ."

His hand crept slowly to the leg of the bed and grabbed hold. Then he took a deep, rattling breath. "Now."

She threw herself backward, jarring him to his knees. Clutching the bedpost, he staggered upright and threw his body across the bed. He landed at an angle, his head pressed close to the canvas wall, his feet hanging over the opposite edge.

Devon put her hand to his brow. He was burning up. She clambered onto the bed beside him. It took her endless minutes to get him on his back. When she'd finally done it, she unbuttoned his wool flannel shirt and tossed it on the floor. Then she unbuttoned his pants and peeled the thick black wool downward. At his thighs the material stuck.

She glanced at his thighs and frowned. Something black had marred the red wool of his long underwear. The discoloration spread nearly to his groin. She tugged harder on the pants.

They wouldn't budge.

"Oh, for goodness' sake." She wiggled backward until she was sitting next to his knees. Taking a firm hold on the waistband, she yanked. The pants, a patch of his long johns, and a layer of bloodied skin ripped away from his body.

A shiver rippled through him, but he didn't move.

Devon stared at his leg in horror. It was one solid mass of dried blood from the inside of his knee to about four inches below his groin. There was something, she thought maybe it was a scarf, tied loosely around his upper thigh, but it was black with blood and as hard as a rock. She used the bowie knife to cut it off.

Fresh blood bubbled from a hole in his flesh. It spurted past the torn red wool of his underwear and slid onto the blankets beneath him. Already it was collecting into a small pool.

A bullet hole! The sight of it snapped her out of her stupor. She pressed a handful of nightgown firmly against the wound. When the blood flow slowed somewhat, she gingerly lifted his thigh and peered at the underside. A relieved sigh escaped her lips. The bullet had gone straight through.

She raced to her armoire and retrieved her sewing basket. Flinging it on the bed, she flew to the stove and set three pans of water to boil.

She watched the water. Her foot started a quick, staccato beat. Panic began at the edges of her mind, and suddenly her whole body was shaking.

Don't be stupid. Think. What do you do first?

Stop the bleeding. She shot back to the armoire and grabbed a muslin summer skirt. Ripping the flimsy material from hem to waist, she twirled it into a rope and wrapped it around the uppermost part of his thigh. At the artery she stabbed a wooden spoon between the fabric and his skin, then turned the spoon clockwise until the tourniquet was tight enough.

While the tourniquet was working, she plucked scissors, silk thread, an embroidery needle, linen, and tweezers from her sewing kit. She dropped everything but the linen into the boiling water.

She waited impatiently for the instruments to sterilize, all the while wiping a cool cloth across Stone Man's fever-hot brow. When she couldn't wait any longer, she poured the boiling water into her big washbasin and gingerly extracted her tools.

With white, shaking fingers she picked up the tweezers and dipped the metallic tip into the red-black hole in his flesh. The minute the instrument touched the frayed, blood-encrusted wound, Stone Man's leg whipped taut. The muscles in his leg corded and bunched.

She soothed him with her voice, and after a few minutes he relaxed. Efficiently she probed the wound for leftover bits of cloth. Finally, satisfied she'd found them all, she set the tweezers down and picked up the scissors.

God, she wished she had something to give him for the pain. But there was nothing. No alcohol, no laudanum. Nothing. She couldn't even risk the time it took to run to the post for the Perry Davis Painkiller.

Gritting her teeth, she lowered the scissors to his flesh and started clipping off the tattered edges of the wound.

When she finished, she glanced worriedly at his face and let out a relieved sigh. He was still unconscious.

She threaded her needle.

It has to be done.

She pulled the smooth edges of the wound together and closed her eyes, gathering her strength. In one sharp jab she sent her needle through his flesh.

Tensing immediately, she waited for his reaction. But there was none. He was out cold. Relieved, she sewed up the entrance and exit wounds quickly, checked her stitches, and then used a pile of turpentine-soaked linen as bandages.

For the next few hours she sponged his hot skin, checked his sheets, and kept him warm. She crooned softly in his ear, talking insensibly of whatever came to mind. But mostly she waited, and the words *please wake up* were never far from her lips.

Stone Man clawed his way through the protective cocoon of velvety blackness. A pinpoint of light beckoned just beyond his reach. He flailed, fighting for consciousness.

"Thank God," came a soothing, liquid voice from somewhere nearer the light. Welcome coolness slid across his forehead.

"Here, drink this. It's cooled moose broth."

He drew his swollen lips together. "Wa . . ." His voice crackled like dead leaves and died.

"Shhh. Here, drink." The words, as soft as a morning breeze, came again, this time accompanied by a hand gently forcing him to lift his head. Too tired to resist, he let the hand control him. A warm drop of wetness touched his parched lips and dribbled down his chin.

He swallowed the rich broth greedily. When his thirst was sated he sank back into the softness beneath him, exhausted.

Everything hurt. His eyes, his mouth, his head, his body, his leg. Everything. The harder he strove to reach the light, the more everything hurt.

The softness of the bed beckoned him to forget the light and to sleep. But there was something he had to do, something that had to do with Devon.

The thought spiraled away, forgotten. He'd think about Devon later, when he was sure he was alive. Right now he was so damned tired . . .

It was two days later when he finally woke. The scorching pain in his thigh roused him. His eyes grated open, and he found himself staring at the smoke-darkened canvas ceiling of his tent.

He blinked, disoriented. What was he doing home? The last thing he remembered, he'd been sitting with Bear. . . .

Memory crashed through his brain, stunning him. Bear was gone. *Oh, God . . .*

He tried to lift his head off the pillow. At the movement a drumbeat of pain burst to life at the base of his skull, and he sank back into the cotton softness, temporarily defeated.

He turned his head to the left and scanned the small tent. The lantern was lit, and its reddish-gold flames illuminated the space.

The place was a mess. Pots cluttered the small stovetop, a ripped-up skirt lay across the table, and clothes and knives were scattered everywhere.

He frowned. Where was Devon? She'd never go to sleep in this kind of mess. Fear seeped through his dazed mind. He struggled to sit up. At the movement a wave of dizziness washed through him. He gritted his teeth and inched himself upright.

She was sitting in a chair at the end of the bed, fast asleep. Her head was lolled over to one side, and her mouth was open. Piles of untamed russet hair haloed her face, wisping airily along her high cheekbones and falling in a tangled heap to her waist. In her lap was a pile of damp rags; at her feet, a basin of water.

Even in sleep she looked tired. There were deep shadows beneath her eyes, and a network of lines on her brow he'd never noticed before. Her skin was a pale, waxy hue, with none of the usual rosiness in her cheeks.

Even so she was the most beautiful woman he'd ever seen. An ache of longing swelled in him, setting off another drumroll of a headache.

He couldn't deny it any longer. He wanted her. And not just for a night. He wanted her for . . . longer.

On his way home all he'd been able to think about was kissing her one last time. He'd never thought about what would happen if he actually survived.

But he had survived, and his death's-door dreaming was just that. A feverish dream. One kiss wouldn't make everything all right. After the kiss they'd still be as different as night and day. A pretty lady like her wouldn't last long tramping through the wilderness with a stubborn old loner like him.

The moment the river thawed he'd lose her.

He sighed. It was a question of pain. Bear's death had made him realize that. In the blink of an eye Stone Man had lost his only friend, and the pain was enormous. But if he let himself love Devon and then he lost her, the pain would be even worse.

Yet lose Devon he would. Come spring she'd pluck up those crisp little skirts of hers and head back to civilization.

Bye bye Stone Man. Hello St. Louis.

It wasn't worth the risk. He'd had enough pain in his life; he didn't need to go courting more. All he had to do was keep a safe distance between them for a few short months. Then she could board the *Yukoner* without a backward glance. She could take her damned bicycle, her alligator gripsack, and her tablecloth with her. His heart was staying put.

He sank wearily back into the pile of pillows and closed his eyes, remembering the feel of her cool palm on his forehead.

Her touch and her voice had been so incredibly soft, so comforting. As a child he'd gone to sleep alone, huddled beneath a flimsy blanket, and he'd dreamed of being touched that way. He'd ached for it.

Now, at the ripe old age of thirty-nine, someone cared enough to sit beside him, to cool his fevered brow.

A grimace darkened his face. Until spring.

Chapter Sixteen

Stone Man awakened with a smile on his face. Lazily he lifted his head off the pillow. For the first time in a week he didn't have a headache. His smile expanded.

The first thing he saw was the woman stretched out beside him. Devon. In his mind the word was a caress. She looked breathtakingly beautiful and oh so desirable.

"Devon," he whispered throatily.

She blinked awake. "Morning," she purred.

He felt himself drowning in her eyes. He reached out to her. She snuggled closer. A lock of burnished russet hair twined around his forefinger, and it felt like a swatch of the finest French silk.

"I . . ." He stopped, suddenly awkward. "I don't know what to say. Words are so inadequate. But thank you for saving my life. It means a lot to me that you cared enough to bother. . . ."

Devon smiled at her whimsical daydream. Since Stone Man's return she'd been unable to control the wanderings of her own mind. At first she'd fought her fantasies, telling herself that it was stupid and childish to pretend. But the more she'd fought the images the stronger they'd become, and finally she'd stopped fighting. It was then that she'd learned something surprising: Dreaming was fun.

But enough was enough.

She glanced longingly at the man sleeping beside her. If only he'd wake up, they could get on with things. There were so many things to be done today, so many things to be said.

She'd already decided that they should spend the winter as lovers. It was a shocking decision, to be sure, but logical. They could hardly live together in a ten-foot-by-ten-foot tent for five months and pretend they were only partners.

It made sense for them to share one glorious winter and then move on. What did she have to lose? She'd be good-old-spinster-aunt Devon soon enough. When the river thawed she was going home. Why not have one good memory to take home with her? A memory to keep her warm on the long, lonely St. Louis nights when she'd be sleeping alone.

She pushed up on one elbow to study Stone Man's profile. For the first time in a week he'd had a good night's sleep, and the effect on his face was startling. He looked carefree, almost young.

Weak winter sunlight filtered through the canvas walls, glancing in flecks of near-blue through the tangled mass of his newly washed hair. She ached to run her fingers through the coarse black strands.

She scooted closer to him. The soft rise and fall of his body brushed her nipples. A delicious shiver rippled up her spine.

To think she'd considered him a friend! He was so much more. She and Bear were friends; she and Stone Man were something else. Something that made her blood tingle when they kissed, something that made her nipples harden at his touch. Something too wonderful to name.

She was ready to begin the winter right now.

His eyes blinked open.

"Good morning," she said eagerly.

"Morning," he answered sleepily.

Stone Man stretched his arms, working the sleep kinks from his muscles. Devon wiggled closer, and he felt the peaks of her taut breasts tickle his ribcage. Without thinking he brought his arm around her body, drawing her closer. His fingers curled around the wool-sheathed curve of her shoulder and squeezed gently.

He half rolled onto his side, and there she was in his arms. For a moment her beauty stole his breath. Her eyes were huge and bright in the morning paleness of her face, and her lips were a beguiling shade of pink. She ran her tongue slowly along her lower lip.

He stared at the trail of glistening wetness, and something in his gut clenched. Hard.

One minute he was looking at her lips, and the next minute he was kissing her. He didn't know exactly how it had happened, and he didn't care. It was a kiss he'd been dreaming about for months, and he took it greedily. His lips possessed hers, moving with a gentle urgency, tasting, seeking. Then he drew back until their lips were barely touching and let his tongue flick teasingly along her upper lip.

One by one his fingers released their hold on her shoulder. His hand slid down her arm, and a thousand tiny goosebumps bubbled to the surface of her flesh. Every nerve in her body leapt to life.

The blunt tips of his fingers traced the soft underside of her breast. She froze, unable even to breathe. His palm glided across the mound, whispering atop her nipples until she thought she'd surely faint.

Just when she couldn't stand the teasing another second, his hand closed around her breast. His strong fingers began a slow, gentle kneading. Devon gasped at the sensations that exploded in her body. She reacted instinctively, arching into his warm palm. A throaty whimper slipped from her mouth to his.

Her quiet moan brought Stone Man back to his senses. His fingers popped open as if scalded.

"Holy shit!" He scrambled backward, putting as much distance between them as possible.

Reluctantly he looked at her. She was sitting across from him, all hunched and waiting. Her face wore the same long-suffering look she used to give him when he belched at the dinner table. Her mouth, still puffy from his kiss, was drawn into a disapproving line.

She was disappointed in him. Again.

Goddamn it! He felt like putting his fist right through the canvas wall. Why in the hell had he kissed her? He'd spent six weeks in the freezing cold telling himself she wasn't for him. He knew damn well she wanted things he could never give her—a home, a family, a goddamn dog, and a white picket fence.

All that running and thinking hadn't done squat. He'd been back in the tent a week—and he'd been half-dead for most of that time—and here he was, kissing her. Wanting her so badly it hurt.

He had the self-control of a rutting animal.

"Goddamn it, Devon. Don't sneak up on me that way."

Her eyes flashed. "Sneak up on you! Why of all the—"

"Okay, okay," he said wearily, "I didn't mean it was your fault. I don't give a good goddamn whose fault it was. But we can't kiss anymore."

A frown darted across her brow. "Why not?"

He groaned at her innocence. "Because I'm too tired to leave again."

"Then stay."

Her sensual voice washed over him in waves. His resolve wavered. "Ah Dev," he sighed. "Just let it be."

She started gnawing on her thumbnail like a nervous rabbit. He grimaced, knowing her analytical mind had found a loose thread; something that wasn't quite right.

Her thumb popped free. She'd solved it.

She looked at him with that "rational" look on her face that brooked no argument. "But you want me, Stone Man. I may be a lady and an innocent, but I'm not stupid."

He groaned inwardly. Another ten seconds and little miss levelheaded would have him so confused he'd probably throw caution to the wind and give her what she was asking for. God knew he wanted to.

He had to change the subject. Fast. He cleared his throat. "Have you unloaded my toboggan?"

"No," she answered crisply, "I've been too busy saving your life to think about keeping your clothes dry."

He was too tired and in too much pain to soften the blow. So he simply said it. "Bear's dead."

Her face went chalky white. "Oh my God . . . When? How?"

"A few days ago." He swallowed the lump of dryness in his throat. "Some half-crazed *cheechako* burst into our tent one night and shot us both. With Bear he had time to aim."

Grief twisted her face. She stared at him, stricken and silent, waiting for more. Tears magnified her eyes, streaking down the milky surface of her cheeks.

Her pain brought his own grief to the surface. Memories crashed through the wall he'd built around them, punching him in the gut.

She opened her arms to him. A tremble seized him. God, it would feel good to be held right now. He'd never been held without paying for it first.

He stared at her small white hands and remembered the delicate feel of them on his fevered brow. All his life he'd waited for her hands, her touch. Only he hadn't known it until this very moment.

He was in big trouble. The space between them was too small, too easily brooked. He eased himself off the bed. His feet landed hard on the floor, and bolts of pain shot up his right leg, throbbing in his thigh. He winced, testing the area with his fingertips.

She was beside him in an instant. "Are you all right?"

The concern in her voice was almost his undoing. He clamped his jaw shut to keep from saying something stupid. Something like *No, goddamn it, I'm not all right. I haven't been all right since the day you came into my life.*

"Are you—"

"I'm fine," he snapped.

She took a step backward, clutching the neckline of her flannel wrapper in shaking fingers. "Of course you are." She gave a short, forced little laugh. "Silly me."

He grabbed his clothes and started dressing. "I'm going to go tell the boys about Bear. It'll take the better part of three days to dig a grave. We'd better get started."

She didn't answer. He turned around slowly. She was still standing beside the bed with her head bowed. Even from this distance he could see that she was trembling.

Her silent pain clawed at his heart. It was all he could do to keep from sweeping her into his arms. He wanted to kiss her tears away. But he couldn't. If he kissed her now, he'd never stop.

He cleared his throat. "Uh, Devon?"

"Yes?" she answered without looking up.

"Uh, thanks for saving my life."

"You're welcome."

The moment he left the tent she sank to her knees.

Oh, Bear . . . The weight of painful memories dragged her slim shoulders downward and bowed her neck.

Cold seeped from the ice-sheened floorboards through her nightclothes and into her knees, but she didn't notice it. The cold in her soul was deeper.

Burying her face in her hands, she let the tears come.

Midas's voice droned on, melting into a meaningless mush in Devon's mind. She stopped listening to his half-baked, stumbling eulogy.

She stared at the gaping black hole in the ground, so deep and dark and terrifying beside the stark whiteness of the snow around it. Tears clogged in her throat and burned in her eyes, freezing on her lashes.

She stood stiff and alone, apart from the miners. Icy blasts of wind buffeted her cheeks, ripping strands of hair across her face. Overhead the sky was a dull gunmetal gray. A fast-moving bank of strafers shielded the sulking sun. All around her spindly, snow-covered trees stood like silent sentinels. The wind moaned and hissed through their whitened boughs.

It felt as if her soul were being twisted by huge, ice-cold hands. Every breath hurt, and her eyes felt raw and swollen from too much crying. Every fiber of her being ached for Stone Man's touch. She longed to throw herself in his strong embrace and be comforted.

God, why hadn't he come to the funeral? It was one thing for him to pay respects in his own way, but couldn't he just once think of her needs? She *needed* him beside her, and she suspected that he needed her. If he'd only reach out to her. . . .

She was daydreaming again.

The last four days had passed in a fog of painful confusion. Not a single word had passed between them. Each morning she woke up, did her chores, cooked their meals, and washed their dishes. All of this she did side by side with Stone Man, and yet she was alone. Achingly alone. She wished the post were still open. That at least would have given her something else to do.

"Hey!" Midas's gravelly voice burst through her thoughts. "Anybody know Bear's real name?"

Devon flinched at the unexpected query; it sparked a memory so strong she nearly staggered at the force of it.

The memory was of one of "their" mornings. That's how she'd come to think of the time she and Bear had spent together. Their time.

"Bear," she'd asked him, "what's your Christian name?"

"Missy, you oughta know by now the Yukon ain't the place to ask a fella his real name."

"I wouldn't tell anyone, not if you didn't want me to."

"Nope."

She'd waited a moment before trying again. "Want to know my middle name?"

He'd grinned at her then. "You're going to dog-and-bone me to death on this one, ain't you? I won't get a lick o' rest till I tell you, will I?"

"Not a wink."

He sighed. "My mammy named me Eugene. Eugene Jedediah Ott. Now, don't you laugh there, missy. I had sixteen brothers and sisters. I reckon by the time I was born all the good names were used up."

She grinned. "I reckon so."

"I'm gonna hold you to that promise, missy. . . ."

"Well?" came Midas's gravelly voice again. "I'm tryin' to make a damn—er, danged marker. Does anybody know his name or not?"

Tears slid down Devon's cheeks and froze solid, lining her wind-reddened cheeks like silver threads. Absentmindedly she plucked the icicles from her face, wincing as a tiny layer of skin was torn away. "He'd want Bear on the marker, Midas," she answered softly. "Just Bear."

"That's what I figured," Midas answered, pounding a whipsawed plank of wood into the ground. At every fall of the hammer, a crack of sound echoed through the still, frosty air.

When Midas finished whittling and pounding, she stared at the marker he'd made.

BEAR
Buried 24, December, 1896
A good man to have knowed

She buried her face in the coarse leather of her gloves and sobbed. Time ceased to mean anything as she stood there, braced against the driving wind. She cried until her soul was parched and her eyes ached.

"Devon lass?"

She heard Father Michaels's voice as if from far away. It took her a moment to realize he was standing beside her.

"Child," came his voice again, "the funeral's over. Ye'll catch yer death o' cold out here."

Devon lowered her hands and glanced around. Everyone was gone except for her and the priest. How like the Yukoners, she thought, to let a person alone with their grief.

She stared at the grave. The black hole was filled in. Now it was merely a brown oval in the midst of a snowfield, and by tomorrow morning even that would be gone. Only the marker would remain.

Bear was really and truly gone.

"I don't think I'd mind catching my death," she said dully.

"Ach, lass, it just seems that way now. Ye're hurtin', and that's to be expected. But ye've got to go on. 'Tis God's way."

She snorted derisively. "Some God. Bear's dead, and his killer is free."

"Now, now. I'll not be hearin' that sort o' talk. And on the day before His birthday, too."

"Sorry, Father."

"Nothin' to be sorry about. I'd expect ye to be a bit angry. But lass, God ne'er takes anything away without givin' somethin' in return. Watch, ye'll see. Somethin' wonderful'll surely happen soon."

"Nothing could be worth Bear's life."

"Ye're right about that. But still . . ." He thought a minute then brightened. "Maybe something good'll happen at the Christmas party."

Devon gasped. "Surely you don't think I'm going ahead with the party. . . . Bear's party?"

"I thought 'twas the Lord's party."

"Yes, but it was for Bear and—"

"And all the men like him who missed home. Ye think they miss their families less since Bear's death?"

"No," she admitted, "but I can't go ahead with it. Not now . . ."

Father touched her forearm. "What about the Indian children ye had me invite? And the men themselves, what about them? Ye sent word they were to be at Joe Ladue's at seven o'clock Christmas night. 'Tisn't exactly the type of surprise ye promised 'em."

She stared blankly at the grave. Thoughts and images and memories chased around in her head. *You just plan that party, missy. I'll be there.* She'd planned it all right; she had enough food prepared to feed the entire camp and more beside.

"Bear would want ye to go on. Don't ye think he'll be watchin' from up there, waitin' for his first Christmas dinner? He'll be a mite disappointed to find out—"

She hiccuped loudly, sniffling. "All right. You win. The party goes on as scheduled."

He started maneuvering her toward home. "That's me girl. I knew ye wouldn't let the children down."

Stone Man stood alone on the hillside opposite town. Around him the wind blew furiously, its mournful dirge an echo of the suppressed pain in his soul. The keening wail was the only sound in the white, muffled world. Overhead the sky was a deep, soulless gray, an uninviting palette that even the hawks had today abandoned. He stared down at the straggling little funeral procession through aching, too-dry eyes. Wrapping his arms tighter around his body, he tried to find some measure of warmth. But it was impossible; the coldness was too deep, too pervasive. And it had nothing to do with the weather.

He sank slowly to his knees. The hard-packed snow crunched beneath the weight of his body. Above his head the wind rattled through a lone spruce tree, and a clump of snow plopped to the ground in front of him. A single flake landed on his eyelash, melted, and rolled down his stubble-coated cheek.

He bowed his head in prayer. The action felt foreign and uncomfortable, but he forced himself to maintain it. It was the least he could do for Bear.

"Take care of him, God. He's a good man." He cleared his throat. "Oh, yeah, and if you could, give him that arm back. He was powerful upset to have lost it."

With a great and determined effort he lifted his head and stared down the valley. The river was a winding strand of white velvet that snaked idly along the row of grayed tents. Behind it the great, frowning hillsides watched in silence.

The funeral was over. The mourners—from this distance a row of black-clad ants—dispersed, each trudging toward his own empty tent. There were only two people left at the grave site. A man and a woman.

If he strained, Stone Man could almost hear the flapping of the woman's black woolen skirts against her ankles.

"Devon." The word came out in a whisper of longing. God, how he wished he could go to her right now. To comfort and be comforted, as he'd never done in his life.

But he couldn't, wouldn't, breach the wall of silent safety he'd built up around himself. If he let her touch him now, when he needed it most, he'd never own his soul again. And his soul, battered and bitter as it was, was the only thing he'd ever had.

It was so damn terrifying, the thought of *needing* her, of not feeling whole without her. It was one thing never to have known comfort; he'd learned to live that way. It was quite another to touch the warmth and then be plunged back into the cold darkness. He could live with not having what he wanted. He couldn't live with needing what he couldn't have.

He pushed tiredly to his feet, and as he stood a white-hot pain sliced his heart. For one blinding moment he thought he was having a heart attack, but then the pain subsided. In its place settled a hard, heavy ache. It felt as if he were being crushed by a wall of granite, the rock slowly stealing the air from his lungs.

God, he wished he were man enough to let himself cry. Maybe *that* would relieve the pain. . . .

* * *

Dinner that night was a tense, dreadful ordeal. Devon sat as stiff as a blade, picking at her food without eating a bite. Stone Man was equally silent and withdrawn.

When she couldn't stand it anymore, Devon dabbed at the corner of her mouth then set her napkin down and stood up, clearing her place.

Her stiff formality irritated the hell out of Stone Man. God, he hated her this way. But what could he do about it? If one barrier came down, they all would, and he couldn't risk living with her without walls. She was too dangerous to his way of life.

He wanted her, but desire didn't blind him to the truth. Once they made love, nothing would ever be the same again. She'd leave him, and whores wouldn't be good enough anymore, and the wilderness he'd always treasured would seem lonely and colorless. Hell, even his tent would seem cramped and dirty.

He carried his plate and cup to the washbasin. They stood side by side, their elbows brushing as she washed and he dried. Not once did they speak.

As soon as the dishes were done they went to their respective places. He sat in his favorite chair, reading silently. She went to the stove; and for the remainder of the tense, uncomfortable evening, they sat silently together. Together and yet worlds apart.

Devon snapped open her pocket watch and glanced at the time. *Oh, God.* It was six forty-five. In another fifteen minutes the guests would begin arriving.

A fresh batch of nerves attacked her. She pressed a trembling hand to her midriff, hoping pressure would calm the roiling in her insides. She wanted tonight to be perfect. For Bear.

She surveyed her handiwork with a keen, critical eye, and a warm sense of accomplishment chased away her anxiety. She'd transformed Joe Ladue's sawmill into a cozy home away from home.

In the far left corner stood a huge fir tree, gaily clad in loops of popped corn and strands of frozen cranberries. Moose-tallow candles winked from the limbs, casting a light, golden glow almost to the center of the room. Scattered beneath the tree were dozens of boxes wrapped in white mosquito netting. Each box held a child's toy; a wooden animal carved by Father Michaels or a doll made by Devon out of her summer petticoats and stuffed with more netting.

In the back right corner was Joe's potbellied stove—the first in Dawson City. On its surface pots of cinnamon-spiced apple cider simmered alongside a large pan of fragrant bear gravy.

Devon closed her eyes and inhaled deeply, savoring the welcome smells of Christmas: cinnamon, apples, evergreen, and candles. She thought about her sister, Colleen, and felt a sharp pang of homesickness.

A sudden, aching loneliness consumed her. Bear was gone; Stone Man hated her. She was so alone in this hard land. Oh, God . . .

Don't think about it. If you do, you'll dissolve into a puddle of mush.

She jerked her quivering chin upright. Swiping the mist from her eyes, she glanced at the window. A small cutout in the log cabin's west wall, the window was made up of empty lightning jars jammed together and chinked with gobs of moss and mud. Boughs of aromatic spruce and fir hung regally across the window top and down its sides. In the corners, holding the evergreens together, were two big white linen bows.

In the center of it all was the table. Or rather, the tables. Sixteen of them, appropriated from every tent in the valley and pushed together to form one long banquet board. Four red wool blankets made up the tablecloth.

Dozens of platters of food ran down the table's center. There were two huge haunches of bear meat roasted to perfection; six bowls of previously frozen whitefish swimming in spiced moose tallow; dozens of squirrel pies; bowl after bowl of canned potatoes, turnips, and carrots; a huge pan of fresh biscuits flanked by rows of blueberry preserves; canned-peach cobblers; and pumpkin pies. The only thing missing were the plates.

A knock at the door shattered Devon's concentration. *Oh my God.*

Stiffening, she wiped the emotion from her face and smoothed the invisible wrinkles from her snow-white shirtwaist. Her hands ran a quick check of the Roman knot curled at the nape of her neck. Satisfied that she looked passable, she walked briskly to the door and opened it.

Two dozen miners and several Indian families huddled outside the door. All she could see were hoods and grins.

Cornstalk surged through the crowd. "Evening, Miss Devon," he said through chattering teeth. "I brung my plate and fork, just like you asked."

"Me, too," Digger chimed in.

"Me, too," came the chorus of a dozen voices.

Devon relaxed. She had nothing to worry about. Not really. Tonight would be a rousing success. She could feel it.

"Come in," she said, stepping aside.

Cornstalk bounded through the doorway and stopped dead. "Holy cow!"

Digger rammed into Cornstalk and bounced backward, tumbling into the people behind him. The crowd collapsed like bowling pins.

"Get moving, you goddamn gnat!" boomed Midas's voice from the rear of the pile. "It's colder'n a witch's tit out here."

Cornstalk plodded forward, his round-eyed gaze fastened on the Christmas tree.

"Oh my God . . ." Digger breathed as he, too, stepped into the circle of holiday light.

Midas elbowed his way through the crowd. "What in the hell is all the . . ." He hurtled to the forefront and came to a crashing halt. His narrowed, angry eyes bugged to the size of platters as he scanned the room. Light radiated from the Christmas tree, dancing atop the foodstuffs and cavorting gaily along the sawdust-covered floor. "Holy shee-it."

He looked up at Devon, and their eyes locked. She saw a softening in his gaze. Before either could speak, the crowd lurched forward, sweeping the old miner toward the table.

One by one Devon took the men's plates, carefully placing them on her red-draped holiday table. She put the children closest to the tree and the miners closest to the barrel of hootch she'd made. She shuddered at the thought of actually drinking that stuff. It had been fermenting less than a month and consisted of water, molasses, a few dried blueberries, and a plop of sourdough.

She wrenched her thoughts back to Stone Man. She couldn't help waiting for his entrance. Time and again her anxious gaze turned toward the door, as if mere wanting could make the portal open. The door remained closed against the driving cold outside.

Around her the party was in full swing. At the tree a half-dozen Indian children were clustered together, pointing excitedly at the presents. Their high-pitched giggles spiked the smoke-filled air. Miners huddled around the hootch table, drinking greedily. The dull roar of their voices, punctuated by spitting, laughing, and the clank of tin hitting tin, filled the room.

Her party was a perfect success. Not a person here was unhappy or lonely or thinking of home. She should have been thrilled. But she wasn't. She was miserable. Of all the people she'd invited, only one hadn't shown up.

She should have known.

A warm arm curled around her shoulders and squeezed. " 'Tis a grand party, lass. Just grand." When Devon looked down, Father Michaels shot her a wink. "And 'tis the best hootch I've e'er tasted."

"Thanks, Father. I'm glad everyone's having such a good time."

The old man's eyes narrowed perceptively. "Ye don't sound happy."

Devon pushed a strand of flyaway hair out of her face. "I suppose I'm rather tired."

"I see," he answered in a tone that belied his words. Reaching behind Devon, he grabbed his parka from one of the hooks in the wall and shrugged into the knee-length garment. "Well, I've got an errand to run; 'tis right back I'll be."

"Hurry back, Father," she said absentmindedly. "We're going to eat soon."

After the priest left she glanced around the room. Everyone seemed to be having a wonderful time.

Loneliness resurfaced, consuming her. God, she missed Bear so much. His death had left a hole in her heart.

Oh, Stone Man, she thought, why didn't you come? I need you so desperately tonight. . . .

"For goodness' sake," she muttered to herself. She was acting like an idiot. He wasn't here, and that was that. Her tears certainly wouldn't draw him.

Forcing her shoulders square, she maneuvered through the happy crowd toward Midas. She stopped beside the crusty old miner. Taking a deep, steadying breath, she tapped him on the shoulder.

"I'm talkin', can't you see?" he flung over his shoulder.

She tapped him again. "Midas?"

When he turned around Devon had to catch her breath. Why, it didn't even look like Midas. A bright, happy smile had transformed his face. When he looked up at Devon, amazingly, his smile didn't die.

"Yeah? Whaddya want?"

"Could I talk to you a moment . . . privately?"

"Sure," he said, following her to an uncrowded corner of the room. Alone, they faced each other hesitantly.

"Midas, I was wondering if you'd consent to play Santa Claus tonight. For the children."

Midas's rosy cheeks paled. It was a moment before he spoke, and when he did his gravelly voice was strained.

"You want me . . . *me* to play St. Nick?"

"If you would."

Warmth seeped into Devon's blood at the telltale moisture shining in the old man's bloodshot eyes. He cleared his throat. "Guess I'm about the only man here who prefers a frozen beard to an icy razor blade."

He didn't fool her this time. It was too late; she'd seen the emotion behind his angry façade. She smiled. A man who was touched by the prospect of helping children couldn't be all bad. No matter how hard he tried to be.

She laid her hand on his sleeve. "I didn't ask you because you have a beard. I asked you because . . . well, I thought there was a soft heart under all that grit and fuss, and I thought you might enjoy it."

"Ha!" He snorted derisively. "Don't go around sayin' such a thing, either."

Devon smiled. "I won't."

He shifted his weight and cleared his throat again. "Uh . . . thanks. I-I haven't played Santa since my boy was the size of a whiskey bottle."

"I didn't know—"

"You still don't."

She decided it was time to change the subject. "I've got some flour to powder your beard and a pair of big red long johns. Find me after dinner."

"Okay. Dev?"

"Yes?"

"You got another guest." He grinned then cocked his head toward the door. "Over there. Big man. Sorta solitary."

Devon clasped her hands together to keep them from shaking. There was only one person who wasn't here. Tilting her chin to a proud angle, she turned around.

In the doorway, standing alongside Father Michaels, was Stone Man.

He did not look happy.

Chapter Seventeen

Stone Man nodded curtly in her direction then promptly turned his back on her.

Devon sighed. Another battle. And on this of all nights. Infusing steel into her spine, she walked briskly to the center of the room and clapped her hands, calling for attention. Almost immediately the revelers stopped what they were doing and turned to look at her.

"Let's eat, shall we?" she said.

A cheer erupted through the throng. They raced to the table, engaging in a quick game of musical chairs before taking their seats. Two chairs were left vacant: one at the head of the table and one at the foot.

Eyeing Devon warily, Stone Man seated himself at the head of the table. She swept past him and took her place at the other end. The red table yawned between them. It was a distance too far for Devon and not nearly far enough for Stone Man.

Father Michaels raised his bony hands for silence. The boisterous crowd quieted immediately. "I'm thinkin' a prayer would sound good."

"That would be nice, Father," Devon said, bowing her head.

"Heavenly Father, we thank ye for this wondrous bounty ye've put on our tables this night. We're—"

"Get on with it, Father!"

"Yeah, my food's coolin'."

Father gave a short sigh. It wasn't much of a flock he had.

Black sheep they were, nigh every one, and hungry grazers at that. "Thank ye, God." He shot Devon a quick wink. "Pass that squirrel pie, lassie."

Throughout the meal Devon was aware of Stone Man's eyes on her, but whenever she looked up he glanced away. His pointed rejection stabbed like a knife. God, she thought, we're so very far apart. How would she ever scale the thick, impenetrable wall he kept between them?

It would take a miracle to bring them together.

When the meal was finished—and it seemed to last forever—Devon rose swiftly and began organizing the leftovers into take-home portions for each guest.

Midas sidled up to her and tugged on her sleeve. "Is it time?"

She had to bite back a smile at his eagerness. "Yes. The costume is in Joe's cache outside. Here's the flour."

A few minutes later the cabin door swung open, smacking into the wooden wall with an earsplitting *crack*. Everyone stopped midsentence and turned. Snow swirled through the open door, dancing like a thousand specks of light above the sawdust floor. Outside the wind whistled and howled.

A potbellied, bowlegged Santa swaggered into the room, leaving a trail of flour in his wake. A gap-toothed grin stretched through the powdered beard and danced in his watery gray eyes.

For a moment Devon actually forgot it was Midas. He looked so different. So . . . happy.

She smiled. Tears formed in the corners of her eyes, and she wiped them away absentmindedly. I hope you're seeing this, Bear. Merry Christmas, friend.

The Indian children stood clustered together around the tree, holding hands and staring at Midas. Their brown eyes were bright with wonder.

"Ho! Ho! Ho! Merry Christmas," Santa hollered.

A wild whispering erupted among the children. They pushed into a tight little circle, their small, black-haired heads bowed together. Talking furiously, they took turns pointing at the man in the red long johns. Finally one of the younger children, a boy of about six, pushed forward.

"Wait, Johnsey—"

The little one ignored his friends' warnings. He marched right up to Midas. "Father Michaels tole us about St. Nick. Are you him?" he demanded.

Midas dropped down to one knee. "I sure am."

The minute the words were out of his mouth, Santa was swarmed. The children were all over him, giggling, teasing, testing his beard, poking his stomach.

"Whoa, kids, whoa," Santa said, laughing. "I got a job to do. I got some presents for you."

It was now or never. Devon glanced quickly around the room. Everyone was caught up in the excitement of Santa distributing gifts. Everyone, that was, except Stone Man. He was sitting by himself in the corner, eating the last piece of pumpkin pie.

She reached under the table beside her and grabbed the present she'd stowed there earlier in the day. Then, steeling her spine, she briskly crossed the room.

He heard the little *click, click, click* of her heels and knew he was in trouble. Burying his chin in the soft folds of his flannel shirt, he offered a quick—and hopeful—prayer that she'd walk on by.

She didn't, of course, and after a long silence he forced himself to look up.

She dropped to her knees in front of him. For the first time in days he found himself face to face with her, and the effect made it difficult to breathe. Her eyes were greener than he remembered, her skin paler. The soft, Christmasy scent of her filled his nostrils.

He quickly cleared his throat. "What do you want?"

Pain flitted across her face, and he felt like the idiot he was. Yet he couldn't trust himself to be nice to her. Not now, not with her lips mere inches from his own.

Her tongue darted out from between her pink lips, leaving a trail of glistening wetness in its wake. "I have something for you. A Christmas gift."

She shoved a little red-wrapped package at him.

It fell in his lap with a muffled thud. He wanted to touch it but couldn't. His fingers were shaking too badly to function.

She laughed nervously. "You don't have to open it. It's

just my old copy of Dickens's *A Christmas Carol*. It's one of my favorites, and, well, I thought you might identify—"

"I didn't get you anything." He knew his voice sounded strained, harsh, but he couldn't change it. It felt like he was being strangled. "I've never given . . . or gotten a present. I didn't even think—"

"It's all right." She laid one small, warm palm against his cheek. "Merry Christmas, Cornelius." And with that, before he had time even to mutter thank you, she was gone.

As his fingers trailed reverently across the bright red paper, a huge, desert-dry lump lodged in his throat.

A present. For *him*. Dear God, it was going to take all the willpower he possessed not to take her in his arms tonight. Every damn scrap.

Several hours later Devon stacked the last plate. Backhanding the sheen of moisture from her forehead, she dried her wet hands on her apron.

The table had been disassembled, the red wool blankets folded and put away. The children and their parents had long since gone home. Only the miners were left, and they were sitting around in small huddles, reminiscing. Not a man in the room wanted to leave.

Well, she amended, maybe one.

Her gaze went to Stone Man. He was sitting all alone in the cabin's corner, half asleep. Her heart skipped a beat. He looked so peaceful with his eyes closed. Almost vulnerable.

Without thinking she took a step toward him.

"Hey Devon!" came a boisterous male voice from the crowd of men at her left.

She swore under her breath. Stone Man's eyes blinked open, and their gazes locked. In that split second before he became fully awake, she saw in his eyes what she'd been looking for. Tenderness.

She flashed him a bright smile.

He immediately scowled. She didn't care; she'd seen the softness, and it gave her new hope for the rest of the evening. Maybe she could find a way to bring that look back into his eyes. She turned toward the boys. "Yes?"

Cornstalk staggered forward. The men closed in around the boy, pushing him forward.

"Mish Devon, we go' sumthin' for ya."

His boozy breath almost knocked her over. The smile froze on her face. She tried not to breathe.

"Me, an' Digger, an' Midas, an' Joe, an' a bunch o' the boys, we go' together an' go' ya sumthin' for Cristmas. Ish our way o' sayin' th—" He hiccuped loudly. "Thanks."

Digger wrenched the pint-sized green bottle out of Cornstalk's hand and shoved it at her. "Crissakes, kid, talk like a human. Here, miss. This is for you. From us."

Emotion squeezed Devon's throat. "I . . . I don't know what to say. . . ."

"Don't say nuthin', just drink it," hollered someone from the back of the crowd.

She examined the bottle's dirty white label. In elaborate black script it read *Farino's Very Dry Champagne*. Spirits! She winced. "I-It's a lovely gesture. Truly. I'll save it—"

"Ain't she gonna drink it?" someone else yelled.

"Course she's gonna drink it. Ain't ya, miss?" Digger said. "Joe Ladue carried that bottle all the way from home."

It took willpower to keep the grimace off her face. As a lady, of course, she'd never tasted spirits, never wanted to. "Now?" At their collective nod, she gulped.

"Here, miss, you can use my cup." Cornstalk swallowed the last dregs of hootch in his battered tin cup then wiped the inside clean with his dirty sleeve and handed it to her.

She suppressed a shudder. Digger grabbed the bottle and the cup and with great ceremony poured the champagne.

Devon's eyes widened. "Oh! You needn't pour it all—"

"Nonsense, miss. Champagne don't keep."

She forced a smile. "Naturally."

When the cup was full to the brim, he handed it back to her. A dozen pairs of eyes bored through her. She was trapped. It would be the height of rudeness to refuse to drink.

She took a dainty sip of the liquid. "Why, it's good!" she exclaimed.

A hearty cheer rose from the men, and they set about clapping each other on the back.

As they congratulated themselves Devon took several unladylike sips, finding the tart taste extremely pleasant. The way it bubbled all the way to her stomach was most delightful.

The men waited patiently for her to finish the champagne (which took a shockingly short amount of time), and then filed past her to the door. One by one they solemnly shook her hand, said thank you, and then left.

The second-to-the-last one to say good night was Midas. He shuffled up to her slowly, his pinched face unreadable. She tensed, waiting for his hatred to resurface now that the party was over.

He surprised her by taking her hand in his. "I done you wrong, and I'm sorry. This here was the first Christmas dinner I've had in twenty-five years, and I can't tell you how—" His gravelly voice dropped an octave. "How good it felt."

Tears sparkled in her eyes. "Oh, Midas . . ."

His face remained earnest as he looked up at her. "Don't let no small-minded old man rattle you again—you belong here as much as any of us. Maybe more." Before she could say a word he bolted out of the door and disappeared.

She turned, instinctively wanting to share her joy with Stone Man.

He was standing in the corner with his parka and mukluks already on. His face was grim and unreadable. "Let's go."

Her balloon of happiness popped. Reality smacked her in the face, wiping away her smile. She may have won a small skirmish with Midas, but the war was still to be waged with Stone Man. Wordlessly she put on her parka and boots and followed him out the door.

They hadn't gone more than ten steps when the champagne kicked in. A flurry of bubbles burst to life in her head. She started giggling and couldn't stop.

"Oh, for God's sake," he muttered. "I knew I shouldn't let you drink that."

She tried to catch up with him, but her feet seemed huge, and her skirts kept tugging at her ankles.

He grabbed her hand, steadying her.

She grinned up at him. "Thanks."

Stone Man couldn't help himself. He smiled. She looked

like a wood sprite, all tousled and flushed and vulnerable. "Don't mention it."

Another giggle erupted. "I already have."

"That's my Dev," he said quietly, "a logical drunk."

My Dev. The words brought Devon to a dead stop. She looked up at him in wonder. "Stone Man, I was thinking . . ."

"Don't!" he said sharply.

She started to ask "Don't what?" then stopped. "Oh, my goodness," she breathed, "my head is buzzing."

He bit back a smile. "That's not your head. Look up."

She did as she was told. A million stars littered the blackest sky she'd ever seen. The moon shimmered against the jet backdrop like a perfect pearl.

A deep, brooding silence fell across the valley, and it seemed for a heartbeat as if they were the only two souls in the world.

Slowly Devon became aware of a strange, formless presence in the night sky. The stars rose and separated, dancing in a thousand specks of light against a billowing silver background. She blinked.

"Are you seeing that?" she whispered. "Or is it the champagne?"

"It's the Northern Lights."

A queer electric crackle rent the stillness, and in an instant bands of shimmering color erupted across the sky.

Devon sucked in her breath, staring in awe at the light show above her head. Every color imaginable flashed across the sky, darting in and out of the darkness like multihued lightning.

It ended as quickly as it began. Within seconds the mid-night blue half darkness of a moonlit night returned.

Devon looked up at Stone Man and found him gazing down at her as if he hadn't been watching the Northern Lights at all. The look in his eyes made her heart skip a beat, and suddenly she knew: the lights were a sign from God. Tonight was the night to reveal her well-thought-out, sensible plan to Stone Man.

She had to act before the spell was broken. Warily, as if he were a wild beast ready to bolt, she lifted her hand to his face. The coarse, cold leather of her glove formed to the stubble-coated planes of his cheek. The champagne had made it impossible to school her features into an emotionless mask. She felt too good to veil her feelings. Everything she felt for Stone Man and everything she wanted from him filled her eyes.

"Devon . . ." His voice was a quiet growl.

Her glove slid to his lips, silencing his protests as she snuggled against his hip. Pressing up to her tiptoes, she wrapped her arms around his neck.

He saw the kiss coming and was helpless to resist it. As her lips touched his he groaned, a sound that was part pleasure, part pain, part defeat. His hands slid around her waist. "Ah, little Dev—"

"Quit talking an' kish me some more. I like it."

Abruptly he released her. "Christ. Let's go inside. You're drunk, and I'm freezing my ass off."

He brushed past her, striding angrily toward their tent. He didn't wait for her or even acknowledge her presence behind him.

She shrugged, unperturbed by his rejection. The champagne made her feel invincible. Jabbing her hands into the big pockets of her parka, she tottered behind him.

Stone Man listened to the quiet crunch, crunch, crunch of her boots in the snow. Each step reverberated through his mind, reminding him of the scene that was coming.

He'd been watching her during the Northern Lights, and he'd seen her expression change. God help him, she'd gotten that "rational idea" look on her face.

He knew precisely how it would happen. The minute they hit the tent she'd launch into it—whatever "it" was. She'd sit primly in her chair with her white hands clasped in her lap and tell him she'd reached a decision.

He winced. She'd probably start off with "You know, Stone Man," and then she'd lay it all out. Her carefully considered, supremely logical plan. He knew it was a doozy—he could tell by the look on her face—and he also knew he didn't want to hear it.

Inside the tent he immediately set about the tasks of building a fire and making coffee. Anything to keep some distance between them.

She sat down at the table. "You know, Stone Man—"

"Not yet," he growled. "Wait till the coffee's ready. I'm not listening to anything you have to say while you're half-drunk."

"All right."

Christ, he thought, she must be drunk. She's *listening* to me.

He knew what he should do. If he had the guts God gave a rabbit, he'd run for the door and never come back. But, God help him, he couldn't leave her again. He was like a child, scared to death of fire and yet drawn irresistibly to stand in its warmth.

So what did he do? Wait until the flames consumed him?

He tried to think but couldn't. He never had been able to think when she was around.

He glanced over at her and almost groaned aloud. She was so damn beautiful. . . .

Pouring two cups of coffee, he walked over to the table and sat down as far away from her as possible.

She immediately scooted close. "You know—" A loud hiccup severed her words. Belatedly she clamped a hand over her mouth.

Horror spread across her face, and Stone Man almost laughed aloud. The champagne had saved him. In her condition she couldn't string a sentence together, let alone lay out her precious plan.

Settling deeper into his chair, he relaxed. Now that she wasn't a threat tonight promised to be entertaining.

Devon stared at her partner, blinking rapidly. His face swam before her eyes. She shook her head, trying vainly to rectify her sloppy vision. It was useless. The tent had begun a slow, lopsided spin. Goodness, she wished she hadn't drunk that blasted champagne. She had a lot of important things to say to him, and right now she could barely remember her name.

Oh, well, she'd simply have to cheat. She maneuvered unsteadily to the armoire and lifted a long, rectangular sheet of paper from its hiding place at the bottom of her shirtwaist stack. Stumbling back to the table, she plopped onto her seat. With slow, exaggerated motions, she smoothed out her Campbell's soup label.

She glanced up and was momentarily disconcerted to find Stone Man smiling at her. "Now then, I've something to say." To her own ears her voice sounded perfectly crisp and clear.

"Huh?"

She frowned, perturbed. "There's something I'd like to discuss with you. Is that . . ." What was that word? Oh, yes. "Acceptable?"

"Sure." He craned his neck to look at her advantage/disadvantage list.

She clamped her hand down on the paper so hard her palm stung. "Now then, I was thinking—"

His mouth twitched. "I'm sure you were."

"Quit interrupting."

"Sorry."

She stiffened. He didn't sound sorry; he sounded amused. Shrugging, she scanned the list. The words were a teeny bit difficult to decipher. Odd, she thought distractedly, usually her penmanship was flawless.

"Now then." She shut her mouth. How many times had she said that in the past minute? She made a mental note not to repeat it. "Now then, I've been thinking, and I've decided that we've a long winter ahead of us."

"Take you long to figure that out?"

She gritted her teeth then added in a meaningful tone, "A long winter in a small tent and an even smaller bed."

"Yep. Digger and Cornstalk were complaining about the same thing at the party. You'll get used to it though, we all do."

It was not going well. She took a sip of coffee. The brew's bitter warmth seeped through her blood, dispelling some of the champagne-induced confusion. Eagerly she took another sip, and then another, until the cup was empty. When she was finished she felt better, more in control.

She set the cup down. "All right, I'll spell it out for you. It makes sense that we share a bed this winter—and I mean that in the most intimate way."

Stone Man's coffee cup hit the table with a clang. He didn't know what he thought she'd concocted in that steel-trap mind of hers, but he damn sure hadn't counted on *this*.

"Y-You mean we should . . ." His words trailed off. What the hell was a nice word for screw?

Heat climbed up her cheeks, but she didn't look away. "Yes. I think we should engage in sexual congress."

Sexual congress? He frowned. Did that take more than two people? Stone Man eyed her uneasily. His every instinct was on full alert. Little miss levelheaded had just tossed a burning match onto a puddle of pure hootch. His voice, when he found it, was unsteady. "You've decided that it's . . . sensible for us to become lovers. Why?"

She beamed, in her element now. Turning her attention to the list, she began reading. "One, close proximity. Two, warmth. Three, you're my last chance. Four—"

"Wait a sec. Go back to three. What the hell does that mean, 'I'm you're last chance'?"

Darn it! She'd meant to skip right over that one.

"Devon?"

Well; there was nothing to do now but answer. "It's nothing, really." She hoped her voice sounded matter-of-fact. "I'm almost thirty years old. It's not likely I'll find a man willing to marry me."

"What does that have to do with me?"

She stared at her hands. When she finally spoke her voice was wobbly and weak. "I want . . . to be loved." She lifted her overbright eyes to his face. "And I want that with you. Only you. Number four, if you're interested, is that I care for you."

Stone Man felt as if he were falling over a precipice. He hoped to God there was a net at the bottom. He reached out, taking her hands in his. "Ah, Dev," he said in a harsh, barely recognizable voice, "do you know what you're asking for?"

"Yes," she answered matter-of-factly. "I read that chapter in Dr. Cowan's book. It was a bit sketchy on details, but—what are you smiling about?"

"A whole chapter. Do you think that's enough?"

"I should think so. I haven't noticed species dying out for

lack of reading matter on the subject. I suspect it comes naturally."

His mouth tilted crookedly. "If done correctly."

She thought about that for a moment. "Is there a wrong way?"

Stone Man's grin faded at the reminder of her naivete. "What are the disadvantages to our . . . sexual congressing?"

She glanced down at her notes. "One, pregnancy—however, Dr. Cowan's section on contraception was quite informative. Two, loss of virginity—just in case I am lucky enough to find a husband."

A white-hot bolt of jealousy stabbed Stone Man. He couldn't help scowling. "Certainly. And number three?"

Her voice dropped. "You could break my heart."

Stone Man swallowed hard. Three was a humdinger, because it worked both ways. Wanting her without having her was one thing, but once they'd slept together he might actually *need* her, and what then? His life wouldn't be worth shit.

Christ, he thought savagely, who was he kidding? It was too late for that thought. Way too late. She'd already wormed her way into his heart, and there was no turning back. Not now.

Leaning forward, he took her face in his hands, holding her as if she were made of spun glass. "Forget the list, forget the pros and cons, and just tell me what you want."

She didn't even blink. "I want you to make love to me."

He squeezed his eyes shut, trying to block out the images her words conjured. His blood burned. "What if I'm not the man you think I am? What then?"

"What do you mean?"

The seconds ticked by as Stone Man tried to find the courage to answer her. He stared at the scarred tabletop, unable to force the words out. For years the memories had been boxed away, shoved into a dark corner of his mind and forgotten, and now when he needed them they were reluctant to come into the light.

Her fingers curled around his forearm and gave a reassuring squeeze.

He winced. Once he told her the truth she'd yank her hand

away, and she'd never touch him again. The thought made him feel hollow and sick inside. But he couldn't lie to her, and his silence was a lie.

Clenching his fists, he said quickly, "I spent five years in prison."

Her hand didn't even flinch. "What for?"

"Murder." He tensed, waiting for her hand to withdraw.

Instead her hold tightened.

The silence stretched between them. Stone Man felt every muscle in his body tighten. Nothing had ever shut her up before. Disgust must have rendered her speechless.

"Aren't you going to ask me?" he asked wearily.

"Ask you what?"

Christ, she must be drunk. He turned his head to look at her. What he saw stole his breath.

Understanding and unconditional acceptance radiated from the dark-green depths of her eyes.

The relief he felt was staggering. He hadn't known until that very second how much he cared what she thought of him. Her silence told him all he needed to know: She didn't believe he was a murderer.

Awe seeped into his voice and eyes. "You aren't going to ask me whether I did it?"

"I know you didn't do it."

That simple sentence, the one he'd waited all his life to hear, shattered the final remnants of his resistance.

Chapter Eighteen

She looked up at him with love in her eyes, and Stone Man was lost. Her loving gaze warmed his cold bones, and for the first time in his life he knew what it meant to be wanted.

That she didn't ask about his past struck a chord deep in his soul. In her silence was absolute trust. "Ah, Dev . . ." The words were ragged, torn.

His arms came around her body, and for the first time in her life Devon knew what it felt like to be held, really held. She lay her cheek against the soft flannel of his shirt and breathed deeply of the familiar masculine scent of him.

Goodness it felt wonderful. Of course, it would be more wonderful to be held and kissed at the same time. She figured he'd get to that, and so she waited.

Unfortunately, patience wasn't something she was good at.

Besides, he was taking too darn long.

Wiggling out of his embrace, she looked up at him with what she hoped was a sultry, inviting expression on her face.

He frowned. "Do you feel okay?"

She gave an exasperated sigh. She should have known better than to be subtle with Stone Man. Closing her eyes, she said, "Kiss me."

Then she puckered up and waited.

Her answer was a low, throaty chuckle. She was just about to open her eyes when she felt the hard, callused tip of his finger brush her jawline. The butterfly-soft touch brought a delightful tingle to her skin.

She decided to keep her eyes shut a moment longer.

He bent forward. She could feel his breath, hot and rapid, flutter against her lips. "Open your eyes, Dev."

She did, blinking slowly. His face was a hair's breadth from hers. She felt the soft strains of his breath against her cheeks.

"Relax your lips," he ordered.

Her pucker faded. Her lips parted, and she wet them expectantly.

"Ah, that's better." His lips brushed hers and then retreated.

Immediately she tilted her head up. "More please."

He smiled. "You can't control everything, Dev—especially not this. So just relax and enjoy."

He had to be jesting. How could one enjoy anything mindlessly? "But—"

His mouth covered hers in a long, lingering mating of lips that stole her breath. A delicious shiver sped up her spine. Dizziness danced at the edge of her mind.

This kiss was nothing like the others. It was hot and yearning and wrenching, and it made every nerve in Devon's body tingle. A strange sense of restlessness seized her.

He pulled away slowly, and as he did Devon frowned. Darn it, why did he always have to stop just when it was feeling so nice? She lifted up to her toes and tried to kiss him. His fingers closed around her shoulders, gently but firmly keeping her at bay.

"Relax, Dev." The words were drawled against her moist, aching-for-more lips.

Relax? When her blood was boiling and her skin was afire? Nothing short of a double dose of laudanum could calm her now. "I don't know if I can. . . . I don't know how."

"Let me show you." He made an infinitesimal move and claimed her mouth with his. His tongue slipped past her parted lips and probed her mouth. The dull throbbing in her loins turned into a slow, burning need. A hunger. It spread through her body like a flash fire. Suddenly she felt as if she'd drunk three pints of champagne.

Her response frightened her; it was so overpowering, so

desperate. The throbbing between her legs was making it difficult to breathe. She was losing control. Oh, God . . .

She stiffened. Her hands, still clasped around his body, curled into tight fists.

"Touch me," he whispered throatily.

"I'm afraid."

He pulled her closer, letting her absorb the safety of his embrace. "Don't be."

She wanted to touch him. God, did she. Timidly she let her fingers unfurl slowly, one by one, until they were splayed across his broad back. His body heat seeped through the damp flannel of his shirt, warming her fingers.

Moving cautiously, she explored his body with her hands, feeling the bumps and ridges and valleys of his broad back. The more comfortable she became with the feel of him the more she wanted, and soon her hands were roving freely down his back, across his broad shoulder, around his waist. Her boldness grew, and suddenly she found herself wishing she were rubbing naked skin instead of worn flannel.

His hands fell away from her shoulders and traveled slowly—oh so slowly—to her back. His touch was feather light, almost a tickle. Her body trembled in response.

Without warning his hot fingers cupped the firm wool-clad roundness of her bottom and dragged her closer. She couldn't have protested if she'd wanted to; her body was like wax in his hands. They came together, hard and completely. Their bodies merged, melted together.

Need propelled her and made her suddenly bold. She stroked his hair, reveling in the feel of the coarse strands twined through her fingers. She rubbed up against him. The metal buttons on his shirt abraded her breasts.

She gasped at the feel of the buttons against her nipples. The taut crests hardened instantly, straining against the wool of her bodice. Drawn by some dark, instinctive need, she rubbed up against the buttons again.

Stone Man groaned, clutching her tighter. "Kiss me," he said in a raspy voice.

Good God, she thought she was. It took her a moment to realize what he was asking of her, but when she did she complied gladly. Her tongue sneaked forward, brushing the warm, wet tip of his. The contact jolted her to her very toes. She heard his sharp intake of breath and knew he'd been as shaken by the mating of their tongues as she. The realization brought with it a heady sense of daring, and she kissed him again, harder, with an urgency and a need that left her breathless.

The harsh fabric of her bodice gaped suddenly. A draft of cold night air slid along her skin, setting off a flurry of goosebumps. She gasped. Before she could utter a word of protest, the flimsy flannel of her winter chemise fell open as well.

Shock ripped through the hazy veil of numbness. She came to her senses with a jolt. Kissing; that's all they were supposed to do right now. Just kiss. She had planned tonight perfectly, and a gaping bodice was most assuredly *not* in the picture for this evening. At least not yet. They had hours of exchanging yet to do.

She pushed him away. "You're not doing it right."

Unprepared for her attack, he stumbled backward. "Huh?" he said when he'd regained his balance.

She started buttoning her chemise. "I said, you're not doing it correctly."

She waited for a response, and when none came she lifted her gaze from her buttons to his face. He was standing not more than a foot from her, studying her intently. And smirking.

"Why are you looking at me like that?" she demanded.

"Like what?" he drawled.

"Like you're trying not to laugh."

"I *am* trying not to laugh."

She tilted her nose in the air. "I don't find it the least bit amusing. You could have told me you had no experience in . . . these matters. I was rather hoping you could be the leader." She sighed. "Now I suppose we'll have to learn together. The blind leading the blind." She started chewing on her thumbnail, thinking. This did put a kink in her plan.

But it couldn't be helped. "Don't worry," she said finally, "it's not your fault you're a virgin, too."

"A virgin? Me?"

She wasn't listening. She was thinking. "It's just too bad Dr. Cowan was so sketchy on details. . . ."

"Devon?"

She looked up at him. "Yes?"

"How do you know I'm a virgin?"

She didn't like the smile that lurked at his mouth. Didn't like it at all. "Well, I suspect you'd know how to do it if you'd done it before."

The smile turned into a grin. "And I don't? Know how to do it, that is."

"Apparently not. Why, here you are going great guns, and we haven't sauntered or exchanged ideas or anything. It's all wrong."

"You lost me, Dev."

"In his treatise on Sexual Ethics, Dr. Cowan explains quite plainly how people make love." She peered up at him. "The right way."

"Of course. There's a right way and a wrong way to do everything."

This time there was no mistaking the amusement in his voice. And his eyes! They were practically dancing with mirth.

She frowned at him. Goodness, one would think he'd be serious—it was, after all, rather a serious subject. But then he'd probably never been much of a student. "Do you care to learn how to do it or not?"

"I wouldn't miss it for the world."

"Good. Then stop grinning and pay attention." She hurried over to the bookcase and grabbed her precious book, opening it to a dog-eared page. Looking down at page 172—the last page of the chapter entitled "The Consummation"—she began to read aloud. " 'An enjoyable walk and saunter, of an hour or more, into the pleasant morning sunshine.' " She flashed him a meaningful glance. "That's step one."

Turning her attention back to the book, she read on, " 'For a couple of hours the husband and wife'—we'll ignore that part—'should lovingly and enthusiastically exchange thoughts, hopes, and desires. Keeping their natures as is the bright sun, with not the smallest cloud intervening to darken their joy and happiness, they enter their chamber.' "

There was a moment of excruciating silence as Devon stared at Stone Man. She was just beginning to get irritated when he broke into a hearty, booming laugh.

"That's it?" he said between laughs. "They enter their chamber?"

Devon tried not to smile, but it was impossible. His laughter sounded so warm, so wonderful. Suddenly the absurdity of Dr. Cowan's advice hit her. She burst out laughing. "I told you the details were a bit sketchy."

He took the book. Setting it down on the table behind them, he swept her into his arms, holding her tight. When she would have spoken he shut her up with dozens of slow, openmouthed kisses on her lashes, her cheeks, her lips, the tip of her nose.

"Dev," he drawled against her throat, "I know you're smarter than I am. But not about everything. My mother ran the most infamous brothel in New Orleans, and she saw to it that I lost my virginity early. If there's one thing I know, it's sex."

"Really? Then you *do* know how it's done?"

"I may not know the 'right' way, but I damn sure know what feels good. And to my way of thinking, if it feels good, it's right."

He pulled back, gazing down at her. There was humor in his eyes and something else. Something dark and burning, almost ravenous. The heat of his stare made her heart hammer against her rib cage.

Suddenly she was afraid. In her innocence she'd danced along a cliff, thinking she could fly. But she couldn't, and it was a long, long fall. A fall that could shatter her soul.

"Devon?"

The rich timbre of his voice sent apprehension skittering down her rigid spine. Nervously she wet her lips. "Y-Yes?"

His hands cupped her face. The warm, familiar feel of his skin on hers slowed the erratic beating of her heart. She took a shallow, shuddering breath and looked up into his eyes.

The ravenous light was gone; it had been replaced by the warm glow of caring. "Do you trust me?" he said softly.

"Of course."

"Then let me love you. Tonight."

She swallowed hard. *Oh, God . . .*

"Dev?" The word was an aching caress, and it reminded Devon that she was not the only one afraid, not the only one vulnerable.

Her fear dissipated. This was what she wanted. *He* was what she wanted. Stone Man was her last hope, her last chance, and she wasn't going to ruin it all over some silly schoolgirl's fears.

"Yes, let's make love . . . tonight," she answered steadily.

He swept her into his arms and carried her to the bed, laying her down on the soft black fur of their blanket.

He hefted the heavy spruce partition that divided the large bed and leaned it against the main support post; then he crawled up onto the bed beside her. Propping himself up on one elbow, he stared down into her face.

"It will hurt some," he said quietly, pushing a strand of hair out of her eyes.

"H-How much?"

"I don't know." He gave a dry laugh. "I've never been with a virgin."

She lifted a hand to his face. He was afraid, she realized, as afraid as she. He may have had his share of sex, but he'd never made love before. She'd stake her life on it.

Perhaps a kiss would calm his nerves, as it had calmed her earlier. Shyly she snuggled closer. The long, hard length of his body fit perfectly against hers. Heat radiated between them, settling into the peaks and valleys of her body. She kissed him softly.

His hand slid over her shoulders and glided down her back, where it moved in liquid, comforting circles. His lips moved against hers tenderly, as if waiting for permission to do more.

She gave her consent by slipping her tongue into his mouth. He groaned at the contact and tightened his hold on her body. Their tongues twined together, moving in a dance as old as time itself.

He kissed her forever. Deep, wrenching kisses that left her breathless and hungry for more.

His hands started moving, slowly at first, and then faster. Then they were everywhere, touching and branding her body in places she'd never expected—her throat, her bottom, her breasts.

The buttons on her chemise gave way easily, and his hand slipped inside. His fingers felt hot and forbidden against her skin. One thumb brushed her nipple, coaxing the peak to hardness. Devon heard a low moan and then another. *Goodness, the sound was coming from her!*

She blushed, thinking it couldn't be ladylike to make such noises. She was just about to ask him when his hand slid down her belly and pushed between her legs.

Her query died in a gasp. He urged her thighs apart, and like a wanton she responded, opening for his touch. His fingers slid through the curly triangle of hair, seeking out that most sensitive part of her body. When he found it he stroked in a slow, circular rhythm.

Need sent her into a frenzy. Without thinking, she started fumbling with the buttons at his throat.

The moment her fingers touched the first button, Stone Man released his breath in a long, unsteady sigh. Then in one quick movement he ripped his shirt from neck to waist and flung it across the room.

Their hot, damp bodies merged. At the contact Devon's tenuous control snapped. She didn't think; she couldn't. Her whole body was alive, her every hair standing on end.

The hand between her legs disappeared, leaving in its place a cold frustration. His fingers, still warm and wet from touching her, slid beneath her chemise. The moisture left a trail along her breasts, a trail that the cold air traced. She shivered.

"Let's get under the covers," he said.

Crawling underneath the fur and wool blankets, they undressed each other eagerly. Devon snuggled up to him. Bringing her hands to his chest, she explored the soft black hair, marveling at its texture.

He took hold of her wrists. "Wait."

She frowned at him. "But I want—"

"I know what you want," he said throatily. "Trust me." He eased her onto her back. Looming beside her, his naked body half in shadow, half lit by the soft golden glow of the lantern's light, he studied her.

She lay there, stiff and unmoving, her naked body stretched full-length on the white sheet, her eyes trained on his. She felt exposed and vulnerable . . . and more alive than she'd ever felt in her life. Her every nerve was tingling in anticipation of his touch.

He brushed the soft underside of her breast with his thumb. It was the only touching of their skin, and it felt like a brand on the coldness of her flesh. An uncontrollable shiver swept her body.

She felt the callused column of his finger inch upward toward her nipple. Her whole body tensed; her breathing stumbled.

The finger traced her aureole, teasing her, tormenting her. Her breath came in ragged gasps. "Please . . ."

He answered her, moving the pad of his finger to the sensitive peak of her breast. She gasped, involuntarily arching into his hand.

One stroke, then another; and then two fingers settled on the drawn peaks of her breasts—tugging, twirling, teasing. She closed her eyes and tried to concentrate on breathing. Oh, but it was difficult. The air in her lungs seemed to have vanished.

The hand on her breast slid down to her waist. A frown darted across her face, and she was just about to open her eyes when she felt it. His tongue! He licked her nipple once, then drew back.

The cold night air rushed in, sweeping across the wet, hardened tip. As the cold faded he took the nipple in his mouth again, this time suckling it softly, laving the tip with his tongue. Devon gasped at the sensation. She arched toward him, her head thrown back into the pillows. Oh, God, it felt so good. . . .

He took her in his arms, maneuvering her body until she was straddling his right leg. With his thigh pressed hard against the throbbing spot between her legs, he forced her to move: a slow, rotating rhythm that ground their bodies together.

A fire burst to life in her loins, and she didn't need any coaching to stoke it. She reacted instinctively. Grinding her hips against his thigh, she moved in a dance all her own, rubbing, pushing, writhing—anything to assuage the excruciatingly sweet ache that pulsed from the epicenter of her body.

"God," she whimpered, "do something. It hurts. . . ."

He rolled her beneath him. Shamelessly she opened her legs, welcoming the hot hardness of his flesh as it pressed against hers. Her knees came up, hugging his hips.

"Christ," he groaned, feeling her legs slide along his body. A shudder racked him. His control was stretched to the breaking point. Slowly, with a gentleness he'd never before possessed, he slid into the warm, wet sheath of her body.

He felt the evidence of her virginity and stopped.

"Don't stop," she moaned, raking his back with her fingernails. "Please . . ."

He gave one hard thrust and ripped the maidenhead apart. She cried out in pain.

He froze then started to pull out. "God, Dev, are you—"

Her hands clutched at his buttocks, holding him in place. "If you stop now, I'll never forgive you," she whispered.

He eased back inside, then stopped, waiting for her body to relax. After a few seconds his hips started moving, a slow, rotating grind against hers.

The fire returned, raged. They moved together. Faster and faster still. He thrust full inside her, then drew slowly back and thrust again.

She writhed against him, moaning his name over and over again, her face buried in the crook of his neck. She could smell their passion; it smelled of sweat and wood smoke and lichen.

The throbbing between her legs intensified, turning into an almost painful burning. She moved faster, wanting—needing—something more. He matched her movements, driving deeper and deeper into her body with each thrust.

Devon moaned. God, she thought, it can't go on like this. Something has to . . .

"God, Dev." Stone Man's harsh, raspy voice penetrated the haze surrounding her mind. "Let it happen."

What? she thought desperately. *What?*

And then it happened. A harsh scream tore from her throat.

Her senses exploded, spiraling out of control in a thousand shards of white-hot light.

Stone Man plunged wildly into her. She closed her legs around him, clinging to his sweat-slicked body. His release, warm and wet, filled her. But it was the ragged whispering of her name that lodged in her heart.

For endless minutes they clung to each other. The sweet smells of lichen moss and spent passion surrounded them.

When Devon finally opened her eyes, she found Stone Man staring down at her. "Did I hurt you?"

The vulnerability in his face squeezed her heart. Too choked up to speak, she shook her head.

"Thank God." He started to pull away.

She clung to him. "Don't go."

He sagged against her, burying his face in the crook of her neck, holding her tightly. She brushed a damp tendril of hair out of his eyes and stroked the side of his face, hoping the gentleness of her touch would speak the words her mouth could not.

You belong with me, she thought.

If only she had the courage to speak the words aloud. . . . But she didn't. If she said it, he'd run. Of that she had no doubt.

He'd never belonged anywhere, and years of isolation and alienation had taken their toll. Even now, in her arms, he couldn't believe he belonged.

Emotion swelled in her throat. God, she'd do anything to erase the pain in his soul.

Suddenly she knew why she'd wanted so desperately to be his lover. It had nothing to do with warmth or proximity or even with the fact that he was her last chance. She wanted it because she loved him.

Chapter Nineteen

I love you. The words burned in Devon's throat, aching to be spoken aloud.

She pressed her lips together. That sentence would send Stone Man screaming into the woods. He probably wouldn't stop running until he hit the coast. And then he'd jump in a boat.

It was too soon to speak. For now she'd have to content herself with feeling. ''Stone Man—''

''Call me Cornelius,'' he interrupted softly. ''I don't feel much like a stone man right now.''

She stretched her naked body full against his. His arms slipped around her waist. Together they snuggled deeper inside their furry cocoon.

Devon looked into his eyes, as warm now as maple syrup, and completely forgot her train of thought. *I love you.* The words leapt into her mind again, and this time the need to speak was almost overpowering.

She averted her gaze quickly.

His finger brushed her chin, urging her to tilt her face up to his. A wave of longing swept through her as their gazes locked. Longing not of the body but of the soul. God, she wanted to touch every part of him, to *know* every part of him.

The thought reminded her of his confession about prison. She couldn't help wanting to ask him about it. But she wouldn't, she vowed; she wouldn't ask him. For once in her life she was going to keep quiet.

"Dev? What's the matter?"

"It's nothing," she said quickly, "nothing at all. I was just wondering about something. Nothing important."

He smiled. "I was hoping a good romp would addle you for a bit longer."

She smiled. "Romp? Couldn't you come up with a more . . . glamorous term?"

"Believe me, I could have chosen worse."

Her smile faded suddenly. She looked up at him earnestly. "Did we make love?"

He flinched, then sighed. Why couldn't she just let well enough alone? He didn't want to answer that question right now. He didn't even want to think about it.

"Cornelius?"

He forced a laugh. In the tent's quiet the sound was harsh and hard. "Did we ever."

Disappointment brought a lump to Devon's throat. She swallowed thickly and looked away. It was what she'd expected, of course. But still it hurt. Why couldn't he admit that what they'd shared was special?

She shouldn't have asked him. She knew better. Why couldn't she *ever* keep her thoughts to herself?

"Dev?" His voice was quiet, and it wrapped around her like rich velvet in the semidarkness, reminding her that even now, even in her aching silence, she had more than she'd ever dreamed of. She had his arms around her, and she had his love. Oh, he might not know he loved her, but she certainly knew it. For now, she told herself, that would have to be enough.

Unfortunately silent acceptance was not one of her strong suits. But this time would be different, she vowed. This time she'd wait patiently—and quietly—until he realized he loved her.

She only prayed that someday he'd feel comfortable enough with her to actually say the words.

"Dev?"

"Yes?"

"What were you wondering about?" He squeezed her playfully. "Some aspect of my stunning technique, perhaps?"

"No . . . It was nothing. Really."

He stopped smiling. "Prison?"

"I-I know it's none of my business, but I can't help wondering about it."

"I was in for murdering a woman." At Devon's sharp intake of breath, he grimaced. "A whore, actually."

"Why did you take the blame for something you didn't do?"

"I never said I didn't do it."

Her gaze was steady on his face. "I know you, Cornelius, whether you like it or not. And I know you aren't a murderer."

Her simple faith in him was stupefying. No one had ever believed in him. All his life he'd been a pariah, an outcast, shut away from society's light by something he hadn't done. And now after all these lonely years here was someone holding up a light, beckoning him in.

If he'd been standing his knees would have buckled. Sweet Christ, but the light looked good. . . .

He was tired of living like an animal, all alone. Once, just once, he wanted to know what it felt like to be at peace. He wanted simply to *be*.

With her he could be whatever he wanted to be.

It was a heady thought; one he'd never had before, and it opened all sorts of doors. Suddenly he felt like a kid again. Young and trusting and free.

Craziest of all, when he looked into the huge, trusting pools of her eyes, he felt as if he'd finally found a home. One that wouldn't vanish in a puff of smoke the moment he admitted he wanted it.

He released his breath slowly. For her he would take the risk he'd never been willing to take for himself. For her he would venture from the darkness.

"Cornelius? Are you all right?"

"Are you sure you want to hear it all?"

"Yes—if you want to tell me."

He tightened his hold on her body, taking strength from the soft, warm feel of her in his arms. A dozen long-suppressed images flashed through his mind. He winced at the memories.

"You don't have to tell me. . . ."

"Yes, I do." He took a deep breath. "Her name was Mibelle—the woman I was supposed to have murdered. She worked for my mother." He remembered Mibelle's flashing black eyes and pouty, dark-red lips, and said, "I fell in love with her the first time I saw her. I was only seventeen, but that didn't matter; not to her anyway and certainly not to me.

"It . . . amused her to become my lover. I was so—" Humiliation wrenched in his gut. "So desperate for attention, I followed her around like an overeager puppy, doing whatever she asked of me.

"I even asked her to marry me and not just once. Every time I asked she laughed and said, 'Ask again next week.' And like a fool I did."

The ache in his voice brought tears to Devon's eyes. She wiped them away quickly, knowing he wouldn't want to see them. Not that he was looking at her. He wasn't. He was staring into space, and she could tell by the haunted, hollow look in his eyes that he was seeing the past.

He saw Mibelle as clear as day. She was standing in front of him, her garish red-velvet gown revealing all but the most expensive parts of her body. He was on his knees. He could hear himself begging, whining for some bit of her favor.

He clenched his fists. God, he'd been so stupid. . . .

Slowly he came back to the present. And felt stupid all over again. Devon was lying in his arms, waiting silently for him to continue.

He owed her the truth. Squeezing his eyes shut against the images, he went on in an expressionless voice. "One night Mother had a huge party in The Painted Lady, sort of a thank-you for all of her prestigious customers. Everyone who was anyone in New Orleans was there—the men, at least—and the whores were strutting their stuff. Mother had me all dressed up like a penguin, serving drinks. She knew it would kill me every time Mibelle 'worked,' and it did. Every time Mibelle took a man upstairs, my heart wrenched out of my body."

"Oh, my God . . ." Devon breathed.

"I'm not telling you this so you'll feel sorry for me."

"You felt sorry for me when I told you about my father," she said quietly.

"That's different."

"Only a man would think so." Devon lifted one hand, pale in the flickering light of the lantern, and pressed it to his cheek. "A broken heart is a broken heart."

Stone Man stared off in the darkness. How had she done it? Ripped through all the pretenses and gotten right to the soul of the issue so easily? Mibelle *had* broken his heart. He'd given her everything: his love, his adoration, his commitment; and she'd thrown them back in his face as if they'd meant nothing.

Yes, the faithless bitch had broken his heart. It was something he'd never admitted before, not even to himself.

But somehow, here, tonight, in Devon's arms, it was all right to admit it. He felt himself begin to relax.

"Tell me about the party."

Her words plunged him right back into the pain. He slammed his eyes shut, trying to block out the memories of that hideous night.

He wished to hell he could just stop talking, but it was too late for that. He sighed wearily then forced himself to continue. "As the night wore on, Mibelle got drunker and drunker. And strange as it sounds the more ridiculous she acted the more I loved her. I thought it proved how much she needed me.

"Anyway, near the end of the night one of New Orleans's most important politicians came down the stairs with Mother's newest girl. Jealousy made Mibelle crazy. She stumbled down the stairs, screaming that she was pregnant with Mr. Big's child.

"The room went stone silent, of course. It wasn't the sort of thing a whore said, especially not in front of the whole town. Everyone in the room had the sense to shut up, to pretend she hadn't said it."

Pain slashed across his face. "Everyone, that is, except a certain seventeen-year-old boy in a penguin suit. God," he said in an agonized voice, "I was so goddamn stupid."

"No, not stupid," Devon said quietly.

Stone Man didn't hear her. All he could hear was the sound

of Mibelle's drunken laughter; it rang in his ears like an off-key chord, vibrating and pulsing.

"I ran to Mibelle and wrapped my arms around her. 'I love you,' I said. 'Marry me and let me be the child's father.' "

Devon waited silently until her curiosity got the better of her. "And?" she prodded.

His blood chilled. "And she laughed at me. Then she walked away."

He heard Devon's gasp, but he didn't respond. He couldn't. All he could think about was that horrible, hideous laughter. It had bounced off the silent walls like breaking glass. God, how he'd wanted to curl up and die.

It happened to someone else. Some other poor fool of a kid. He said the words over and over in his mind until he almost believed them. Then he forced himself to go on. He kept his voice calm and matter-of-fact. "Mibelle was found dead the next day. Murdered. Everyone in town knew who'd done it, but Mr. Big couldn't be expected to go to jail. Certainly not for killing a whore.

"But someone had to pay for the crime. After all, the local judge—who, by the way, was at the party—had promised to keep the 'good' citizens of New Orleans safe. Oh, yes, someone had to pay, and for the right price, my mother was willing to give them a patsy. Her son."

His lips thinned into a grim line. "I was perfect: naive, expendable, and stupid. I'd told a room full of people that I loved her. And best of all, no one cared whether I lived or died.

"They had a fifteen-minute trial, and that was it." He gave a harsh, self-deprecating laugh. "Fortunately the cost of killing a whore was relatively cheap. Only five years of my life. When they let me out of that stinking, rotten hole, I ran as far from 'civilization' as I could. I'll never go back." He shuddered. "Never."

In his voice Devon heard the echo of a young man whose only crime had been to love. She felt a sudden, almost blinding anger at all of them: the mother who'd sold her son's freedom, the woman who'd taken his innocent love and stomped it beneath her heel, the crooked court. They'd taken so much from him—his pride, his ability to trust, his willingness to love.

It all fit into place now. The anger he wore like a suit of armor; the drifting, solitary life-style he espoused; the disgust he felt for his fellow man. They were all walls that protected his heart from further injury. The falsely convicted boy had grown into a man who refused to let himself be hurt again. A man who refused to care whether he belonged.

No wonder he refused to leave the refuge of the wilderness. Everyone he'd ever loved had betrayed him.

She sighed. There was nothing she could say that would ease his pain. All she could do was love him as deeply and as well as he'd allow. Maybe someday, if she loved him long enough, he'd realize that his exile was over. Maybe he'd even realize that she wasn't like Mibelle and that his love was safe with her.

With that thought she curled up against his chest and closed her eyes. She was asleep in seconds.

Memory's icy grip eased slowly. He'd made it, he realized suddenly. He'd made it through the darkness and into the light. His eyes slid shut in a moment of silent thanks. He felt better than he had in years: freer, more relaxed.

And all because of Devon.

The woman he loved.

He could no longer deny his own feelings. He needed her: her wit, her laughter, her strength. More even than that, he needed her simple faith.

She made him believe in himself. Because she saw in him more than a reclusive, angry murderer, he became more.

For the first time in his life he wanted something, and he wanted it with a desperation that twisted his gut. He wanted the welcome her eyes promised. He wanted the home her arms offered.

No wonder his stomach was in knots. He wanted something that didn't exist. The home he'd felt in her arms was a false home. Like one of those storefronts on Circle City's main street. It was a home that existed until spring, and then it was gone.

How many times had she promised to leave Dawson City when the river thawed? It wasn't an idle threat either. It was a plan of action. And, God knew, Devon never turned her back on a plan. As soon as she had enough money for boat fare she'd leave. She couldn't wait to leave the uncivilized Yukon backwater behind her—and the filthy Neanderthal whom she'd slept with because it was "sensible."

Oh, she cared for him. He knew that. But it wasn't enough; not for either of them. They were both stubborn, pigheaded people, and they both knew what they wanted out of life. He wanted to tramp around in the wilderness taking pictures for the rest of his days.

Not so Devon. She might say she'd never marry, but it was what she wanted. It was what every woman wanted: a nice house in town, a husband with a steady job, children, and a dog.

He didn't want any of those things, and he couldn't ask her to adopt his isolated life-style. He loved her too much to turn her into a recluse.

He couldn't leave, and she wouldn't stay. So they'd spend the winter together, laughing, sharing, loving, caring. Pretending spring wasn't coming.

But how could he love her all winter and then return to his old, lonely, meaningless life? For one frozen, magical heartbeat, he would have *belonged*—and that brief moment would make the return to isolation almost unbearable.

Maybe it would help if he never actually said "I love you." Maybe if he didn't say the frightening, irreversible words aloud, he could pretend he didn't love her. Then he'd make it through the winter with his soul intact.

Silence wasn't much of a shield. But it was all he had.

Besides, he rationalized, it was better for her if he kept silent. She deserved more out of life than a broken-down old man who was terrified of love. Yes, he'd keep his love a secret. It was better that way. Better for both of them.

Devon snuggled closer against the warmth of Stone Man's body. It didn't help. She rolled onto her back, clutching the blanket to her breasts. Her teeth started chattering. Goodness, she thought, it must be fifty below.

Oh, why did the fire always have to die out in the middle of the night just when it was needed most?

Bemoaning the fact wouldn't change it. Unfortunately. She was simply putting off the inevitable. In one determined movement she flung back the fur bedspread and jumped out of bed. Her bare feet hit the icy floorboards with a jolt of pain. Wincing, she raced to the stove. With shaking fingers she crammed the frosted logs into the little sheet-metal opening and dropped a lighted match onto the pile. The flames started slowly, inching their way along the icy wood. Devon rubbed her hands together. It wouldn't be long now. . . .

She sat down at the table, wincing the moment her bottom hit the hard wood. Lordy, she hurt.

Moving slowly to alleviate the pain, she scooted her chair closer to the fire. As soon as she was warm, she'd crawl back into bed. It didn't hurt so bad when she was lying down.

Behind her the bed creaked. Then a foot hit the floor.

"You don't have to get up," she whispered. "I already started the fire."

She felt him behind her. The warmth of his body encircled her, chasing off a bit of the chill that clutched her bones.

Then his hands were on her shoulders. She lolled her head back, resting it against his body.

His fingers moved to the buttons at her throat. They fell open one by one. A draft of frigid air slipped through the opening, breezing across her nipples.

He slid his hands underneath the flannel, splaying his fingers across her collarbone. Each digit was like a column of fire on the icy coldness of her bare skin. The very tip of one nail brushed her hardened nipple. Her breasts tingled in anticipation of his touch. She tensed, waiting.

He didn't disappoint her. His hands moved slowly downward.

She felt the callused skin of his fingers on the soft mounds of her flesh and shivered uncontrollably.

Then his fingers moved again, this time coming together at her nipples. He put a thumb and forefinger around each peak and tugged gently.

Sensation exploded in Devon's body. There was something so erotic about it all: the darkness, the man standing unseen behind her, her ice-cold flesh, and his hot fingers on her nipples—only her nipples.

She moaned softly, "Oh, God . . ."

He swept her into his arms and carried her back to the bed, laying her on the cold, rumpled sheet. The scent of their previous lovemaking clung to the cotton, wrapping her in the promise of passion.

He stretched out beside her. Taking her in his arms, he pulled the covers tight around them and kissed the velvet-soft lobe of her ear. "Better add frostbite protection to the list, Dev."

She shuddered as his lips loitered at the base of her throat. She wrapped her arms around him. "To hell with the list."

His soft chuckle floated in the darkness, disappearing in a quick intake of breath as Devon's forefinger slid down his chest. She trailed her fingertip past his waist, past his navel, through the second thatch of hair, and still downward.

Reaching her target, she smiled softly to herself. He wasn't the only one who could talk with his hands.

Stone Man stared at the sagging ceiling, watching as the first tenuous strands of sunlight illuminated the dirty-gray canvas. He stretched languidly, drawing the fur blanket up around both of them. God, he felt good. He hadn't felt this good in years. For the past seven mornings he'd wakened with Devon snuggled up against his hip. Whenever he wanted to he could just reach out and touch her.

Something in his blood stirred at the thought. Hell, he wanted to right now. He rolled onto his side and studied her. God, she was beautiful. So beautiful it made his heart stop.

She blinked awake. Their gazes locked, and immediately she smiled.

"Morning." Her voice sounded harsh, brackish.

He kissed her forehead. "Morning."

She started to get up. "I'll start the fire."

The fur blanket fell away from her naked body. The sunlight slanting through the canvas dappled her skin, rippling across her breasts. It caught in her hair and transformed the corkscrew strands into a halo of fire.

He took her in his arms. "Let's make our own heat," he murmured throatily.

Her soft laughter knocked at the door to his heart. Her

hands slipped around his body. His skin felt warm where she touched him. They kissed, a slow, lazy kiss that bespoke of time and love. They pulled slowly apart, and Cornelius stared down in the dewy pools of her eyes.

I love you. The words erupted in his brain, bringing with them a white-hot stab of longing. God, how he wanted to say the words, to believe in them with his heart and soul. Maybe, he thought crazily, maybe this time he could find the courage to say them.

He opened his mouth to speak, but before he could force a single word out she caressed his cheek and said, ''Kiss me.''

He swallowed hard. Later. I'll tell her later. For now kissing her was so easy. It was what he always did when he thought about how much he loved her. He kissed her until they were both senseless and numb. And in the languid aftermath of their passion the need to speak receded.

They made slow, passionate love, and when they were both spent they lay curled in each other's arms.

''Cornelius?'' She wiggled upright until her face was right next to his. He could feel the whisper-light tracings of her breath on his cheeks. ''Cornelius, I've been thinking about something.''

''How surprising,'' he said with a teasing smile.

''I tried to be patient, but I can't anymore. I just can't.''

He frowned. ''What is it, Dev?''

''I love you.''

The words fell between them. Every bone in Cornelius's body seemed to dissolve. His throat closed up. All he could do was stare into her huge, overbright eyes, and dream. God, the words sounded so good . . .

''Don't worry,'' she said quickly to cover the silence. ''I'm not asking for marriage, and I know you'll never go back to civilization. I just want to hear the words. I know it's silly, but I want to pretend you love me, too. I know it's only until spring, but . . .''

Until spring. She kept up a nervous babble, but he didn't hear anything past *until spring*. At that something in his soul ripped away. Pain cut through his heart like the sting of a frozen lash.

How could he have been so stupid, so blind? He'd done it again. In the past week he'd let himself fall deeper and deeper in love with her, let himself believe she was really different than Mibelle and his mother. That she loved him enough to stay with him forever.

He grimaced. He'd been wrong. Just like before. Oh, she wasn't like Mibelle or his mother, not in spirit. But the differences between them didn't much matter to his heart.

Damn her, he thought angrily. Damn her for making him think she was different, for making him want something he couldn't have. Ache for it, in fact.

Well, he wasn't seventeen anymore, and he wasn't stupid or naive. He wasn't about to give her his heart and soul on a silver platter and then watch her walk with it. No way.

"Cornelius?" Her voice wobbled. "Aren't you going to say anything?"

"I can't." He closed his eyes, and after a few moments of heart-wrenching silence, Devon buried her face in his chest. Her hot tears streaked down his skin. Every one felt like a brand.

But he wouldn't let himself speak the words she wanted to hear. God help him, he just wasn't strong enough. He couldn't tell her he loved her and then watch her walk away.

"Devon, stand still!"

Her clear, happy giggle rang through the silent, deserted hillside, and Stone Man couldn't help smiling with her. It felt so good, so *right*, just being alive on this first day of spring.

"I can't take your picture if you don't stand still."

"That's exactly the point." She stopped dancing just long enough to flash him a bright smile. "I wouldn't be caught dead having my picture taken in these clothes."

He stared at her with an almost painful sense of pride. She was his. *His*. Even now he couldn't believe his luck. There hadn't been a single morning during the long, lightless winter months when he hadn't wakened with her in his arms.

He crunched through the snow toward her, his hand outstretched. She took it without hesitation, curling her thick, leather-and-fur-sheathed fingers in his. Around them the world was crisp and clear and mantled in white. "You look great in anything."

She leaned up against him. The soft gray cloud of their breathing mingled, rising in a mist around them. "Or nothing," she teased.

"Especially nothing."

She kissed him once lightly then twirled away. "Then take my picture naked. But not in these clothes."

He repositioned himself behind the camera, determined to get at least one photograph of her today. Somehow it seemed important that he have a picture of her, his first real love, on the first day of spring. He hunkered down, peering intently through the icy, brass-mounted lens. She flashed in and out of the little round circle of his vision.

"Cornelius, I—Oops!"

She'd fallen. He shoved down hard on the front end of his camera then moved it side to side until he had her in his sights. In the blink of an eye he had the shot. Devon, up to her pretty little butt in the snow, wearing a shortened skirt; wool bloomers; fur-lined, knee-length mukluks; and a huge fur coat. His only wish was that the camera could capture color: the bright pink of her cheeks and nose and the deep, inviting green of her eyes.

"Don't you do it, Cornelius. I mean it."

He moved out from behind the camera to help her up. A huge snowball immediately slammed into his chest. White flakes fluttered everywhere, clinging to the fur of his parka. He advanced.

She lurched forward, sped past him. Smiling, he watched her run. She looked so young, so free. He could watch her forever. Right now, in moments like this, he could admit how much he loved her. In his mind the words came easily, almost effortlessly. So easily he could almost say them aloud. Almost, but not quite. Every time he started the words congealed in his throat, mired in a hopeless tangle of fear and dread. Soon, he told himself for the thousandth time. Soon.

Chapter Twenty

The twenty-fourth day of May dawned just like all the early spring days before it—crisp and clear. There was nothing at all to distinguish it from yesterday or the day before.

Devon sat alone at the table, drinking her morning tea. Outside the now-familiar sounds of construction and newly burgeoning civilization rang out. The clang of falling hammers, the squeak of poorly played violins, the tinny jangle of a saloon piano, the high-pitched whine of the sawmill. Even though it was barely ten o'clock in the morning, the streets, she knew, would be crowded with men restless for the thaw. Aimlessly they'd be drifting along the newly fashioned streets, their spike-bottomed boots clicking atop the weathered boards.

It had all started last August when George Carmack had first whispered the word "gold." That single, magical word had been carried on the wings of the Yukon wind, its utterance a lure too strong to deny. They'd come from every corner of Alaska and the Yukon, the gold seekers, and almost overnight they'd transformed Dawson City. Where before nothing had existed but a few dilapidated tents, there now were hundreds of sturdier, newer tents. And every day log cabins were being built. Stone Man had been right. It was spring, and Dawson City was an honest-to-God town.

Devon set down her teacup. She could feel it somehow, the miners' restlessness. Or was it her own?

Today was the first day in two months she hadn't gone to the post with Cornelius. She couldn't say exactly why she'd decided to stay home today except that she was edgy and nervous.

Something was going to happen today; something bad. She felt it in her bones. The premonitory feeling had risen with her this morning, and with every breath she took it grew stronger.

The last five months had been the happiest time of Devon's life. She and Cornelius had spent every waking and sleeping moment together, and day by day their love had grown.

At least *hers* had, she thought with a sad sigh. His feelings were still locked inside his heart; the word "love" had never once eked past his lips. Not even in the throes of their considerable passion.

She told herself it didn't matter, that words were meaningless next to actions. His actions said "I love you" in a thousand and one silent ways. He was so loving with her, so gentle.

But no matter how many times she tried to convince herself, she didn't believe it. She'd waited silently all winter for him to admit he loved her. But after that night when she'd declared her love, the word had never again been spoken by either of them.

Her hand strayed to her midsection. Absentmindedly, as she sipped her tea, she stroked her stomach. It had become an unconscious gesture in the past month. One she did whenever she thought about the future, about the man she loved more than life itself.

If it were up to her she'd gladly spend the rest of her life following Cornelius through the world's uncharted wildernesses.

It was, however, no longer up to her. God had seen to that. She glanced down at the minuscule swelling beneath her canvas shirtwaist. Now she had someone else to consider.

She felt a wave of almost unbelievable wonder at the thought of the child within her womb.

The miracle. That's how she thought of the child, for she'd carefully followed Dr. Cowan's advice on contraception. On even the coldest nights she had risen from bed and injected herself with warm water.

Cornelius had often commented on her dependability.

Her smile faded at the thought. He'd seemed so glad that she was "responsible." What if he didn't want the baby? What if—

No. She refused to give in to panic. She'd successfully put off thinking about the future for a month. There was no reason she should make herself sick thinking about it now. Tomorrow was a bridge she'd cross when she had to.

And besides, he'd want the baby. He *would.*

But she didn't really believe it. Not of a man who'd never once said "I love you."

A chilling sound wrenched her out of her thoughts.

She jumped to her feet. The tin cup slipped through her fingers and fell to the floor with a clatter. *Oh my God! The river!* Hiking up her heavy spring skirts, she rushed out of the tent and dashed toward the river.

Her heels clipped along the wooden planks of Dawson City's newly constructed boardwalk. All around her the sounds of building rang out: the clang of falling axes and banging hammers; the steady whine of Ladue's overworked sawmill machinery; the thunk of falling boards. But Devon heard none of it as she sped past a dozen new tent establishments. She heard only the frightened, erratic pounding of her heart.

At the muddy, gray-brown banks of the Yukon she came to a breathless halt. Clutching her aching side, she stared, wide-eyed, at the river.

Please God, not yet . . .

It came again suddenly, the sound that had drawn her there. An eerie, thunderous rumble followed by a terrifying *snap*. She stared at the river in horror, watching a huge, dirt-colored block of ice heave upward. The *snap* echoed again. The earth beneath her feet shook.

Then it happened. A ghostly block of ice, as big as a house, broke free and started inching downstream.

Tears stung Devon's eyes and blurred her vision. The river became a shifting muddle of grayish-white chunks. She pressed a hand to her stomach.

Tomorrow had come.

Now she had to face the future, squarely and without little-girl fantasies, for if there was one thing she'd learned from her mother it was the price of viewing the world through rose-colored glasses. Her mother's blind, illogical belief that her husband would change after marriage had brought suffering upon them all.

Devon refused to make that mistake.

Everything hinged on Cornelius's willingness to change his life-style. She knew he was capable of loving the child, knew he would make a wonderful father if only he'd let himself. But she also knew she couldn't demand it of him; he had to offer it. Otherwise it wouldn't mean a thing.

That was the issue. Would he *willingly* accept the responsibility of supporting a wife and child? If he would, everything would be wonderful. And if not—

If not, she would have to be strong for the baby's sake. The thought sickened her, made her feel lost and alone.

But she wasn't alone. Her hand strayed again to her stomach, and the wonder came back, this time chasing away the fear. She'd never be alone again. The realization gave her strength. With strength came honesty.

She could no longer afford the luxury of waiting for Cornelius to come around and express his love. She had to know now whether he loved her enough to change his life-style. Because if he couldn't allow himself to be part of a family, she had to get moving. If he wouldn't accept the responsibility of having a wife and child, she had to leave Dawson City in time to have the child in St. Louis, among family and friends.

Unfortunately "How do you feel about children?" wasn't the sort of question one just asked, especially not of a man like Cornelius. A man who probably hadn't spent ten seconds in his whole life thinking about kids.

No, she decided, she couldn't simply ask him. A sneak attack would be much more effective. She brushed aside her discomfort at the method; this wasn't the time to worry about tactics. She needed answers.

A good dinner, a cup of hot tea and some popcorn, and maybe a little romance would work for starters. Then, when he was nice and relaxed, she'd sneak in an unexpected question. One that would get him started thinking about home and hearth and family without being overly obvious. After a few lead-in questions, she'd slip in a quick query on whether he'd ever wanted a child.

If she made him comfortable enough and asked just the right questions, he might actually think about what it would be like to be part of a family. A real, loving family.

Wouldn't that seem wonderful to a man who'd always been on the outside looking in? Why, he might just realize he *wanted* a family all his own.

She grinned. It might work. For the first time in a month she felt hopeful for the future. Things always looked brighter when one had a plan.

Stone Man stood on the banks of the Yukon, his arms folded across his chest, his narrowed eyes focused on the river.

"Goddamn it," he hissed as a wagon-sized boulder heaved through the ice floe and eased its way through the thawing water.

Spring had come.

He stomped back to the post. Halfway there he saw her. She was marching up the boardwalk like an invading general. Even from this distance he could see the determined set to her jaw. And she was gnawing on that damn thumbnail again.

God help him, she'd seen the river break, and now she was thinking. He winced. It had to be about leaving him.

He stopped in front of the post. She brushed by him in a swirl of blue skirting, her eyes trained on the brand-new planks beneath her feet.

"Dev?"

She spun around. The moment their eyes locked, a furious blush swept her cheeks. He frowned. What the hell was she so skittish about? "What are you doing?" he asked in a harsher voice than he intended.

"I-I was thinking."

"I can see that. Blood is dripping down your thumb."

The thumb popped out of her mouth. She stared at him blankly. It was disconcerting to face him before she had her plan set. All she could think of was to ask him if he'd ever wanted a son. She gave herself a mental shake.

"What were you thinking about?" he demanded.

She said the second thing that popped into her mind. "The river."

His eyes narrowed almost imperceptibly; his face hardened. "I see."

Devon frowned, confused by the coldness in his voice. "What's the matter, Cornel—"

"Stone Man," he corrected sharply.

"But—"

"The first boat should be here in a few days."

His interruption stopped her. She didn't know how to respond. There seemed to be undercurrents in his sentence; angry, swirling undercurrents she couldn't quite grasp. "I-I know," she finally answered, "Cornstalk told me that the boats were probably lined up upstream, just waiting for the thaw."

"So you've asked." He folded his arms across his chest. Stepping back, he leaned stiffly against the post's support beam and eyed her. His face was chillingly void of emotion. His eyes were hard. "What now?"

Devon was totally confused. What in the world did he mean, what now? "I . . . don't follow you."

"That's what I figured."

Devon gave an exasperated sigh. Granted she had things on her mind, and she wasn't paying perfect attention to what he was saying, but he wasn't making a darn bit of sense. "Oh, for goodness' sake, what is the matter with you? You're talking in circles."

"You want direct? How about this: When are you leaving?"

"Right now."

His jaw dropped. "Now?"

She winced at the loudness of his voice. "Cornelius, I don't know why you're so upset, but we'll simply have to discuss it tonight. Right now I've got things to do, and I'm going home. I'll see you for supper?"

"Fine."

"Good." She started to leave, and suddenly his hands were around her waist, drawing her into a fierce hug. Lowering his head, he kissed her with an urgency that left her gasping for air.

As abruptly as he'd grabbed her he let her go. Reeling from his burst of passion, she stumbled backward. Without a word he disappeared inside the post.

Devon thought about following him then changed her mind. Talking to him in his present state of mind would only give her a headache. Besides, she had a lot of cooking to do for tonight.

After she'd gone Stone Man peeked outside the post flaps and stared at their tent. Gray wisps of smoke spiraled up from the metal stovepipe, giving the sorry canvas structure a quaint, homey look.

A strange thickness swelled in his throat as he looked at the only home he'd ever known. Not that it would be a home for long. As soon as she left the tent would become once again four wood-and-canvas walls and a plank floor. No longer would there be a soul to the place, a heart.

He had a home and a love for another few days. After that he'd be alone again. Only it would be a new kind of aloneness. Cold, forbidding, and full of memories. In short it would be hell.

A bell clanged, wrenching him out of his melancholy thoughts. He brought his head up suddenly. Damn them—couldn't they do anything quietly?

Another miner had bought a round of drinks for the house, and naturally everyone in town had to hear about it. They rang that ridiculous bell every time anyone tossed a poke on the bar.

He glanced down the boardwalk. At the end the Pioneer and the White Elephant saloons sat like two dirty-sailed ships. He didn't have to look inside to know that both tents were chock-full of miners and whores.

He gave a disgusted sigh. They'd ruined everything, the damned miners.

His peaceful valley had been murdered. Buildings, both log and tent, were sprouting willy-nilly along the boardwalk and through the valley. The old rules and customs had been forgotten, and the old-timers no longer felt free to leave their cabin doors ajar. There were upwards of two thousand people in the town now, and less than a dozen Yukoners. It was a gold town now. A boom town, to be raped and plundered and ultimately forgotten.

He should be packing his things and looking for another wilderness to record. But he couldn't move on—not this time. She'd ruined it for him. The isolated life-style no longer held any appeal for him. Now all he wanted was a little cabin in the middle of some remote valley. A place for just the two of them, a place to call their own . . .

As always the realization brought with it an almost blinding sense of loss. How could he go back to merely existing now that he'd lived?

He wandered back inside the post. If only things were different. If only there was a way they could compromise. . . .

But there wasn't. He couldn't live in a goddamn city. He just couldn't; and he couldn't ask her to spend her life in his backwater wilderness. He loved her too much for that.

Not that she'd stay if he did ask her, he reminded himself harshly. She'd made that point often enough. She couldn't wait to leave him, and now that the river had broken there was nothing to keep her here.

He loved her, and she was leaving. It was the past all over again.

A headache pounded through his skull. He closed his eyes and rubbed his temples. He'd thought about a compromise a thousand times, and it always ended up the same. A dead end. Now the time for thinking was gone.

A cold, icy dread spilled through his body. She was going to hit him with it when he got home tonight.

Good-bye.

Devon buzzed around the stove, tasting, testing, opening and closing the door. A myriad of pungent, mouth-watering aromas floated in the air above her head, making the small tent smell like home. Every food Cornelius had ever expressed a liking for was simmering somewhere on the little stove.

She glanced at the table. It was perfect. The red tablecloth, now faded from many washings, draped the old table in color, and a Campbell's soup can full of wild arctic poppies added a splash of yellow.

She smoothed the hair out of her face, wishing she'd put it in a roman knot after all. Cornelius liked her hair down, liked to run his fingers through its coarse, curly strands; but she much preferred it back. When it fell in her face she felt untidy.

She'd pull it back, she decided suddenly. It wouldn't do tonight for her to feel at a disadvantage. Just as she turned toward the armoire for her hairpins the door creaked open, and Cornelius walked into the tent. She stumbled to a halt. A sudden, overwhelming fear clutched her by the throat, making breathing difficult.

So much was riding on tonight. . . .

"Hello," he said, doffing his mackinaw and hat.

His greeting broke Devon's frozen spell. She forced her arms to her sides and offered him what she hoped was a bright smile. Moving mechanically toward him she said, "Hi. Sit down, I'll get you some coffee."

She started to turn back to the stove, but he caught her midspin and pulled her into his arms. "I don't need any coffee. What I need is you."

Devon's heart lurched into her throat. *Need.* It was a word he hadn't used before, and it carried with it a wealth of meaning. Hope surged through her. Her forced, tense smile melted into the real thing. "And I need you," she replied softly.

Their gazes locked, and time came to a crashing halt. The tent spiraled out of focus, blurring into a pale-gray backdrop. There was, for one heart-stopping moment, nothing in the world but the two of them.

Say it, she thought.

Don't say it, he thought.

Neither of them spoke. Slowly, like a flower left too long in the shade, the moment died. The tent came back into focus.

Devon felt suddenly awkward. Smoothing the hair out of her face, she pulled out of his embrace and said shakily, "Wash your hands, dinner is ready."

Stone Man felt her absence like a cold north wind. Stiffly he moved to the washbasin she kept filled with water. His sense of impending disaster swelled. She was tense, edgy. The burden of holding back her thoughts was killing her.

After washing his hands he sat down at the little table and put the carefully folded napkin in his lap. He no longer even thought about it; the action was as natural as breathing.

A knot twisted his throat as he stared at the bright yellow flowers. How much longer before he was eating off a dirty, scarred wooden table again—without a napkin, without a tablecloth, without even utensils?

Amazingly the poppies blurred. He swiped angrily at his eyes and jerked his gaze over to the stove.

She was doing her sparrow in a glass box routine again. The sight brought a bittersweet smile to his lips.

She turned around suddenly. Bustling to the table, she swept up their plates and hurried back to the stove. In an instant their plates were piled high with food.

He stared down into his plate, and as he did the full impact of what was happening hit him all over again. Sweet Christ, she'd cooked all his favorite foods. Every goddamn one of them.

The condemned man's last meal.

"Cornelius? Is something wrong? I thought you'd be pleased . . ."

He lifted his head slowly to look at her. "Nothing's wrong. It's a wonderful meal. All my favorites."

She beamed. "Good."

She started eating, counterclockwise, one food item at a time. He stared at her a long time, feeling a hollowness spread through his chest. Then, reluctantly, he began to eat. Even the roasted bear meat in chutney tasted like ashes on his tongue.

After dinner, as they stood side by side washing the dinner dishes, Devon tried to study him covertly. She couldn't see his face, but when their bodies brushed she could feel the tension in his arms.

Around them the air seemed charged with undercurrents of disaster. She had to clench her fists constantly to still the trembling of her fingers.

"Shall I make some hot cocoa?" she said in as bright a voice as she could muster.

"No. I don't want chocolate."

"But I'd planned—"

"I don't give a good goddamn for your plans, Dev." He threw down the soggy dishtowel and swept her into his arms. "I've got plans of my own for tonight—and they don't include listening to your logical babble. Not tonight."

"Logical babb—"

He silenced her with a kiss that left her breathless and trembling. "Now," he drawled against her moist, parted lips, "would you like to hear my plans for this evening?"

A wave of desire washed through her body, chasing her calm, rational thoughts into the dark corners of her mind. She could ask him later. . . .

"I believe I'd rather feel them," she murmured back, arching into him.

She thought she heard a muffled "Thank God" as he lifted her in his arms and carried her to the bed.

They undressed each other eagerly. Naked, they came together like new lovers, with a pent-up passion that left them both reeling.

Afterward they lay twined in each other's arms. For the first time all evening Cornelius allowed himself to relax. He was safe for tonight. He knew Devon well enough to know that if she'd planned on saying good-bye tonight she couldn't have made love first. When her mind was on something there was no getting through to her body.

Devon felt his skin against every hot, sweaty inch of hers, and she reveled in the feel of it. The smell of his body, as familiar now as the smell of her own, filtered to her nostrils. They were so perfectly matched, so *right*. How could he not see it, how could he not feel it?

He had to, she told herself.

She chewed nervously on her lower lip. It was time to find out. Her first instinct was, of course, to blurt out the question burning in her mind. She refrained, reminding herself of her plan to go slowly, to start with a few innocuous, leading questions.

She laid her cheek on the soft, slightly damp mat of hair on his chest. Her forefinger trailed lazily through the black hairs, her touch slow and feather soft.

"You know, Cornelius—"

Laughter rumbled in his chest. She halted, peering up at him. He was smiling broadly.

She frowned. "What are you laughing about?"

His hand stroked her face. "Just memories, love. It's nothing."

Love. He'd called her love! Hope soared in her breast. Her plan was going to work. She could feel it. He already loved her; he just didn't know it. All she had to do was get him to realize it, slowly and in his own way, and then everything would fall into place. If he loved her, really loved her, he would want their child. He would ask her to stay and make a life with him.

She took a deep breath, forcing herself to follow the plan. She still had to go slowly. "Cornelius, I've been thinking about your work."

"My work?" He chuckled. "We make hot, exciting love, and all you can think about afterward is my work? How unflattering."

She caught the teasing in his voice and smiled. "Well, I'd been thinking about it for a while," she admitted. "I have an idea."

"Fire away."

She scooted upright for a better look at him. She didn't want to miss any nuance of emotion that crossed his face.

Her expression was too earnest, too eager, she knew, but she couldn't seem to change it. Excitement tinged her voice. "You know how much I hate you stomping off to the gulch, dragging that horrid sled."

"Yeah."

"Well, I know you have to carry all that stuff with you, and I thought . . . Well, I thought a dog might help." She smiled at him expectantly, waiting for his agreement.

It didn't come.

In fact he didn't say anything; he just looked at her strangely, a lazy smile lurking at the corners of his mouth. She frowned. He certainly didn't seem to be thinking about the merits of home and hearth.

Maybe he needed a little more convincing. "Plus it would be nice to have a pet, don't you think? Especially a dog. He could sleep on the floor, curled up in front of the stove. It would make everything so . . . homey."

He propped up on one elbow to look at her. "You want me to get a dog?" He sounded incredulous.

Devon felt the first stirring of apprehension. It wasn't going right. The plan had barely begun, and already he wasn't following it. He should have agreed by now. Why was he smiling?

"I'd take care of him," she added as an afterthought.

That smile again, a little bigger. "You would, would you?"

"Y-Yes." She nibbled nervously on her lower lip. Oh, why didn't he just agree? How hard could it be to say "Yes, Dev, a dog would be nice. A malamute, maybe." That's what he'd always said in her thoughts.

When she couldn't stand the silence anymore, she started talking again. "A dog would be nice. At least, *I* think it would. I mean, it would make us more like a family—" She looked at him meaningfully. "You know, a *real* family. You know it—"

He pressed a finger to her lips. "You're babbling, Devon."

"I know, but—"

"Shhh. I appreciate the thought, Dev. Honestly I do. But if I'd wanted a dog, I'd have one."

"But—"

"But nothing. A dog is too damn much responsibility. Hell, what if I forgot to feed the damn thing and he died? I'd feel like shit. No, it's a nice thought. But I couldn't take the responsibility."

Devon sucked in her breath as the implication of his words hit home. Tears seared her eyes. She blinked them away rapidly then sank into the mattress, burying her face in the pillow.

"Devon?" She felt his hand on her bare shoulder, stroking it gently. "What is it? Did you really want a dog that much?"

She shook her head, grateful now for the russet curls that shielded her face. "No," she answered in a muffled voice. "I'm just tired. Let's go to sleep."

He snuggled alongside her, his arms coiled around her naked body. One warm hand slid beneath her body and settled against her navel.

When she felt his hand on her stomach, she lost control. Tears poured from her eyes. She didn't try to stem their flow, for she knew it would be useless. Every dream she'd ever had had just been shattered.

God help her. She was pregnant by a man who couldn't accept the responsibility of feeding a dog.

A child was certainly out of the question. There was no choice left to be made. She loved Cornelius too much to make him accept a responsibility he didn't want. She'd seen firsthand how forced responsibility affected a man.

Not that Cornelius was anything like her father; he wasn't. He was an honorable, loving man. So honorable in fact that if he knew about the child, he'd marry her. A marriage he didn't want for the sake of a child he didn't want.

No, she decided grimly, that kind of marriage wasn't what she wanted. Not for herself, not for the child, and certainly not for Cornelius. There was no choice to be made. She had to leave before Cornelius found out about the baby—and that wouldn't be much longer.

When the boat left Dawson City, she'd be on it.

Chapter Twenty-one

In her sleep Devon snuggled closer to Cornelius. Beneath her bunched-up nightgown, she felt the welcome, familiar warmth of his legs intertwined with hers; a quiet, contented snore escaped her lips.

She became aware of it slowly: his sensuous, lingering kiss. Without thinking she parted her lips, allowing her lover free access to her mouth. The kiss—a building, magical caress—deepened. She felt his tongue graze her teeth then move on, tangling with her own. A knot of sweet, aching pleasure formed in her loins.

The hard skin of his palms slid across her breasts, making her shiver in anticipation. She blinked awake.

"Hi," he said.

The sound of his voice brought a lazy smile to her lips. A smile that faded the moment she remembered last night.

The memory hit her with the force of a physical blow. Oh God, she thought suddenly, if the boat came today, this would be the last time she'd waken in his arms. The last time she'd feel his loving touch on her body.

She threw her arms around him. A sob welled in her throat; she felt the hot sting of tears in her eyes.

"Love me," she whispered shakily. "Now . . ."

It was slow and quiet and almost bittersweet, their love-making. Afterward, as Devon lay in his arms, she tried to block out the memory of last night, but it was useless.

"Devon?"

She heard his voice as if from far away and wrenched her

thoughts back to the present. Pulling out of his warm embrace, she looked up at him. The concern in his eyes twisted her heart. "Y-Yes?"

"What's the matter?"

She bit down on her lower lip to stop its tremble. Her gaze plummeted. God help her, if he kept looking at her like that she was going to crumble. . . .

"Dev?"

"Nothing's the matter. I was just thinking about—" *About last night. About our child.* Her voice wobbled. "—about the post. Shouldn't one of us get down there? The men are counting on us."

He sighed, a worn, weary sound that said he knew exactly what she'd been thinking about—and that it wasn't the post. "Yeah," he said finally, pushing away from her body. "I'll open up. You come on down when you want."

The minute their bodies separated, Devon felt coldness sweep the length of her exposed skin. A coldness of the soul.

She forced herself to remain in bed as he dressed for the day. It was the only way she could keep from flinging herself into his arms.

When he'd finished dressing he sat down on the bed beside her. The wooden planks supporting the bed groaned beneath his weight, as they did every time he came to bed. For the first time the noise sounded melancholy to her ears. She felt an almost overwhelming sense of loss.

Stop it! her mind commanded. Quit being so maudlin.

She had no reason to cry. For one brief, glorious winter, God had given her what she'd never even dreamed of having. A piece of heaven.

True, it was only a handful; and true, she didn't get to keep it; but she'd had it, and that was more than most people could ever say. And more than that, she had a piece of it to take home with her; a living, breathing memory of her love. She had her child.

It was greedy to ask for more.

She looked up into his face, and her sense of melancholy melted into manageable proportions. She was lucky, she told herself. Lucky to have known him at all. He'd changed her, softened her, and without even knowing it he'd given her the two greatest gifts of her life—his love and their child.

She took his face in her hands. The freckled, milky white flesh of her fingers was a pale contrast to his dark skin. Their gazes locked, and in the golden depths of his eyes she saw what she'd always seen. Love.

"If only you could admit it," she said wistfully.

"Admit what?"

"That you love me."

His face hardened. "You put so goddamn much stock in words, Dev. But if you don't know how I feel about you by now, you're not as smart as I thought you were." With that he bounded off the bed, grabbed his mackinaw, and bolted out of the tent.

As the door clicked shut, a steel weight settled on her lungs. Tears pricked her eyes.

He was right. She knew he loved her; it was in his eyes every time he looked at her and in his hands every time he touched her. He just couldn't say the words—and that wasn't surprising, given his past. She even knew that, in time, he'd find the courage to speak.

Unfortunately they'd run out of time. It was all well and good that he loved her, but it wasn't enough. She needed a commitment.

If he'd asked her to stay with him, even once, she'd risk it all. For an invitation would mean he wanted to change his isolated life-style, wanted to build a home with her. It might even mean he wanted to be part of a family.

Normally she wouldn't need an invitation. In fact, if things had been normal, she would stay whether he asked her to or not. But the child changed all that.

Now she needed the security of that invitation, and it hadn't come.

She'd reached the right conclusion last night. She had to leave. It was best for Cornelius. He had his life as he wanted it: solitary and isolated. Without responsibility or commitments. Being tied down to a family would kill his spirit, and his spirit was what Devon loved most about him.

Yes, it would be better for all of them if she left. Now.

Before he found out about the child and forced himself to take an action they'd all regret.

Stone Man noticed her coldness the moment she stepped into the post. It swept across his flesh like a winter wind, chilling him to the bone.

It had begun, he realized wearily. She had begun the grim, determined separation of their lives.

Regret churned in his gut. The acrid, angry taste of a thousand *what ifs* burned on his tongue. What vengeful God had done this to him, he wondered bitterly. Taken an isolated island of a man and thrown him under a brilliant beam of light—a transitory brightness that, when it died, would leave in its wake a darkness colder and more complete than a midwinter Yukon night.

If only he had the courage to ask her to stay. Hope surged at the thought, flaring brightly for several agonizing heartbeats before it died.

He couldn't do it. He'd done that once, with Mibelle, and that little naivete had cost him five years of his life. With Devon he'd be risking more than his freedom. Much more. If he asked Devon to stay and she said no, it would kill him. He'd given up his emotional armor months ago, and he had no shred of it left. He was naked to her attack.

It all came down to self-preservation. If he didn't ask her to stay, then she couldn't turn him down. And if he'd never heard the refusal, he could, in later years, tell himself that perhaps she would have stayed. He could cherish the memory of her.

Besides, why should he have to ask her? He knew Devon; if she wanted to stay with him, wild horses couldn't drag her onto the sternwheeler. She was a woman who did as she pleased; a woman who knew her own mind.

So why should he embarrass himself by groveling? She'd just turn the tables on him like she always did. She'd get that perfectly logical look on her face, gnaw on her thumbnail, and ask him why he didn't come to St. Louis with her.

Why didn't he? The thought came out of nowhere with stunning force.

Why didn't he?

He didn't because he couldn't. Years ago, when he spurned society, he vowed never to look back. It was a vow he'd kept easily, and after a few years, civilization had come to mean hell to him. The thought of going back, of having to fit in, was terrifying. He'd lived on his own, like a wild animal, for the last twenty-two years. How could he possibly go back?

Even more frightening than the thought of trying to be something he wasn't was the thought of disappointing her.

And he would. Oh, sure, he'd mastered the rudiments of table manners, and he'd even given up chewing tobacco, but he wasn't exactly church-social material. He'd embarrass and disappoint her. Then she'd get that pained, pinched expression on her face—the one that said he'd failed.

She was too big-hearted ever to say a word, but he'd know he'd failed, and he'd want to crawl under the nearest rock and die.

He refused to set himself up for that kind of pain. He much preferred one swift stab in the heart to a lingering, drawn-out bloodletting.

"Miss Devon. Miss Devon!" Her name echoed down Front Street.

Stone Man felt a jab of apprehension. His gaze cut to Devon. She was still sitting at the table, knitting on that silly pink tablecloth.

Just outside the tent a shadow loomed. It appeared to be a single man dragging a sled. "Hang on, Miss Devon, I'm a-comin'," yelled the voice again.

Devon turned to Stone Man. "Who was that?"

"How should I know?" Stone Man retorted in a harsher voice than he'd intended. He couldn't help himself; something about the shadow made the hair on the back of his neck stand up.

The distorted black figure tossed his pull-lines to the ground then hefted something—a sack, maybe—off the sled. The object hit the boardwalk with a loud thunk.

Digger Haines plowed through the tent flaps, dragging a burlap sack behind him. The sack burped and slid across the uneven plank flooring.

Digger stopped beside the table. Swiping the sheen of

sweat from his dirty brow, he flashed Devon a bright grin. "I done it, miss! This here sack's full of gold."

Devon jumped to her feet. Her knitting needles clattered on the tabletop, forgotten. "*That's* full of gold?"

"Chock-full, and it's all yours."

Devon's jaw dropped. For the first time in her life, she was speechless.

Digger cackled. "You didn't think that grubstake'd amount to anything, did you?"

"What grubstake?"

Devon heard Stone Man's too-quiet voice, heard the ominous note of warning in it, but she didn't respond. She couldn't. She was stunned. Ideas and possibilities and realizations crashed together in her mind, tumbling over one another. She was rich. *Rich.*

"While you were off tramping through the gulch," Digger answered good-naturedly, "your partner here grubstaked my claim on Eldorado."

"Oh, she did, did she?"

"*I* didn't," she answered distractedly. "The post did. Good heavens, Stone Man, we're rich."

"You're both rich!" Digger patted the sack proudly. "And this ain't all of it. I still got a pile of muck left to sluice and dozens o' shafts left to dig. Hell, we're all gonna be rich as kings. We can live anywhere we want. Paris, London, San Francisco. Hell, miss, you can go to Boston and have your pick o' husbands."

Devon's smile faded. Stone Man's scowl intensified.

"Thanks, Digger," Stone Man said evenly, "go buy yourself a drink. You deserve it."

Digger looked from Stone Man to Devon and back to Stone Man. They were standing like statues, just staring at each other. He loosened his collar, which suddenly felt tight. This was the strangest damn reaction to wealth he'd ever seen. Why, he almost felt bad. . . . "I-I'll just leave it here in the corner. If you got any questions, I'll be stayin' at that new boardinghouse next to the Pioneer Saloon." He turned to leave.

"Digger?" Devon said as he reached the flaps, "thanks. I knew I was right to trust you."

He beamed. Now that was more like it. "Sure, miss. 'Bye." With that he scurried out of the tent.

"So," came Stone Man's mocking voice, "we can live like kings in San Francisco."

"Or St. Louis." The words slipped out of Devon's mouth before she had time to think. Immediately their gazes locked. Her throat constricted. Time seemed to dwindle away to nothing as she waited for his answer.

Oh, God, she thought desperately, don't make me leave you. All I need is an invitation. . . .

Stone Man's fists clenched and unclenched. A knot twisted around his windpipe. She was asking him to come with her. To her tidy, well-ordered little life in St. Louis.

The Neanderthal and the lady. He winced at the thought. He couldn't do it—not to either of them.

He forced a scowl. "What good is money if you have to live like sardines? You keep the gold, Dev. It's too much responsibility for me."

Devon's knees buckled. She clutched the table edge with shaking fingers to steady herself. He'd done it; he'd turned her down. She glanced down at the tiny pink blanket she was working on, and an unaccustomed bitterness assailed her. "I should have figured that," she said sharply.

"What's that supposed to mean?"

"You figure it out, Stone Man. I'm tired of thinking for you."

His lips compressed into a hard line. "Whoever said gold doesn't change a person is full of shit."

"Oh, it changes things."

"I know. Digger's goddamn grubstake made you picket-fence rich. You don't need my money anymore to leave. You can buy your own goddamn ticket."

Devon felt like wilting into the floorboards. But years of training with an abusive father stood her in good stead. She'd learned not to show her pain.

Clutching the baby blanket to her breast like a shield, she stared at Stone Man through cold, expressionless eyes. "Your relief is showing, Stone Man, but you needn't worry. I'll be on the first boat out of this sorry, godforsaken pile of mud."

Stone Man watched her leave him. Her heels clicked atop the plank flooring. Every footfall was like a nail in his heart.

God help him, he thought. It was all over.

The next sixteen days—and nights—were the longest of Stone Man's life. He watched Devon from a distance, never daring to get close enough to touch her. They lived in a world of walled silences and resentful glances. At night he slept pinned to the canvas.

Who would have thought a ten-by-ten tent could seem so goddamn big?

He was afraid to get near her, afraid to touch her. Most of all he was afraid to look at her. The few times their gazes had accidently locked, he'd seen pain in her eyes. Stark, bitter pain.

It was like having a red-hot knife shoved into his gut. He knew the pain mirrored his own, knew they both felt it keenly. But what could they do about it? She hadn't offered to stay. He couldn't offer to go.

He grimaced. No matter how much he thought about their problem, the answer never changed.

Lifting his head, he stared at her. She was sitting at the table, knitting on that damned pink tablecloth again. Her ramrod-stiff back was to him. She'd been sitting in that precise position for two hours, knitting. Not once had she spoken.

Her pointed silence was wrenching. He hadn't realized until last week how very much he enjoyed talking with her. Or, as she and Dr. Cowan would say—a bittersweet smile tugged at his lips—exchanging thoughts, desires, and ideas.

She hadn't spoken to him since Digger's announcement. They'd lived like enemies in an armed camp—distant, angry, wary—and it was tearing Stone Man up inside. With every silence he remembered the laughter. With every separation he remembered the closeness. God, he couldn't live this way any longer.

Mornings were the worst. When he woke up the first things he noticed were the fresh, clean scent of her and the warmth of her body beside his. For a heartbeat, before his sleepy mind focused, he was in bed with the woman he loved.

Then came remembrance and pain. The scant inches between their bodies yawned like miles, and the feeling of loss assailed him. His first waking thought was always: You don't belong in her bed anymore.

He groaned, running his fingers through his hair and shaking his head. He'd wanted to say *I love you* a hundred times this week, but each time the words lodged in his throat. The past had taken its toll. He wasn't strong enough to say the words, not when he knew she was leaving.

A blaring whistle ripped through the tent's premeditated silence.

Devon's head snapped up. "What was that?"

Stone Man didn't answer. He couldn't.

She turned to look at him. "Stone Man? What was that?"

He swallowed hard. "You should recognize it—it's the sound you've been waiting for. The sternwheeler's here."

She paled. One hand flew up to cover her mouth.

His whole body tensed. After a few minutes of excruciating silence, his patience snapped. "Say something!"

"W-When is the next one?"

Icy fear spilled down Stone Man's back. She couldn't. She wouldn't. He'd had sixteen days of pure hell, waiting—just goddamn waiting—for the boat to come. He refused to spend the whole summer wondering which boat she was going to wander aboard.

No way. He'd geared himself up for her to leave. He was ready for the pain. Hell, a part of him welcomed it. "Don't even think about it," he said harshly.

"About what?"

"About waiting for the next boat."

She crumpled forward, her elbows slamming onto the table in front of her.

Instinctively he surged toward her and pulled her to her feet. "Dev? Are you all right?"

Her answer was a high, brittle laugh.

His forefinger forced her chin up. "Dev?"

She looked into his eyes for the first time in days. Her skin looked paler than he remembered, more fragile, and her lower lip was red and raw. Without thinking he ran a finger along its puffy surface. "You shouldn't bite your lip."

She tried to smile. It was a trembling, dismal failure. "My thumbnail's almost gone. I was desperate."

"Ah, Dev . . . Why are we hurting each other so much?"

Tears sprang into her eyes. "Because we love each other but not enough."

Stone Man squeezed his eyes shut. He'd told himself the same thing a thousand times. So why did it hurt to hear her say it? He knew she didn't love him enough to stay. Still, hearing it from her own lips . . . Sweet Christ, it hurt.

It took him a moment to summon the courage to speak, and when he finally found his voice it was ragged and hoarse. "The boat will only stay long enough for the crewmen to cut a couple of cords of wood. You'd better get packing."

"But—"

He grabbed her by the shoulders. "Don't make it worse. If you're going to leave, then just goddamn go."

"Take your hands off me, please," she said quietly.

He did.

She plucked up her precious pink tablecloth and pressed it to her stomach. She stroked the soft yarn, seeming to draw some solace from it, and after a few seconds her chin edged upward.

He might even have believed she was in control of her emotions if he hadn't been close enough to see the trembling of her mouth.

"Don't worry, Stone Man, I'm leaving. I can't live like this anymore either."

His next two words were the hardest he'd ever spoken. " 'Bye, Dev."

She smiled grimly. "Eager?" Swiping the tears from her wet cheeks, she hiked her skirts off the ground and marched toward the flaps. At the canvas opening she stopped. Without looking at him she said, "I'll be back for my share of the gold."

Then she left him.

Chapter Twenty-two

Devon stood outside the post, trying to gather her composure. She pressed one small, gloved hand to her midsection and tried counting to ten. The old trick didn't work.

Dear God, she wanted to bolt. To simply hike up her skirts and run—as long and as fast and as far as her Curacoa kid walking boots would take her. Anywhere as long as it was away from the sternwheeler.

She looked down at the scrap of paper in her hand. Her lace-sheathed fingers closed tightly around the ticket, obliterating the hastily scrawled sailing time.

It was too late to change her mind. Her things were packed; Cornstalk had taken all of her trunks down to the dock. Everything she owned was on the boat. All that was left was good-bye.

Her stomach twisted into a knot. *If only he'd asked her to stay . . .*

"Enough," she said through clenched teeth. He hadn't asked her, and that was that. She'd made a decision—a smart one—and it was time to stop whining about it. It was best for Cornelius and the baby that she leave, and they were the people who mattered.

Setting her jaw at a determined angle, she lifted her pinstriped serge traveling skirt and entered the post. What she found inside stopped her cold.

Everyone she knew was inside.

"She's here!" Digger cried from somewhere within the throng.

The men surged toward her. They were all talking at once, and Devon couldn't distinguish a single voice in the buzzing, excited chatter. She scanned the crowd. The bright-eyed, grin-wreathed faces blurred, melting into one another.

An elbow jabbed her, and she glanced sideways. Father Michaels was standing right beside her. He was looking at her with an odd, disappointed expression on his pointy face. He cocked his head to the left. Her gaze followed his.

To Stone Man. He was behind his precious counter, his barrier to the world. He stood motionless, his big arms folded across his chest, his eyes trained on her.

The heat in his whiskey-colored eyes made her stomach somersault. He was looking at her as if they were alone. . . .

No. She couldn't think like that anymore—not if she wanted to make it out of this post with some modicum of pride intact. She broke eye contact. "What's this all about, Father?" She hoped her voice sounded light.

Midas and Cornstalk pushed to the front of the crowd. Midas cleared his throat, and the men around him quieted. "When we heard you was leavin', we all got together and decided to give you this." He shoved a small piece of wood at her.

Oh, God, not a going-away gift. Her fragile self-control couldn't handle it now. The last thing in the world she needed was for someone to be nice to her.

Reluctantly she took the brown square. It shook in her hands.

"Turn it over, miss," Cornstalk prodded.

After a heartbeat's hesitation, she did, and the moment she saw the other side a huge lump lodged in her throat. It was a makeshift plaque, and carved onto the dark surface were the words: *To Devin. The furst womun to winter among us. We'll miss you.*

The words blurred. Her throat constricted. "Oh, my . . ."

"Read it out loud!" yelled someone from the back of the crowd. Immediately the crowd started buzzing in agreement.

Midas put up his hands for silence. "She don't have to read it. We all know what it says."

Devon offered the old man a grateful smile then turned her attention to the men around her. "I-I don't know what to say

. . . except thank you." She pressed the plaque to her breast. "I'll treasure it always."

The sternwheeler's horn blared. The sound sliced through the men's boisterous cheers. Devon felt its impact right down to her toes.

Midas clapped her on the back. "We'll wait outside for ya, Devon. We want to walk you to the boat. No need to hurry. It don't leave for an hour yet."

She nodded distractedly. "All right. I'll only be a minute."

The men shuffled out, leaving in their absence a groaning silence. She stared at Stone Man. He stared back.

"Nice plaque," he said finally.

"Yes, isn't it."

Again the silence. The awkward, yawning silence that was a slap in the face to everything they'd shared. Devon pressed her hand to her stomach, forcing herself to remember why she was going. How noble her reasons were.

Right now she didn't feel noble. She felt cowardly and lost and alone. She swallowed hard, keeping the tears at bay by sheer force of will. "I guess I've got to go . . ."

"Guess so."

"Are you going to walk me to the ship?"

He looked pointedly at the shadows huddled just outside the flaps. "Looks to me like you've got a whole bunch of escorts. One more wouldn't even be noticed."

She forced a shrug. "Guess not."

He pulled a small brown package out from under the counter. "Here," he said gruffly, "this is for you."

"I didn't get you—"

"Just take it." He looked away quickly. "You've given me plenty."

He handed her the gift. She untied the knot with shaking fingers and ripped off the brown paper wrapping.

Her breath caught in her throat. It was a framed photograph of her dented Campbell's soup can full of wild poppies. The picture wobbled in her hands; the flowers blurred. She swallowed hard. "It's perfect. Thank you." Even to her own ears her words sounded horribly stilted and distant.

"You're welcome."

"Well," she said awkwardly, "I'd best be going."

He nodded.

She tried a lighthearted smile and failed. "I'd say I'd write, but a letter would never find you."

"Nope."

"So, I guess this is good-bye."

"Good-bye, Dev."

She meant to walk out the door, to walk away. But she didn't. Instead some deep, instinctive need drew her to him.

He didn't back away. He just stood there, waiting for her. The minute she stepped into the circle of his arms, he hugged her with a fierceness that left her breathless. She fitted her body to his, reveling in the wonderful, welcome feel of him. The achingly familiar smell of him surrounded her. His heart hammered beneath her cheek.

"I'll miss you," he said above her head.

His words, spoken in a broken, whisper-ragged voice, severed her final shred of self-control. That was it; the only declaration of love she'd ever get from him. He'd miss her—but not enough to ask her to stay. God help her, it wasn't enough.

Tears streamed down her cheeks, burrowing into the corners of her mouth. She wrenched out of his embrace. Clasping the photograph to her breast, she rushed headlong out of the tent.

She pushed through the flaps and landed smack in the middle of the crowd. The men squished in around her, cutting off her every avenue of escape. The thick, pungent odor of unwashed bodies clawed at her nostrils. Panic seized her.

An arm curled around her waist, squeezing. "It's all right, lass. Take a deep breath. Relax."

She sagged against Father's small, comforting body, letting him protect her. Concentrating on each breath, she felt some small amount of control return. "Sorry, Father," she said with a trembling laugh, "I don't know what came over me."

"Don't ye?"

"Come on, come on!" Cornstalk's voice rose above the men's chatter. "Let's go, miss."

She pulled away from the priest slowly, unfurling until her

back was ramrod stiff. She pasted a thin-lipped smile on her face and then faced the boys. "All right, fellas, let's go."

Tilting her chin, she took her first step toward the sternwheeler. Her first step away from Stone Man.

Around her the men chattered like locusts, but she couldn't hear a thing over the pounding in her chest. She was surrounded by a dozen friends, and never in her life had she been more alone.

Every step took her farther away from the man she loved. With each footfall she thought *it's not too late. Just turn back around . . .*

But it was too late. Way too late.

"Good-bye, miss." Cornstalk's high-pitched voice sliced through her jumbled thoughts.

She jerked her head up. She'd reached the end of the boardwalk, and Digger and Cornstalk were right beside her. Both were grinning. She offered them a tremulous smile.

"Good-bye, Cornstalk. I'll miss you." She laid a hand on Digger's dirty sleeve. "I'll miss you, too, Digger. You changed my life."

Digger's Adam's apple did a swift bob. "You changed mine, too, miss. Your share of the gold I've found is already on board. I'll send the rest of your gold to San Francisco. I'll send you a telegram when it gets there."

Before Devon could respond, Midas pushed Digger aside. " 'Bye, Devon," he said in a gruff voice.

"Good-bye, Midas. Thank you for the plaque. I'll treasure it always."

"Yeah," he grumbled, melting back into the crowd. In an instant the whole crowd was talking at once, yelling, shouting, wishing her well on her journey.

Father materialized at her side. Taking her hand, he walked with her across the newly-constructed wooden dock and up the wobbly ramp to the sternwheeler. When they reached the puckered metal decking, he stopped.

"You don't have to do this," he said quietly. "He loves you."

The tears she'd been holding back squeezed past her lashes and slid down her cheeks.

"Oncc this boat pulls out . . ."

Devon pressed a finger to his lips. "Please, Father, don't," she begged in a ragged whisper.

"Ach, ye're a stubborn one, ye are. Come here, lass, give an old man a hug."

His gentle touch shattered her self-control. She sagged in his embrace, letting tears course unchecked down her cheeks.

"God be wi' ye, lass."

Sniffling, she pulled out of his embrace. "And with you, Father."

Long after he'd left, Devon remained at the sternwheeler's rusted railing, her fingers curled like talons around the rough metal. Wind buffeted her cheeks, whipping her hair into a disheveled mess, and still she stood alone. Waiting.

The footsteps had finally died away. Stone Man sagged forward. His elbows hit the counter hard.

Every little *click, click, click* of her heels on the boardwalk had hit him like a lead pipe in the gut. But it was over now. She was gone.

Closing his eyes, he massaged the throbbing ache at his temples.

"Well, Stoneyman, I always knew you were stupid. Now you've proved me right."

Stone Man's head snapped up. Seeing Midas's wizened little face, he growled. God, it would feel good to smash the old man's face right now. "Don't give me any of your shit today, Midas. I just might give you the pounding you deserve."

"You'd like that. It'd give you something to take your mind off her."

Stone Man scowled. "Who?"

Midas spat a big glob of tobacco on the floor. "There ain't a man up here'd let her go."

"I know that."

"You don't know shit," Midas said harshly. "If you did, you'd be runnin' after that gal, promisin' her the moon if that's what it took to keep her."

"If all she wanted was the moon, there wouldn't be a problem."

"Christ, you're stupid," Midas snapped.

"Now, wait a minute, I don't have to listen—"

"Yes you do. This time you do. I know about screwing up, Stoneyman, and I wouldn't wish that on anyone. Even you." He spat then cleared his throat. "I left behind a fine wife and child to find gold. Only you know what I found out? They *were* the gold—I was just too stupid to see it. 'Course, by the time I figured it out, they were gone."

"Goddamn it," Stone Man roared, "I don't need to listen to this shit. Keep talking all you want. I'm leaving." Without bothering to grab his coat and hat, he stormed out of the tent.

He marched across the street to his tent. Yanking on the latchstring, he flung the door open and barreled into his sanctuary.

The change hit him like a slap in the face. He stopped dead.

It was as if she'd never been there. There was no tablecloth on the table, no flowers in a dented Campbell's soup can, no frilly undergarments hanging on the clothesline.

The tent walls crept in on him. Suddenly the place felt small and cramped. Lonely.

Something white winked at him from the center of the table. Dully he walked toward it. It was a piece of paper. Real, honest-to-God paper; not some scrap of linen from her sewing kit or an old petticoat, but paper.

He picked it up. It was, of course, folded in exact quarters. Opening it he found that one side of it was jagged, as if it had been torn from a precious book.

He glanced at the bookcase she'd made for him. There were only a few books left—his books.

He swallowed thickly, forcing his attention back to the paper in his hands. Staring hard at the note, he tried to read her words; but in his shaking hands the letters leapt and danced.

He squeezed his eyes shut, damning himself for being a fool. After a few moments he opened his eyes and tried again.

I love you. Good-bye.

Simple. Direct. To the point. Just like the woman who wrote it.

Only she'd been crying when she wrote it; he could tell by her uneven, almost palsied penmanship, and by the puckered watermarks that splattered the page. The thought of her crying over him was like a hot knife in his throat, making breathing difficult.

He opened his fingers, letting the paper flutter to the floor. It landed silently, a crisp white square against the dark wood.

He stared unseeingly at the canvas half-wall as he sank unsteadily onto the nearest chair. It took him a moment to realize what was missing.

The damned armoire was gone.

A depression unlike any he'd ever experienced engulfed him and sapped his soul. Mechanically he pushed to his feet and shuffled slowly to the corner of the tent. Dropping to his knees, he reached for the wall. His shaking fingers glided across the rough-hewn planks, feeling for nail holes.

She'd ripped it right out of the wall.

Just like she'd done to his heart.

Failing to speak the words of love hadn't protected him. If anything the forced silence had made his love grow stronger and more invincible, like a flower that blooms against all odds in the shade.

Now, having brought love into his life, she was leaving it, leaving him with memories that would haunt him until the end of his lonely, wandering days.

He had his old life back.

Life. He almost laughed at that. He had no life. He hadn't had one before she landed in Dawson City, and he sure as hell didn't have one now. He had an existence, nothing more, and from now on he doubted like hell he'd even have that.

What he would have were doubts. Huge, aching doubts. All his life he'd wonder *what if*. What if he'd told her he loved her; what if he'd asked her to stay?

Memories careened through his mind in a shifting, spinning kaleidoscope of images. He and Devon lying together in the mud, laughing, that damn petticoat sign flapping in the wind above their heads. Devon, sitting butt-deep in snow, her face all flushed with happiness, her green eyes bright. Him, standing alone on a windswept hillside, watching Bear's funeral.

With the memory of Bear's death came a bolt of pain so strong he nearly staggered. It had happened so quickly. One moment he'd been laughing with his old friend; the next he'd been holding his ice-cold, lifeless wrist.

So quickly. So many things left unsaid.

Like now. There were so many things he'd never said to Devon; so many things he should have said.

The sternwheeler gave two long blasts, the sign that it was pulling out. At the sound something in Stone Man snapped.

He lurched to his feet. By God, he refused to live with the doubt, refused to go back to his old life. Pride be damned. Solitude be damned. For once in his life he was going to fight for what he wanted. And he wanted Devon.

He shoved through the tent's narrow wooden door and raced down the boardwalk. When he got to the end, he was panting and breathless. The sternwheeler had pulled out. It was about two feet from the shore and just beginning to chug downstream.

He saw her instantly. She was standing at the back railing, staring at him. He put his hands to his mouth, and yelled, "Devon!"

His words rose above the whispering of the wind and the chugging of the ship's engine.

"What?" she shouted back.

He took a deep breath. "I love you!" The minute the words were out of his mouth, ice slid through his blood. She could crush his soul with a single word or with no words at all. The memory of Mibelle's sharp, cutting laughter pealed loud and clear in his ears. The breath in his lungs died.

"What?" she screamed.

"Sweet Christ," he muttered, then sucked a load of fresh Yukon air into his lungs and tried again. "I love you! Stay with me."

Her hands flew to her mouth. She glanced at the bright red bicycle beside her then at the sack of gold. "What about the gold?"

He rolled his eyes. "Screw the gold!"

She waved him closer with her hand. Frowning, he stepped into the river. The brownish water swirled around him, slapping his thighs.

She started hiking up her skirts, and before he could holler a warning she'd jumped over the railing. She hit the blue-brown glacier water with a loud splash. Water splattered everywhere. He watched in horror as she started bobbing downstream.

Cursing under his breath, he surged toward her, fighting the river's grip. Water smacked his thighs and washed across his waist as he swept her into his embrace.

Her wet arms coiled around his neck. He held her tightly, trying like hell to maintain his balance in the swiftly moving water. "Say it again," she demanded.

"Good God, Dev," he said between gasps, "wait till I can breathe." Turning, he slogged through the water and staggered up the slick muddy bank.

"Say it again," she said as soon as they reached the dock.

He gazed into her wide, earnest eyes, and felt the bitter casing on his soul break free, float away. He was home. Kissing the droplets of water from her nose, her lips, her eyelashes, he murmured, "I love you." Once spoken, the hoarded words reeled one after another. "I love you, I love you, I love you. . . ."

A cheer went up around them.

Stone Man tore his gaze from hers and glanced up. The miners were clustered around them, clapping gleefully and yelling like the madmen they were.

Father Michaels stepped forward. "Will ye be needing a priest?"

Stone Man heard Devon's sharply indrawn breath. He looked down at her, into the finely sculpted face that held his future, and he smiled. "We will. If she'll have me."

Love filled Devon's heart to overflowing. It spilled into her throat, making it impossible for her to say a thing. Tears burned behind her eyes.

"Dev?" She heard the aching fear in his voice. "I'll go to St. Louis if that's what you want. I'm ready to be a husband and a father, ready to build a home. I'll even let you get a goddamn poodle. Just say we'll be together."

"St. Louis won't be necessary—" At his relieved sigh her smile turned into a grin. "But if we're going to spend another winter here, we'll have to discuss the tent."

The rich, melodious timbre of his laughter encased her, rumbled all around her. Reveling in the warm, wonderful sound of it, she thought to herself, *tonight*. I'll tell him about the baby tonight. Burying her face in the warm, water-dappled crook of his neck, she gave a deep, contented sigh. And began to plan the evening . . .

Author's Note

The Science of a New Life by Dr. John Cowan, M.D., was first published in 1874 by Cowan & Company Publishers. Some of the headings and chapter titles have been reworded for easier modern interpretation. The sexual "how-to" information offered to curious virgins, however, remains exactly as Devon would have read it.

About the Author

Kristin Hannah received an undergraduate degree from the University of Washington and a degree in law from the University of Puget Sound. It was during the first magical—sleepless—nights of motherhood that she began writing fiction. Two years later A HANDFUL OF HEAVEN won the Romance Writers of America's prestigious RITA award for Best Historical Romance by an Unpublished Author. Two months after winning the RITA, the book won the Georgia Romance Writers' coveted MAGGIE award. Kristin lives with her husband and young son in the Pacific Northwest and is currently working on her next historical romance.